The Shingle Weaver's Picnic

Patti C Smith

ISBN 978-1-964097-45-9 (softcover)
ISBN 978-1-964097-46-6 (hardcover)
ISBN 978-1-964097-47-3 (ebook)

Printed in the United States of America.

The Shingle Weaver's Picnic

Patti C Smith

TABLE *of* CONTENTS

ACKNOWLEDGEMENTS

I've heard it said that it takes a village to raise a child, perhaps. But I know for sure that it takes a village to write a book. It's the continuation of encouragement from family members who read draft after draft and cheer you on anyway. Thanks, Mom; my sister, Mary K; my son, John, and his wife, Sandi; my daughter-in-law, Cindy. It's a loving husband who shares you with your computer when he would really love to have your company and attention. Thanks, Vern. It's approval from longtime friends who also read drafts and make you feel the Pulitzer Prize is coming around the corner with your final rewrite. Thanks, Bev and Pam. Then come those who take your fumbling, beginning writing exercises and guide your rewrites from scribble to possibilities with the patience of an angel and that special touch that corrects and teaches without crushing the newborn talent that strives to bloom and grow inside you. Thanks, Carole Bugge, my multitalented second teacher. Your encouragement stays with me to this day. Last but not the least is my very first teacher, Season H. Fox, who has become one of my best friends over the years since I took my first online class in creative writing from her so many years ago. She gave me the strength, determination, endurance, and inner confidence to become the writer I want to be. She taught me the A through Z of creative writing, and even her editing became a learning exercise, and she also became the literary midwife that brought this book to life. For her efforts and those of my friends, family, and other teachers, I will be forever grateful. I also want to thank my publishing team from Page Publishing Company for their assistance in bringing this book through the publishing process.

CHAPTER 1

The Long-Awaited Summer

THE WARM MIDDAY SUN filters through the ivy-covered sunporch. This cozy room was added a few years before her mother's death. She wonders, *Why had Mom stayed in this small cottage long after Grandpa George died, leaving her the entire ranch and the large main house?* Cricket knows the reason. This was the place where her mother and father had spent their last days together, the place where Makie stored all the memories of her short life with her husband. This was the place where she raised their children, Annie and Max Jr., the place where Makie had grown old. Cricket sits surrounded by all the neatly tied boxes from the attic. Each is filled with a multitude of lovingly touched, tattered pieces of the past: mementos of family events, Max Jr.'s accomplishments from kindergarten through his graduation from medical school, his wedding, the birth of his three boys. Other boxes celebrate Cricket's childhood through all the milestones of her life: a lock of her hair and a baby tooth, both carefully mounted on a card and placed in a now-tarnished silver frame; all her school report cards, tied with a gold ribbon; a finger painting of two small handprints in blue saying, "Happy Mother's Day! Love, Cricket"; diplomas; a deteriorating pink tutu; a tiny pair of shabby ballet slippers; and even her high school cheerleading outfit. Cricket's mom seemed to have saved everything pertaining to her family like a collection of precious gems placed in neat cubical time capsules. How can she condemn to the dumpster all these things that her mother had so carefully boxed and stored for all these years? She has been dreading this final sorting of personal items, knowing full well they will be the most difficult and emotional. She looks up as the door opens. Max stands, leaning against the doorjamb, smiling down at her. The resemblance to their father is uncanny, from his mannerisms and sense of humor, to his spirit and striking good looks. "The spitting image," their mother used to say.

"Max, you startled me. What on earth are you doing here? I thought you were on your way to the airport?"

"I didn't have anything really pressing right now, and . . . well, I just couldn't let you do this last piece of business all alone. So . . . I canceled my flight, called Julie and the kids, and I'll stay a few days. We could use a little brother-sister time together anyway. It's long overdue."

He removes his jacket, tosses it over the back of a chair, and settles into the sofa next to Cricket, sliding his arm around her shoulders and giving her a loving squeeze. Then he slowly rummages through a few of the boxes, laughing at the petite size of Cricket's ballet slippers, the pictures of himself missing a front tooth. He smirks at high school photos taken of him in his football uniform, growing serious as he contemplates the bronze-covered baby shoes with an engraved name and date.

"Look, Cricket, my baby shoes." He holds the tiny shoes next to his present-day size 12s. "Can you believe my feet were ever that small?"

And they laugh at the absurdity. Cricket's laughter soon turns pensive as she observes the objects surrounding her.

"I don't think I have the heart to toss all these memories, Max. You should take the box of things Mom saved of yours. Your boys will get a kick out of seeing you at their age."

"Good idea, sis. I'll ship them home before I leave. Is this all there is?"

"That's it," says Cricket. "Our lives in a nutshell. Or should I say in cardboard?"

Reaching into the bottom of the last carton, she retrieves an antiquated photo album, one she hasn't seen in decades. She folds it in her arms. She can still smell the faint scent of oiled leather. She and Max start to turn the pages that contain pictures of family birthday parties, Christmas mornings, vacations, Easter egg hunts, of them building snowmen in the mountains. They experience nanoseconds frozen in time of their mother and father as young lovers sitting on a rock at the beach, horseback riding in the mountains, barbequing with their friends. Of their dad dressed in his Air Force uniform. Of their grandparents and all the treasured memories of time spent with them as children. They are all gone now, their parents, all their grandparents. Only she and her brother remain, and Cricket feels a sudden wave of sadness as she lingers over these pale, forgotten photos of loved ones and bygone days, this kaleidoscope of family events that chronicles the aging process of an entire generation with the flip of each page. In the midst of this sentimental journey, Cricket stops at a page of photos taken on her last trip to visit her grandparents in Everett, Washington, just before Max was born. Her eyes travel to one particular photo of herself and seven of the friends who had lived in her grandparents' neighborhood. The photo captured Cricket and her friends standing arm in arm in their youthful exultation and naïveté; some were curly-headed moppets, others gangly-legged preteens, with Marvin and Mary Frances physically developed beyond their years. *How incredibly young we were!* thinks Cricket. She gently runs her fingers over the faded black-and-white photo. Incredibly young, credulous, and totally oblivious to the evils in this world that would change every one of their lives forever before the sun set on the very day this photo was taken.

Max examines the picture. "What happened that summer, Cricket? You and Mom never wanted to talk about it. Even Grandma Bane would break into tears when I would ask. And that bracelet made from Dad's aviator wings, I've never seen you without it. Don't you think I'm old enough now to know what went on?" He gives Cricket a wink and a smile.

"If you feel up to it, that is. How about I fix us a cup of tea and then you can tell me all about it?"

Cricket pauses a moment. "Okay. It's long overdue, and tea would be nice." Max hurries off to the kitchen, and Cricket leans back into the cozy, pillowed sofa and lets her mind wander back to that long-ago place. She is amazed that she remembers with such unabridged clarity that one particular summer many decades ago, when one unexpected event would be the beginning of her lifelong collection of moments, hours, or days that could forge a path that could either enrich the spirit or inhibit the soul's ability to soar. It was the summer of her seventh year, an epilogue of her unquestioning acceptance of all things magic, fairy tales, and happily-ever-after. She was about to be deported from Never-Never Land, and her life would never again feel as absolute.

Although Cricket loved school, with every approaching summer vacation, she found that she could hardly wait to be released from the tethers and bonds of the school year with its routines, structure, and dress codes. It would be the beginning of three glorious months to spread her growing wings, to explore and investigate her broadening world. At the start of each summer, Cricket and her mother would usually board a train from wherever her father was stationed. Their summer adventures would take them away from the stifling valley heat, the mosquitoes of the Gulf Coast, or the mugginess of the Eastern Plains and into the beautiful, cool, mountainous Pacific Northwest to visit her grandparents. This summer would be different from past summers, and rather exciting, Cricket kept telling herself. They were expecting a new baby, so she would be traveling alone and staying with her grandparents for the entire summer, until sometime in early September, after the baby was born. The summers of Cricket's youth had no television, DVDs, iPods, iPhones, or much airconditioning, for that matter. These warm, sunny months she spent almost entirely outdoors, tending to lemonade stands, building forts, or going on bike picnics into the nearby parks, attending the local movie house for the continuation of the Saturday-afternoon matinee cliffhanger, and spending endless hours in and around the favorite swimming hole. Summers also brought with them an incredible menu assortment of delectable foods. These scrumptious, seasonal delights, unavailable any other time of year, would present themselves at breakfast as juicy, cold sliced peaches that sent a tiny river of delight slowly flowing down the back of Cricket's throat, freshly picked oranges juiced by hand, or warm apple slices sautéed in apple cider and cinnamon. Lunchtime often offered ice-cold melons of all shapes and colors. Their cool cubes burst in her mouth with an ice-cold splash to diminish the midday heat. Dinner's finale might be strawberry shortcake with hot homemade baking powder biscuits sliced in half, buttered, and covered with fresh crushed strawberries and whipping cream. Another berry delight was Grandma Bane's special blackcap dumplings with the dumplings gently spooned over the top of a hot, bubbling blackberry mixture and cooked until the pot looked like a gathering of white snowballs floating on a sea of dark berry-colored lava—yum! These were just a few of the tastes of summer that were cataloged into Cricket's childhood remembrances, along with picnics of crispy fried chicken, home- churned ice cream, real maple syrup on steaming hot cakes, and oh, yes, Grandma Bane's hot peanut butter cookies. As the evening replaced the oppressive heat of the day with a soft, cool breeze from the river, backyard sleepovers would take place, with young girls giggling into the wee hours of the morning under homemade tents designed of old blankets. As the new day began, sunburned noses and shoulders were the fashion statement and accessories of this magical season. "Annie Elizabeth Jordan, stop your wiggling! I'll be done in just a minute." "But, Mom, it hurts." "I know, sweetie," said Makie, kissing her daughter tenderly on the neck. "Maybe next time you'll listen to me and wear a T-shirt over your bathing suit so you won't get so sunburned. Now hold still and let me finish."

"I'd look pretty dumb being the only one wearing a T-shirt in the water."

"Well, maybe you might look dumb during the day, but you'll feel absolutely brilliant come nightfall, when you're the only one with no sunburn and you can sleep comfortably. Think about that. There now. All done."

"Thanks, Mom. That feels better already."

Finally, the cool, soothing effect of the aloe gel began to work its magic, and the pain and sting started to disappear. Sliding very slowly down into the soft cotton sheets that had hung drying in the sun that morning, Cricket was immediately surrounded by the scent of the freshly washed linen—another one of those bygone events that can instantly transport the memory to match the moment.

"Your grandparents called today," said Makie as she tucked Cricket gently into the sheets. "They were very excited and are looking forward to your visit."

Makie fidgeted with the blanket and sheets as she wistfully looked down at her daughter. "This is the first time we'll be apart for more than a day. I'm sure going to miss you, my little Cricket, and I'll miss seeing my parents too."

"I'll miss you too."

"This should be a wonderful adventure for you, traveling by yourself." She brushed the curls back from her daughter's eyes. "You're not nervous about making the trip, are you?"

"Oh, Mom, it's not like I've never done this before. It will be fun, honest."

"You know, if it weren't for the baby, I wouldn't dream of missing our annual trip. Hope you understand."

"Please don't worry. Everything is just fine, okay?" Cricket wondered if telling such a whopper of a lie was a sin. Everyone had told her she must be strong for her mom and the new baby, that she must help Mom through the tragedy of grief. But how could she do this? How would she mend her own heart, let alone someone else's? How could she help someone else to not feel sad? Cricket couldn't ask Grandpa George, because he was the saddest of them all. Perhaps Grandpa Bane would have the answers for her when she got to Everett.

"Do you want to see if we can feel the baby kick?" Mom asked. "Oh, yes, let's!" Makie lay down next to Cricket, who gently rested her hand on her mom's tummy. They lay there for a minute or two. Then a sensation like a hundred little butterflies fluttered beneath her hand, and then a little bump appeared on the right side. Cricket placed her hand gently over the bump, and just as if the baby and she were holding hands, the tiny bump stayed beneath her palm for a few seconds then gave her hand a hardy thump. "Mom, did you feel that? He kicked me!"

"Wow! I sure did, Cricket. He's getting stronger every day. But don't forget, sweetie, it could be a girl too. Would you be disappointed with a little sister?"

"No. Boy or girl would be just fine with me." Cricket flinched slightly, since her answer was another whopper of a lie. She really desperately wanted a little brother that would be named after their dad. She could only wonder if adults did this all the time, telling lies to make a loved one feel better. Another question for Grandpa Bane. "Oh, Cricket, I almost forgot. I contacted the office of the Travelers Aid today, and I talked to a very nice lady about your trip. She assured me that someone from Travelers Aid would come aboard at every stop to check on you to make sure you are all right.

Does that make you feel a little better about traveling alone?" "Mom, I'll be just fine. Stop worrying."

"Okay, sweetie. Sleep tight. I love you!" She bent over to kiss Cricket good-night, adding the flutter of her eyelashes to Cricket's cheek. Butterfly kisses, Makie called them.

When the lights were turned off and Makie closed Cricket's door, her classic scent of lavender soap lingered lovingly and mingled with the night-blooming jasmine growing outside the bedroom window. The crickets and frogs cued up their evening crescendo, and the room slowly filled with the mysterious luminescence and silhouettes of the moonlight. Interpretive shadows danced on the walls and ceiling as the curtains caught the river's breeze and joined in the ballet. "Dear God, this is Annie Elizabeth Jordan," Cricket whispered as she began her prayers. "I think we have been friends long enough now that you can call me Cricket. That is, if you want to. Everybody else does except Grandpa Bane. I think it's nice when friends are on a first-name basis. Besides, I call you by your first name, don't I? I guess I could call you Supreme Being, but I like just plain old God a lot better. Let me know what you think on this matter. In the meantime, please bless my mom and our new baby and take care of them while I'm away. Please watch over Grandpa and Grandma Bane and Grandpa George too. Thank you for another wonderful day, and I'm really sorry I called Jimmy Wallace a horse's ass when he pushed me into the water. Grandpa George says that even though he says that all the time, I'm not supposed to do it until I grow up, but somehow it just slipped out. I'll try to do better tomorrow."

Cricket hesitated for a moment to reach under her pillow and retrieve a man's handkerchief. She carefully unwrapped it, one corner at a time. She looked lovingly at the treasure folded inside, a pin made of a set of flier's wings with her dad's name and rank engraved on the back. A few warm tears slid down her cheeks as she recalled the day her dad gave her these wings. Clutching them in her small hands, Cricket continued her prayers. "God, please take good care of my dad. Tell him we said hello and that we all miss him something awful. Grandpa George doesn't say much, but I've come to know him pretty well, and his heart may be even more broken than ours, I guess, because he's such a big man. "One last thing, God, I'm not sure what is and what isn't a lie anymore. I think if Mom knew just how sad I really am about losing my dad, she would be even sadder than she is already, so I didn't tell her the truth and I said everything is just fine when it isn't. Is that a bad lie? I'm also a little nervous about this traveling-alone thing, so . . . if you could please give me a little extra courage or send an angel to watch over me, I sure would appreciate it. "I need to have a talk with you about our new baby. I'm really happy to have the new baby in our life— please send a boy if you can—but I'm wondering, will Mom love that new baby so much she won't have any love left over for me? Or do moms have an endless amount of love all lined up like measuring cups and each kid gets a big cupful whenever they need it? Please have Grandpa Bane give me your answer. We have some great talks. He's very smart and knows just about everything. Well, that's about it for tonight, God. I hope you had a good day, and I'll see you in the morning. Thanks, God, and good night." Cricket placed her dad's aviator wings gently on his monogrammed handkerchief and wrapped it snuggly and put it back under her pillow. It wasn't long before she surrendered herself to the night. With heavy eyelids, she floated deep in dreams filled with the endless possibilities of the adventure she was about to take. Cricket was more than eager to see her grandparents. She adored her grandmother, but her grandfather had stepped up to be a surrogate father after her dad was killed, and their bond became deep and precious. Her dreams encircled all the wonderful things she and her grandfather had shared in past summers: the long walks in the woods, trips to the ice cream parlor, sailing around the San Juan Islands on Grandpa's boat, the *Miss Makyla*, and picnics on the beach. So many cherished memories she was eager to repeat. But nowhere, not even in the darkest corners of those dreams, could she have begun to imagine the sinister, horrifying events that lay hidden in the shadows of the summer to come, a summer that would demand she leave the innocence of childhood behind and face the adult world, its scars, its flaws, and the dark side of its sometimes-demonic nature that changes fairy tales into nightmares.

CHAPTER 2

Makyla Lara "Makie" Bane

MAKYLA LARA BANE WAS born in a lumber camp in the mountains above Everett, Washington, on a sunny June morning in 1913. She figured out at a very early age that it was necessary to hone her skills in mountain climbing, skiing, horseback riding, and any other sport that ensured her tomboy status as a means of survival in dealing with her older brothers, Franklyn and Donald, and her younger brother, Ken. Makie, as she became known, was doted upon by her mother, who, although loved her sons beyond measure, had long dreamed of adding a daughter to their family. It was a matter of balancing out their household's abundance of testosterone with three sons. Even the family dog, an independent little Scottie named Bardie, was male. Makie's father fell under her spell on the day of her birth. He swore Makie reached for his finger, held it tight, and smiled at him. Nobody had the heart to tell him that a newborn doesn't possess those abilities so early on, and if they had, he wouldn't have believed them, anyway. He, too, adored his sons, taking great pride in their every endeavor, but with Makie, there was a special bond that lasted all during their lifetimes. Being the only girl of the family had its drawbacks and advantages. Makie had not only the advantage of two devoted parents but also the disadvantage of older brothers who believed their single most important task was to protect, defend, and shelter their baby sister from all things worldly and dangerous. They extended this same protection to their baby brother, Ken, until he was age ten, and then they recruited him into the Circle of Sister Protection. He made a wonderful spy and talked Makie into taking him just about anywhere with her, including her dates to the movies, picnics, and church socials. On the subject of protection for the "baby" of the family, Makie concurred with the Brothers and wholeheartedly participated. No one at school dared bully little Ken, or they had to answer to Makie or, God forbid, one of the older brothers. By the time Makie was in the sixth grade, she could outrun, outride, and ski and hike better than every one of her brothers. Against her constant protests, they made her and little Ken spend endless hours after school learning self-protection for that just-in-case situation when they weren't around. She became so skilled at these maneuvers that the Brothers (Franklyn, Ken, and Donald), as they became known, decided perhaps they had been a little too diligent in her training. She was now capable of beating the crap out of any of her classmates, which she proved on several occasions. The Brothers decided a little feminization was in order, so they insisted she get involved in ballet classes. At first, Makie was appalled at the very idea of giving up her dungarees for a dumb tutu, but soon she discovered dancing was her bliss. During her early school years, she only had to deal with brotherly escorts to and from school, dance class, or athletic events. As she grew into a young woman, however, the brotherly escorts took on a more serious nature, as their idea of danger expanded to include any and all males, putting her personal romantic life in dire jeopardy. Sending little Ken as a tagalong, not-so-undercover spy also became one of the rules.

"Who was that guy we saw you talking to at the malt shop?" asked Franklyn, the eldest brother, who was the usual spokesperson for the Brothers Inc.

"Tall, good-looking, well dressed, great smile . . . that guy?" said Makie.

"Yeah, that guy," chimed in Ken.

"That was Arnold Webster, Margie's cousin from Boston." Makie crossed her arms and gave the Brothers a stinging glare.

"He's very nice. I met him at the Strawberry Festival, and we dated most of last summer while you Neanderthals were in the mountains, fishing and swinging from trees. Mom and Dad think he is a very acceptable young man."

"What's he doing in town now?" asked Franklyn.

"Arnold is going to the university in Seattle, and he's in town staying with Margie and her family for the weekend, if you must know." Makie straightened her posture, a giveaway sign that she had dug in her heels and was prepared for an argument. "He asked me to be his date for the end-of-the-year dance, and I said yes. I'm not a baby anymore, and Mom and Dad said it's okay, so I don't want any trouble from you clowns, understood?"

In the past, a young man inviting Makie to a picnic, school dance, or even a church social without the Brothers' permission could be seen sporting an unexplainable black eye the next day. To make matters even worse, all three of her brothers were natural- born pranksters and took great pleasure in the harassment of many potential suitors. They got away with their impish behavior because it was still the era of "boys will be boys," and they wore this mantle with great pride. When the Brothers heard the malt shop rumors that this out-of-towner, who had yet to seek their approval, had publicly declared his admiration for their little sister and planned to ask her to wear his fraternity pin, they decided it was time to step in. One weekend, on the pretext of getting to know the lad, the Brothers took Arnold out on the town and got him roaring drunk. Arnold was in a total fog when he awoke the next morning to find himself sleeping in a trash bin down by the docks, a place no one went to alone. Arnold never could explain his brand-new tattoo that read "I LOVE CHUCK." Needless to say, the pinning was called off. Makie was livid, but her brothers avidly claimed that the last time they saw Arnold, he was happy and well, having a drink with a very nice young lady in a red boa who, coincidentally, had a tattoo on her thigh just exactly like the one Arnold had gotten on his upper right arm. The Brothers swore an oath they had nothing to do with the misadventure that befell Arnold, but a very dark cloud of skeptical doubt hung over their heads for years. Not long after the Arnold Webster incident, *the* event of the entire school year was fast approaching: the end-of-the-year dance. Adder Toomey, the cliché quarterback of the football team, decided to test his self- perceived popularity against the Brothers' well-known reputation for making rubble out of any young man who dared approach their sister without permission. He would ask Makie to be his date for the dance. Granted, Adder was tall and rather good-looking, but he was also a loudmouth braggart and consummate party animal who considered himself a true gift to all womankind. He prided himself on how much he could drink on any one occasion. Makie grew up just down the street from the Toomeys and was well aware of his boorish reputation, and wanted nothing to do with him. He had never been under consideration as any sort of dating material. When Makie politely turned down Adder's invitation, he couldn't believe his ears. No girl had ever turned him down before. He was dumbstruck, irate, and determined not to take Makie's rejection for an answer. Who did she think she was, anyway? He could have any girl he wanted, and he had chosen her. Didn't she realize what an honor that was? He knew he could bring her around to his way of thinking, so he began his misguided campaign of pressure and pursuit. He would change Makie's mind. Adder harassed her walking to and from school, followed her from class to class, and threatened to trash-talk about her in the boys' locker room. If that weren't bad enough, one early evening, when she was walking home from babysitting for a neighbor, Adder swooped up next to her in his bright-yellow jalopy, picked her up and dumped her in the front seat of his car, and sped off in the direction of the local lovers' lane, a deserted bluff overlooking the city. "Addergoole Toomey, what do you think you are doing? Stop this car right now!" protested Makie.

"I'm not taking you home until you say you're going to the dance with me," said Adder, slurring his words and drinking from a bottle in a brown paper bag as he upped the speed of the car.

Makie felt uncomfortable and nervous. Adder was obviously drunk, driving like a wild man. She had heard the rumors, on more than one occasion, that he had gotten very rough with some of his dates. Then her ire took over.

"Look here, Adder, I've tried to be nice about this, but you're not getting the picture. I wouldn't be seen with you at a mud-wrestling contest. You're a loudmouth, supercilious, alcoholic jerk. Now, stop this car—and I mean *now*—or you'll be sorry, I promise you!"

"Ah, Makie." Adder whipped the car, tires screeching, toward a secluded section of the parking area near the end of the bluff. "You don't know what you're missing, but I aim to show you, darling . . . oh, yes, I aim to show you."

Pure panic spread over Makie as she gripped the door handle, ready to launch into her escape. When the car slammed to a stop, throwing her against the seat, she lost her hold on the handle. Adder grabbed her by the hair, yanking her to him. He pulled her close and kissed her hard and roughly. She could barely breathe as she twisted her head away to avoid his disgusting advances and foul breath. All those past hours of self-defense training she had received from her brothers flashed in front of her eyes. She began kicking, scratching, and hitting him with her fists, but she was no match for his superior strength. He pinned her arms behind her back and slid his free hand under her skirt to her crotch. With one forceful jerk, Adder ripped her panties from her body. He began a drunken attempt at foreplay as Makie struggled to free herself. Adder pushed a button on the side of the passenger's seat. It flopped back flat, and he climbed on top of Makie, almost crushing her with his full weight. He kept her arms pinned, slow and clumsy with the use of one hand, but managed to unbutton her blouse and bra. He kissed her neck, her breasts, her belly, breathing heavily.

"Oh, baby, you smell good enough to eat. I know you want it," moaned Adder.

Makie was beyond panic. She knew if she couldn't think of something fast, she'd be in deep trouble. She could feel the hot tears on her cheeks but couldn't let him know she was so scared. *Stop crying and think,* she lectured herself. Adder continued his solo erotic journey between her legs, where he was totally lost in his depraved fantasies, kissing, invading untouched territory with his tongue. Overcome with his passion, Adder released Makie's arms and reached down to unbuckle his belt and unzip his pants. This gave her just enough room to free one arm. She doubled up her fist. With one swift move, she bashed Adder with an unexpected force, right in the nose, followed by a knee to the groin and deep scratches on his face. Adder released her and sat up in shock and surprise, his face frozen in disbelief. He doubled over in distress. He let out a scream of pain as his nose bled all over his prized school letter sweater. He looked at his bloody hands for a moment while the shock of what had just happened sunk in.

"You bitch!" Adder screamed. "You broke my fucking nose . . . you goddamn bitch!"

"It's just a bloody nose, for crying out loud, not the loss of a limb. And that's just a small example of what's in store for you if you ever put your grubby hands on me again!" Makie slammed the door so hard making her exit that the side mirror broke off.

She pulled her clothing together and started her long walk home in the dark. She was shaking inside—and outside as well, she noted—as she wiped the tears from her face with trembling hands. This time, Adder Toomey had picked on the wrong girl, and she had done as much damage as she could. The Brothers prepared her well, and she was grateful now for all those hours of forced practice in self-protection. Adder, on the other hand, did not come out of the encounter on the winning side. He sported a blackened eye, broken nose, scratched face, painful groin, and a very badly bruised ego.

Makie headed for town, with Adder's screams and curses echoing through the bluffs.

"You'll be sorry, Makie Bane! I'll get even with you, bitch, just you wait and see!" Adder's slightly battered condition wasn't anything compared to what was coming for him once the Brothers got wind of how he had molested their sister. The boys just happened to be sitting on the back stairs when Makie finally returned home and eavesdropped as she angrily related her horrific story to her best friend, Gladdie More, on the kitchen phone.

"It was truly disgusting, Gladdie," said Makie, fighting to hold back her tears. "I was really terrified. I'll never know how I remembered all those things my brothers taught me about selfdefense . . . but I did."

"No, I've decided I'm not going to tell the family," whispered Makie. "In the first place, my mom would be appalled. My dad would likely have him arrested, and who knows? My brothers would probably kill the slimeball and spend the rest of their days in jail. I don't think he'll ever try anything with me again. He's got scars to prove he lost this one. Got to go, Gladdie. Talk to you tomorrow."

Makie hung up the phone and sat in the darkened kitchen to gather her thoughts; waves of sobs welled up and poured out, followed by a river of tears, as she released all her fears and humiliation. She grabbed the dish towel, placing it over her mouth so she wouldn't be heard, and ran to her room, closing and locking the door. Eavesdropping until they had heard every last sordid detail of Adder's assault, the Brothers looked at one another and agreed upon what must be done without having spoken one word.

The next day, after Adder's "Come to Jesus" meeting with the Brothers, he was mysteriously out of school for three weeks and conspicuously absent from the end-of-the-year dance. The story was that an old football injury to his knee had caused him to stumble and fall down a rocky cliff behind the school grounds. Everyone in school had already heard the true story of how 105- pound Makie Bane had beat the shit out of Adder for getting fresh with her, followed by a total trouncing by her brothers, but Adder never mumbled a word about the cause of his injuries, and the humiliation of this experience heaped upon him by the Bane family would boil beneath the surface of his false bravado well into his adult years. Like all young people, Makie had her dreams. Her tall graceful stature fit perfectly into her aspirations to become a professional ballet dancer. She had danced locally all through her school years, and upon graduation, she auditioned for the famed Seattle School of Ballet and was accepted. She was ecstatic about the opportunity to study at such a prestigious school of dance. She planned to become accomplished there, with her final goal being New York City. In the fall of 1931, Makie tearfully said goodbye to friends and family and began her new life as a hopeful prima ballerina. There was no doubt she was in her element, for her talent shone bright among many fine dancers, and soon she was being looked at for starring roles. Her schedule was grueling. She took ballet technique class daily, did rehearsals for upcoming performances, and had studies in music, painting, sculpture, and ballet history. Five nights a week, Makie waited tables, and she loved every minute of her new life. The night of Makie's first solo performance, she stood in the wings watching every move, every arabesque, jeté, and pirouette. She inhaled each moment like the sweet air of a summer night. The music cued. Her moment was arriving. Then it was here. Makie burst onto the stage. Her grace of movement, beauty of expression, and artistic talent lit up the entire stage and garnered her a rousing applause, standing ovation, and four curtain calls. Thad and Arvilla Bane were filled with pride at their daughter's accomplishments. To watch this lovely young woman's hopes and ambitions come true in front of their eyes was breathtaking, a moment they would never forget. This special occasion even touched the Brothers.

They said to one another, "What a wonderful job we did in raising this kid!" They all showered Makie with compliments and flowers. She noticed her dad held her in a hug for longer than usual.

When she pulled back to look at him, she saw tears of pride and love roll down his cheeks.

"I love you too, Dad," said Makie as she returned his long, warm hug with one of her own. Makie was halfway into her second year, with her first starring role coming up in December in *The Nutcracker*, when her dreams came smashing down around her.

The Great Depression, which began not long after the stock market crash of 1929, had gathered a bleak momentum with its decline in industry output and rising levels of unemployment. Failing businesses laid off workers that were beginning to number in the millions, banks were failing left and right, the unemployed had no way to feed their families, and there were no unemployment benefits, food stamps, or welfare payments. There were just families banding together to help one another survive. When Makie's father called to tell her there was no more money for school, Makie was brokenhearted, not only because of the loss of her fantasy, but also because of the pain she heard in his voice and the tears she could tell were falling even over the phone, for he had wanted this journey for her as much as she did, and telling her he couldn't help her reach it anymore nearly killed him. By the time she reached home and stepped off the train, she had managed to pull herself together. She pushed her way through the crowded railway platform, stopping only to adjust her grip on her luggage. When she looked up, there was her dad coming toward her. She dropped her suitcase and raced into his open arms, and they held each other for what seemed like forever. Behind them stood her three strong, handsome brothers. They also hugged her like there was no tomorrow.

"It's okay, little sis," said Franklyn. "Everything will be all right, I promise." "You bet," said Makie.

"We're together, and that's all that counts." "Where's Mom?"

"She's home, fixing your favorite meal," said Ken. "Where else?"

"Well, let's get going, then. I'm starved!" said Makie.

Arm in arm, the Banes left the Seattle Train Station and headed to Everett and home. The next day, Makie was energized by the security of being with her family. She gathered her strength to do what she had to do and never looked back. In the months that followed, she waited tables, worked in the kitchen of the local hospital, exercised horses and cleaned stables, worked as a maid, and eventually landed a job as a reporter for the local radio station, the place where she would meet the love of her life. Maxwell "Max" Calder Jordan stole Makie's heart before she even knew it was missing. He was in town with a traveling air show put on by the US Army intended to interest young men across the country into enlisting in the Air Corps. After his breathtaking display of air maneuvers, he was scheduled to be interviewed at the local radio station.

The minute he walked through the door, Makie's knees began to wobble and her heart pounded out of control. She could barely keep her composure during the interview. Somehow, she brought it off, but she was totally embarrassed, thinking that surely everyone had noticed she was not acting like herself. But Max made her feel so at ease that in no time at all, they were talking like they had known each other for years. Makie invited him home for dinner that very evening. Her mom and dad were charmed by this handsome young fellow, but Makie knew something special had happened when even the Brothers were caught up in Max's charisma and effervescence. Long into her senior years, Makie could close her eyes and vividly recall every moment of that first evening. She remembered Max's insatiable appetite, which pleased her mother no end. She remembered the room filled with laughter and the exchange of fishing and hunting stories as they all acquiesced to the charm and affability of this gregarious stranger with the warm smile and dancing eyes. She remembered that first kiss, when she gave him her hand to say goodbye. He raised her hand to his lips and held it there for what seemed like minutes. His lips were warm and moist. Then he gently turned over her hand and kissed the inside of her palm from fingertips to her wrist. He curled her fingers, pressing them into a tiny fist.

"I'll leave this kiss with you," he said, "and collect it when I take you to dinner tomorrow night. It's a date?" Makie thought she might have nodded, or perhaps she answered yes, although she had no memory of movement or hearing her voice.

She saw his hand wave from the driver's side window as he pulled away and disappeared from sight. It was in that moment that Makie knew this man, this total stranger, would one day be her husband, but what she couldn't possibly know was this rare and precious gift was not one she would be allowed to keep.

CHAPTER 1

The Romance

MAX JORDAN WAS A lean, tall, incredibly handsome young man with a brilliant smile that instantly put everyone he met at ease. His casual nature, tousled flaxen hair, and intense sky-blue eyes mesmerized and captivated any audience of men or women. The evening Makie first invited Max to dinner, he had the family's full attention before the first course was finished. He was all man through and through, enjoying flying, hunting, the out-of- doors, and all sports, but when he gave a woman his attention, she felt like the radiance and warmth of his sun was shining on her and her alone.

After dinner, they strolled out into the backyard and sat in the swing, talking until almost dawn. Makie felt like she had known this man all her life. He was like an old friend that had just come back into her life after a long absence. Max had one more air show to perform in Seattle, and then he had two weeks' leave coming. Upon his return, he took a room in Mrs. Blackwell's boardinghouse, and for the next fourteen days, he and Makie were inseparable. They took the family boat, the *Miss Makyla*, and spent their days investigating the coves and shores of the San Juan Islands.

They both loved the out-of-doors—hiking, picnicking, skiing— but their favorite activity was horseback riding along the cliffs and beaches of the coast just south of Everett, sloshing around the shore, digging up clams.

Then, as the sun floated on the horizon at the end of the day, they enjoyed a good, old-fashioned clambake. Afterward, they snuggled down into the soft sand near the blazing campfire and talked of their dreams and hopes, surrounded by the distant trill of seagulls and the lapping surf. The Brothers truly liked Max. That, Makie assumed, would save him from any of their not-so practical jokes, or so she thought. One warm, sunny afternoon, the Brothers, Makie, and Max went hiking through Coyote Canyon. They finally reached Parson's Meadow, where Makie began spreading out the picnic lunch while the boys cut off to the river for a quick swim. The Brothers had decided to wait until Max was swimming and then steal his clothing, leaving him stranded stark naked in the woods. That would certainly show the true color of the stripes of this young Adonis who was showing big interest in their baby sister.

Max, being wise to their reputation and having overheard part of their scheme, was looking for the perfect opening to teach these three clowns a well-deserved lesson. On the pretext of attempting to undo a huge knot in his boot laces, Max managed to hang back just long enough to let the Brothers strip down and get distracted in their water games, waiting for their chance to hijack Max's clothes. Max watched for his opportunity, and when their attention was completely given over to their games, he gathered up their clothes. When he got back to the meadow, he told Makie, and they laughed so hard their ribs hurt.

"It's high time someone got even with those jokesters," said Makie between fits of laughter, "and oh, do they ever deserve it! I only wish I could see their faces."

"I sure hope they have a sense of humor," said Max with a smile of pure pleasure. "I wouldn't want to take on all three of those bozos at once."

Makie and Max waited until late afternoon, and still no sign of the "three musketeers." They finished their picnic, packed up everything, and headed for the car. Thinking the boys had learned their lesson and not wanting to really leave them stranded totally naked, they festooned the path with pieces of the Brothers' clothing on the bushes, trees, boulders, everywhere, right down to the main road, ending by placing all three sets of boots in a neat row along the roadside. The Brothers finally made their way home well after dark, exhausted, mosquito-bitten, and sunburned in places that had never seen the sun before. They had decided to bypass the path where Max and Makie had left their clothes in favor of an unmarked route home to avoid being seen in the buff. They stood on the porch looking contrite, dressed in three of Mrs. Tucker's abundantly sized dresses they had snatched off her clothesline. Max and Makie had a case of ice-cold beer waiting along with a lumberjack-size steak dinner. Makie's dad couldn't hold back his laughter at the sight of his pranksters finally getting one pulled on them. After the boys showered and dressed, the family sat around the dinner table devouring the feast, talking and laughing into the night. Max had passed the test for family membership in the eyes of her brothers, and Makie loved him all the more for the lasting bond he had created with all the beloved men in her life.

The Halloween Festival was coming soon, and Max wrangled a weekend pass for the event. It would likely be his last leave for a while, because he was to start a monthlong flying tour in the Midwest. The evening of the festival was next to perfect. The night air had begun its journey from crisp to cold. A full harvest moon hung in the sky, lighting the area like a giant backdrop in a play, while dew-laden pine trees scented the air. The Brothers accompanied Makie and Max to the dance, but this time, they were scrubbed and polished and had their own dates. Taking care of Makie's well-being, this unspoken agreement between them, had been enthusiastically turned over to Max, an honor Makie had always thought might never be bestowed on any living male. Makie and Max danced every dance, cherishing every moment they had before his leave ended. They were totally lost in their intimate world.

When the band took a break, they sauntered down to the lake, hand in hand, enjoying the crisp night air and the huge moon that lit their path. By the lake's edge, they took in the mystical beauty of the moon's luster dancing across the water in competition with a thousand stars, and Max pulled Makie to him, holding her face between his hands.

"Makie Bane, I love you more than ice cream on a hot summer's day . . . more than the smell of hot coffee and muffins on a Sunday morning . . . more than my very life. You make my heart race faster than any plane I've ever flown. I can't imagine opening my eyes every day for the rest of my life and not seeing your beautiful face, feeling you lying there in my arms. Will you take all this love that is about to make my heart burst? Will you be my heart's song? Will you marry me?"

He bent down on one knee, reached into his jacket pocket, and produced a lovely gold ring made up of a garland of roses, with a diamond in each rose. Makie's eyes filled with tears as she experienced a joy and tenderness she had never known.

He lifted her up past tiptoe range until she and Max were face- to-face, and all she could say, in a hushed whisper, was "Yes."

Max scooped Makie up into his arms and kissed her slowly, intensely, passionately, and Makie's world would never, ever be the same again. Maxwell Calder Jordan and Makyla Lara Bane were married that Christmas in a quiet, at home ceremony with just close family and friends in attendance. For the next four years, Makie lived every girl's dream with the man she adored, and every day was a celebration. One crisp fall morning in September of 1935, Anne Elizabeth Jordan was born. Her parents finally had their prayers answered, the start of their family.

Max's love affair with his new daughter was instant and deep. "Listen to her tiny voice," whispered Max.

"She sounds just like a little cricket."

And from that day forward, Cricket became her name. By 1939, the world had begun to churn with unrest and danger abroad. Germany invaded Poland and Britain. France had declared war on Germany. There were blockades and shoot-on sight orders for any ship threatening US ships. The air shows were discontinued, as war for the United States was starting to look inevitable. The conversations among young men had changed from sports to the rising threats from Europe. More and more of these spirited young pillars of our future talked of joining the fight, protecting democracy. Cricket's mom, the perfect Air Force wife, never complained; she simply followed Max's assignments wherever they led. He was eventually posted at Pearl Harbor, Hawaii, under the command of Lieutenant Colonel James Doolittle, training young fliers in the B-25 twin-engine bomber.

These normally land-based planes would go on to carry out a daring surprise attack on Tokyo in April of 1942 from the deck of the aircraft carrier USS *Hornet*. By the end of September 1941, after eight months of the Germans blasting London nightly by dropping more than 190,000 tons of bombs, Germany gave up its attempt to conquer Britain by air, with German losses of more than twenty-six thousand planes. That was more than enough for Cricket's dad. He made arrangements for Cricket and Makie to return to the States to live with his father, who owned a large cattle ranch in the San Joaquin Valley, in California, a safe distance from the coast. Max was sure war was just a matter of time, and he didn't want his wife and child stranded away from the safety of the United States when the carnage began. To this day, Cricket can close her eyes and recall the smell of the flower-scented Hawaiian breeze that washed over her as the three of them stood on the dock in Honolulu, waiting for Cricket and her mother to board the vessel that would take them away. Max kept a cheery mood about him as he tried to make the departure as painless as possible. But Cricket could feel her mom's heart breaking. Makie held Max so close they seemed to become one. When it was Cricket's turn, Max lifted her up into his arms, holding her unusually tight and close. When they were face-to-face, Cricket could see his eyes fill with tears as he looked at her with an intensity she had never seen before. Neither one of them could hold back their pain and sorrow. "Always remember, my little Cricket, I love you and your mom more than fresh air and sunshine, and no distance between us will ever change that. Do you believe me?" Max attempted to choke back his tears, to no avail.

"Yes, Daddy, I believe you. But can't we stay, Daddy? Please don't make us go . . . please." She threw her small arms around his neck and began to sob.

Max held Cricket even closer, rocking her back and forth. "Here, here," he said, pulling an initialed handkerchief from his pocket. "Let's wipe those tears away."

He removed his aviator wings from his uniform, wrapped them in the hankie, and pressed them into Cricket's small hand.

"Anytime you feel lonely, look at my wings and know that wherever I am, I'll hear you, and even though you can't see me, I'll be there with you, okay?"

"All right, Daddy. But you'll come home soon, won't you?" "You bet, my little Cricket." He smiled. "I promise. But until

then, remember I'm always here in your heart . . . no matter what." The ship's horn let out a loud blast, and the smokestacks sent billows of clouds upward, signaling its imminent departure. Max and Makie threw their arms around each other in one final embrace, then Makie grabbed Cricket's hand, and they scrambled up the gangplank and squeezed themselves into a spot along the railing.

They searched for Max's face in the crowd below.

"There he is, Mom," said Cricket, pointing between the rails toward a large stack of boxes along the dock's edge.

She began to call out her father's name, waving her arms to get his attention. Max spotted them too and returned their wave. The ship began to slowly move along the pier, its horn blasting so loudly they could barely hear the people yelling goodbye to their loved ones. Makie held Cricket up so she could see over the railing. There they stood, watching Max, the dock, and the harbor slowly disappear as they set out to sea. They squinted at the horizon until they lost sight of land and were surrounded only by the boundless ocean and undulating waves. A thick shroud of loneliness kept Cricket and Makie in place, their eyes searching the horizon for the vanishing island long after it had disappeared from view and the sun had begun to set. That first night at sea, Cricket climbed into bed with her mother, and as they snuggled close, she closed her eyes very tightly, trying to hold on to the memory of her dad's face and the sound of his voice. But all she could see was the space between herself and her dad widening as their ship began its journey across the Pacific.

Could there ever be any space or distance as vast, wide, or lonely as the expanding space created by the leaving of someone you love? *I don't think so,* thought Cricket. And so she had her first experience as a neophyte in the club called Reality.

"Hello, God, this is Cricket here," she whispered, so as not to wake her mom. "I thought you might not be able to find me because I'm on a big ship in the middle of an ocean. We're headed to my grandpa's ranch in California. You can find me there for a while until my daddy comes to get us. I know you're busy working out this awful thing that's going on all over the world, but I sure would be grateful if you could keep an eye on my dad, because he's alone now, miles and miles away from us. I don't understand about war and why people have to hurt one another to win an argument. Oh, look, God, my dad gave me this before we left." Cricket reached under her pillow and pulled out the hankie that contained her dad's Air Force wings. "See, God? Wings, just like your angels. Does that make me sort of an angel too? I hope so. I'd love to be able to help you with all you have to do. Well, God, I just wanted you to know where I am, you know, just in case. Bless my dad, my grandparents, and good luck with this war thing. You're going to need it. Good night!"

Cricket and Makie arrived in the States in the early fall of 1941. Max's mom had died when he was a teenager, so he was raised by his father and his five uncles. Cricket had never met her grandfather on her dad's side, and her curiosity began to build as they came closer to the end of their journey. As Cricket stood on the dock in the midst of the pushing and shoving of a plethora of people arriving and others rushing to greet arriving passengers, her vision was only of legs and luggage rushing in all directions. Soon, a pair of long- legged jeans wearing a large pair of cowboy boots stood before her. A deep male voice greeted her mother, and before she knew it, she was being lifted up into the arms of this total stranger.

"I'm your grandpa George," he said. "Nice to meet ya! Let's head for home."

Grandpa George was a tall rugged-looking man with sandy gray hair, a face of weather-worn wrinkles, bushy eyebrows that arched over his squinted blue eyes—eyes the color of her dad's— and rough, well-used hands, scratchy like sandpaper.

"Are you my daddy's dad?" asked Cricket with some trepidation. "Yep," he answered.

That was about all the conversation for the time being. His nature was pleasant, but the man wasted no words and wasn't given to meaningless chitchat. It was difficult to gauge his mood by his expressions, which were inscrutable and often hidden in the shadow of his large Stetson hat. But there was no doubt that behind this gruff exterior was a man who loved and adored his only son. Cricket and Makie were given a small but adequate cottage near the big ranch house, and Makie had it feeling like home in no time at all. It had a cozy little living room with a well-functioning fireplace that kept out the fall chill and the damp gloom of the San Joaquin Valley's thick winter fog. The kitchen overlooked a garden path that led to a large pond surrounded by tall wispy willows and was often occupied by a family of ducks and the occasional regal snowy egret. The second story of the cottage held two comfy bedrooms with dormer windows and down filled beds and pillows. The furniture in Cricket's room once belonged to Max's older sister, who had died in a car accident many years earlier. There was a white wrought iron canopy bed, a small white desk and chair, a tall white dresser, and a stand-alone oval full-length mirror. Some of the ranch hands helped Makie paint the inside of the cottage and refinish the wooden plank floors.

Grandpa George hung a large two-seater swing on the front porch. It had soft cushions and big comfy pillows. A place Cricket and her mom would sit in the evenings, exchanging talk of their activities of the day and reading Max's letters. Max's uncle Jeb owned the local newspaper, the *Valley Post*. He was delighted to have Makie as a member of the staff and placed her in charge of a daily column directed at the challenges of running a household, raising children, and keeping the home fires burning during these hard times. Mrs. Munos, Grandpa George's longtime housekeeper, enjoyed having a young girl around the house and kept an eye on Cricket while Makie was at work. Cricket also spent a great deal of her time with her grandpa George. He bought her a pair of cowboy boots and taught her to ride a pony. When he needed to leave the confines of the ranch on horseback, he would set her snuggly in front of him in the saddle, and they would ride the outback of the ranch, checking fence lines, or ride to town for an errand that always included a trip to the ice cream shop. On these rides, he would tell Cricket all kinds of wonderful stories about her dad when he was a small boy and the times the father and son spent together.

"Before your dad was fifteen years old, he could beat anyone in a barrel race, calf-roping, and wrestling a steer to the ground for branding." The pride in her grandfather's voice rang loud and clear, even to Cricket's young ears.

"He had a wonderful sidekick, a red-white-and-black Australian shepherd named Sheila. The two of them were inseparable. Her ample multicolored coat served as a blanket for both of them on the coldest of nights. Sheila's intense blue eyes were a match for your dad's, and there wasn't a living thing that walked, crawled, slithered, or flew that could escape Sheila's keen sense of sight, smell, or hearing. When the two of them spent days and a few nights in the outback of the ranch, camping and looking for strays, Sheila's nights were spent keeping watch over her friend and master." Max knew every inch of the ranch and planned to be a rancher one day, until he fell in love with flying. Max's uncle Jake took him to the county fair one fall when he was almost sixteen. A friend of Uncle Jake's was a crop duster and stunt pilot and made some extra money traveling to the fairs around the county, taking fairgoers on rides. Max coaxed his uncle into letting him go on his very first plane ride. That did it! From that day on, all Max dreamed of was flying. He saved every cent he earned to take flying lessons. Then when he turned eighteen, he joined the Air Corps and eventually became one of their top ace pilots. Cricket could sense some sadness in Grandpa George's voice when the story came to the part where Max left the ranch for a flying career, but she could also feel the esteem, respect, and love he had for his son. Makie and Cricket were doing pretty well in their new life on the ranch, under the circumstances. Makie loved her job at the paper, and Cricket was doing well in school, and she was making new friends.

The Indian summer had passed, and the crispness in the air gave notice of the winter to come. One day just after Halloween, Cricket was playing in her room when she heard her mom on the phone downstairs. She sounded giddy with joy as she called out to her.

"Cricket, hurry down here! It's your dad on the phone! He wants to talk to you."

Cricket jumped up, running so fast down the stairs she almost tripped when she reached for the phone.

"Hi, Daddy, how are you? Where are you, Daddy. Are you coming home? When?" Max could barely get a word into the conversation, but finally, he managed to tell her that yes, he had been given a short leave and would be home in a few days.

Makie and Cricket were ecstatic with joy and dizzy with excitement. Without even stopping to grab a sweater, they dashed to the big house to tell Grandpa George the great news. It was the first time they had seen his face actually register a broad scope of emotions as he broke into a huge, wide smile, picked Makie up and twirled her across the kitchen, and gave them both one of his big bear hugs. The seconds, minutes, hours, and days seemed to move in slow motion, each one longer than the last. Then finally, the day that Max was coming home arrived. Makie got all dressed up, adding a new red flowered hat to her attire that matched her lipstick. Cricket had new hair ribbons, and Makie spent all her rations stamps to get her a new pair of patent leather shoes. Grandpa George loaded all of them into his 1941 Ford truck, and off they went to the train station, a forty-five-minute drive from the ranch. They all stood on the station platform, awaiting the train's arrival, too excited to sit down. At last, from a long way off, the wail of a train whistle announced its imminent appearance.

Then suddenly, there it was, the huge black engine chugging and steaming its way toward the platform. It felt like all of them were holding their breath as they watched one passenger after another exit the train.

Then as the steam began to clear, there he was, tall and so handsome in his uniform, standing on the last rung of the train steps, ready to launch in their direction. Makie raced to Max and into his waiting, outstretched arms.

Grandpa George caught Cricket's hand as she started toward her father and quietly whispered in her ear, "Let's give them a minute to themselves, Button Nose, just a little minute."

She tried to restrain herself, but that minute seemed like hours. Finally, she couldn't wait any longer. Ripping her hand from Grandpa George's grip, she ran to join her parents, calling, "Daddy, Daddy!" Max scooped her up, and she threw her arms around his neck, and the three of them stood there in a trio hug she wished would last forever. Grandpa George stepped up, gazing at his son's face like he was drawing a treasure map. He reached out to shake Max's hand then grabbed it, pulled him close, and gave him one of his famous bear hugs.

"Welcome home, son," he said in his deep, throaty voice. "Welcome home!" Were those actually tears Cricket saw in the eyes of that gruff old gentle giant? That night was better than Christmas, birthdays, and Easter put together. Mrs. Munos prepared a hearty roast beef dinner with all of Max's favorite side dishes. Grandpa George pulled out two hidden bottles of wine he had saved for a special occasion just like this. Even Cricket was allowed to have a small shot glass of wine mixed with water to celebrate with the adults. Mrs. Munos surprised Max with his favorite dessert, too, her special double- crusted apple pie. The candles on the dinner table almost burned to a puddle of wax before everyone finished talking. Cricket fell asleep snuggled deep into her father's arms. He gently lifted her and carried her to the spare room next to Mrs. Munos's room, where he tucked her into bed.

Max stood for a minute, looking down at his daughter in her slumber. He gently brushed the curls from her eyes, kissed her on her forehead, and whispered, "God bless you, my little Cricket. We've handed you a lousy world to grow up in, but I'll do what I can to make it a little better. Sleep tight."

Max and Makie strolled under a full moon, headed toward the cottage for some time alone. His leave was short, and time, a precious commodity. The moonlight lit their way. A lone coyote was heard in the distance calling his mate. Reaching the porch, Max stopped, turned toward Makie, and stared into her questioning eyes.

"God, I love you, Makie. Sometimes I don't think I can bear being away from you and Cricket for one more minute, but . . ."

Makie slowly placed her fingers against his lips. "I know, Max, I know."

Max kissed Makie long and hard with a hunger their separation had brought both of them. It was like the first time all over again for Makie. Then Max picked her up, cradled her in his strong arms, closed the porch door behind them, and slowly climbed the stairs. The next five days were wondrous. Max, Makie, and Cricket spent every minute together. They all bundled up like snowmen and had a picnic down by the pond. They went riding on Max's favorite trails around the outback of the ranch, with him showing Cricket some of the places he and Sheila had camped in when he was a boy. They took in a movie in town and even had dinner at a fancy restaurant with white linen tablecloths and waiters in black tuxedos.

Grandpa George gave a large party for Max's friends and the family, and Makie heard stories about her husband she had never heard before. These last days were filled with love, with laughter, with them talking into the early morning hours, recalling the joys of the past and hopes and dreams of tomorrow, making memories that would have to last for a lifetime. The time was passing way too fast. November 8, the date of the end of Max's leave, rushed toward them and, before they knew it, they all stood on the station platform, in solemn silence, just where they had stood a few days before in total jubilance.

"Max, any chance you can get back for Christmas?" asked Makie.

"I don't know. Things aren't looking good. It's a real mess out there, and I don't see how we can avoid getting into this damn war." Max shook his head in disgust. "But you know, if I get the chance, I'll grab it in a second." He took her gently in his arms.

"You be strong for our girl, Makie, and know I love you both beyond measure. I'll always be near you, right here in your heart, no matter where in hell they send me. Kiss my little girl for me and kiss her often, for she's the best part of both of us, understand?"

Then he kissed her in a long and tender embrace that lifted her feet slowly off the platform floor as they disappeared into the billowing steam that exploded from the train's engine. The train began its journey away from them. Max stood on the open platform of the caboose, waving until he disappeared from sight. They stood staring into the blank distance as if they were glued in place. The quiet of the now-empty station platform was deafening, the ride home solemn and silent. That night, Cricket could hear her mom crying into her pillow, the same pillow where Max had laid his head that morning. Makie held the pillow close, straining to retrieve any detectable scent of Max's Bay Rum aftershave.

Cricket tiptoed into her mother's room. "Please don't cry, Mom. We'll be okay." They wrapped their arms around each other, and Makie fell asleep with unused sobs still throbbing in her chest.

Before sleeping, Cricket reached into her pajama pocket, pulled out her dad's aviator wings, and began her silent prayers.

"Hello, God, this is Cricket speaking. I hope you had a good day. I know how busy you must be with all that's going on. Thanks for letting my dad come home for a few days, but I wish he could have stayed a little longer. Mom and I feel awful sad now that he has gone. He said he had a lot to do to make this world a safer place for Mom and me, but if you don't mind me saying so, I thought that keeping the world in order was your job. "I've been reading the papers when Mom and Grandpa aren't looking, and I've tried, but I just don't understand this war thing. It's very confusing, scary, and it worries me a lot. How can people be so mean to one another? Killing one another with bombs and guns. And why? Maybe you could have Grandpa George explain it to me. He has a way with words that makes everything seem all right, whenever he decides to talk, that is. "Oh, remember that A I promised I would get in spelling? Well, I did it just for you. It's sitting right on my desk, if you would like to see it. After your birthday, when I go back to school, I'll try for another A, this time in math, which is my hardest subject. "One more thing, God. I hate to ask for a favor, with you being so busy and all, but I need to find a way to help Mom not feel so sad all the time while Dad is away. That would make Dad happy too, because he says her smile lights up the world, and that should please you a lot. Give it some thought, and we'll talk tomorrow. God, bless Dad, Mom, my grandparents. Thank you, God. Good night!"

December wasn't the usual cheery month it had always been. Oh, yes, the Christmas decorations were up, a beautifully decorated tree stood tall with ornaments and twinkling lights in the corner of the big ranch house living room, the house was filled with mistletoe, boughs, and ribbons. But something was missing, and there was a wide hole in everyone's heart that no one knew how to fill. Sundays were always special, a friends-and-family sort of day around the ranch. Mrs. Munos didn't work on Sundays and was usually off attending early Mass. Grandpa George loved to cook, and a Sunday brunch was his favorite meal. Most of his brothers and their families would show up to join the table along with any ranch hands who weren't working. It was around midmorning, and everyone had just returned from church. Grandpa George was starting to prepare his famous Sunday meal. Makie was setting the table as Uncle Jake's car skidded to a stop in the driveway.

"Turn on the radio! Turn on the radio!" he hollered as he ran up the porch steps and through the kitchen door.

Everyone pulled up chairs, gathering around the now-blaring radio in the living room. They all sat like mummies, listening to the unbelievable, horrific broadcast. It seemed surreal and nightmarish. "The Japanese have bombed Pearl Harbor," the announcer proclaimed. One by one, the large living room filled with uncles, aunts, and friends until the kitchen was empty. No one said a word as they all sat there in a trance, staring at the radio. Cricket searched the faces of the adults around her for any familiar expression that would tell her what had happened, but no one moved or spoke. They acted like they were expecting someone to announce this was a play, a joke, another Orson Welles production designed to terrify the public. But it wasn't a joke or a play; it was real, and everyone in that room knew Max was probably right in the middle of all this horror and devastation. It wasn't until days later that the whole story, with details, came out. At 7:55 on the morning of December 7, 1941, 360 Japanese planes attacked the Pacific Fleet in Pearl Harbor, Hawaii. The United States lost the battleships *Arizona*, *California*, *Oklahoma*, *West Virginia*, and *Utah*. The attack also destroyed 174 planes and damaged four battleships, three cruisers, and three destroyers, and hundreds of lives were lost.

Grandpa George's face was expressionless and stoic, as usual, but there was something in his eyes that gave away his underlying fears. Makie had lost all color from her now-ashen white face and needed to steady herself by holding on to the back of a chair. A few seconds later, she collapsed, motionless, on the floor. Cricket felt the breath go out of her body seeing her mother lying there pale and seemingly lifeless. She raced to her side and began to cry and held her mother's head in her lap, stroking her hair.

"Mommy, Mommy, wake up! What's wrong?"

Uncle Jake's wife, Aunt Penny, wrapped her arms around the terrified Cricket. "Come on, child, your mother will be all right. Let's go outside for a breath of fresh air."

Cricket struggled to stay by her mother's side, but Uncle Jake came to his wife's rescue, picking up the hysterical child and taking Cricket out to the swing on the front porch. Aunt Penny comforted Cricket, hugging her warmly, and offered an age-appropriate explanation of the situation. Meanwhile, Uncle Jake returned to the living room and carried Makie to the guest room, where Doc Perkins, a usual guest for Sunday brunches, attended to her. The rest of the day was abuzz with phone calls, people coming in and out, and constant updates on the radio. Aunt Penny had assured Cricket everything would be all right, but she sensed the adult tension, fear, and disbelief.

Aunt Penny was sweet but not realistic when it came to fooling a child. Cricket knew things were not going to be okay; nothing so awful could become okay all of a sudden. Where could she turn to get the real truth? It wasn't a good time to ask her mom, who seemed to have picked up a flu bug and wasn't feeling very well, and Grandpa George was totally distracted trying to get in touch with Max. So Cricket turned to her trusted old friend. "Hello, God. It's Cricket. We heard the bad news this morning on the radio. Something this horrible must have been a big surprise to you too! All those soldiers, sailors killed in the bombing. What on earth could have made the Japanese so angry that they would do something as horrible as that? I heard people saying that my daddy must be in the middle of this mess. It scared Mommy so bad she fainted. Could you please find a minute to check on my dad for us? Everyone around me is very, very upset, and I don't know what to do to help. Any suggestions would be very much appreciated, and if there is anything I can do for you to help out, just let me know. God, please bless my daddy, wherever he is, Mommy, and my grandparents. Thanks, God, and good night!"

Cricket took out the hankie from under her pillow, unwrapped the aviator wings, and held them tightly in her small hands. "Daddy, wherever you are, Mom and I miss you something awful and pray you are safe and will come home soon. Can you hear me, Daddy? Good night."

Days later, Cricket, who had been able to read since she was four years old, began a secret and relentless search, devouring each page of the newspaper in an attempt to understand this catastrophic event that had changed her world. Her vocabulary expanded to include such words as *carnage, butcher, slaughter, hostility, horrendous, appalling, annihilation* and *bloodshed.* On December 8, 1941, the United States declared war on Japan. On December 11, 1941, the United States declared war on Germany and Italy, and World War II was in full swing around the globe, and the dark predictions that Max had spoken of became factual, with devastation to a degree that no one could have imagined. Max was killed during the bombing of Pearl Harbor in an attempt to get his plane off the runway and into the air to fight the Japanese. He was deemed a hero and received, posthumously, the Medal of Honor. Makie took to her bed, for the grief was intolerable. Grandpa George retreated into his work around the ranch, and Cricket just sat and waited for something to happen to bring her loved ones back into her life. That would take a miracle, she thought, a really big miracle. She prayed for it every night, and then on Christmas Eve, just like the three wise men had believed, it happened. A miracle. The family was sitting around the living room, exchanging gifts and trying to pretend it was a normal Christmas Eve, just for Cricket's sake. Uncle Eli was playing Christmas songs on his guitar, and Mrs. Munos was serving hot cocoa and a huge plate of homemade Christmas cookies. A real Currier and Ives portrait, at least on the surface.

"Cricket," said Grandpa George, "there's something your dad wanted me to ask Santa about, something he wanted Santa to bring you, but I decided I'd like to do that myself, so come on over here, Button Nose, and open this here box by my chair."

Something from my dad, thought Cricket, and then a big smile crossed her face for the first time in weeks. "What is it, Grandpa? What did Daddy want me to have?"

"You'll just have to open this box and find out," said Grandpa, with an equally broad smile.

She removed the big blue ribbon with great care, peeled back the paper, and slowly raised the lid. Then, as all eyes in the room were on her, she removed the lid, and there it was, an eight-week- old ball of fur, an Australian shepherd puppy, mostly white, with multicolored markings and eyes so blue they looked transparent. Just like Max's dog. Cricket picked it up and held it close to her chest, hugging and kissing the wiggly little thing.

"Oh, Grandpa, it's beautiful! Is it a girl or a boy?" "It's a girl," he said.

"Can I name her Sheila, like my daddy's dog?"

"You name her anything you please," said Grandpa, kissing Cricket on the forehead.

Sheila was passed around the room, to everyone's delight, with a reaction only a fuzzy little puppy can bring. The gloomy undercurrent of the room was changed instantly to the joy, hope, and warmth this holiday usually brings. "Look, Mom, look what Dad wanted Santa to bring me! Isn't she just wonderful?"

"She's definitely the most beautiful pup ever," said Makie, giving her daughter a huge hug. "Merry Christmas, darling."

"Cricket," she added, "I have something your dad and I wanted to give you too. It had to be special ordered, so it won't arrive until sometime in September this coming fall. It's a baby brother or sister."

The room fell suddenly quiet for a moment, then the whole family got to their feet, smiling, laughing, and congratulating Makie on the wonderful news. A new baby, a new life, an affirmation of joy and hope. What a gift, not just to Cricket, but to the entire family as well. Grandpa George looked down at Makie, with huge tears rolling down his weathered checks.

"God bless you, girl, God bless you." He gave her a gentle kiss on the cheek.

That night, Cricket's prayers were full of joy and gratitude. "God, happy birthday to your Son, and thank you so much for a wonderful Christmas Eve. I just knew you could think of something to make my mom smile again, and you sure picked a winner. I never would have thought of a baby brother or sister, but then you're God, and you think of everything. I'd like to put in my request for a brother, someone like Dad we can name Max. I don't know how long it takes to make a baby, so I hope I'm not too late for this request. Say hello to my dad for me. Ask him if he needs his wings back now that he's a real angel. Tell him about the new baby and my puppy and let him know that I love him very much. God, bless Mom and my grandparents. Good night, God."

Cricket's dreams were a mixture of joy and sadness. The new puppy and the prospect of a baby brother or sister were more wonderful than she could have ever imagined, but the loss of her dad left a deep wound in her heart that she doubted would ever heal. The war continued on, with the news getting worse every day. Other families had begun to receive notices of the loss of a loved one. *What a stupid thing,* Cricket thought, *fighting and killing people over a piece of land or a political philosophy. I hate war, and I bet God does too. I hope whoever started this thing is in deep trouble with him, and I hope he grounds them with no dessert for . . . well, forever.* Cricket's view of the world and adults, seen through the eyes of a child, would take on a more personal nature in her very near future. She would begin to understand the true meaning of the word *fear*, the real meaning of evil, and the painful senselessness of the taking of an innocent life.

CHAPTER 4

The Train Ride

CRICKET HAD AN AWFUL time falling asleep the night before the "big day." Her excitement about her impending train trip to visit her mother's parents, Grandpa and Grandma Bane, was overwhelming. It was somewhere in the same category as Christmas Eve or the day before her birthday, mixed with the anxiety of an unexpected test at school. Under all this excitement lay Cricket's growing fears concerning the expanding war, her inability to grasp the meaning of this savagery and its effect on her family, plus her apprehension over her uncertain status once the baby was born.

"Dear God," Cricket started her prayers, "Cricket here. I wish you were here where I can see you. Maybe sit on your lap and have a nice, long talk. There is so much I don't know. When someone you love dies, can your heart really break? I miss my dad so much it sure feels like something is broken. Mom is both sad and happy. Not having Dad around makes her very sad, but the thought of the new baby makes her happy again. Grandpa George doesn't say much, but at Dad's memorial, I saw the tears rolling down his face, and his body was shaking with sadness when they handed Mom the flag from his coffin. Remember Dad gave me his aviator wings before he went away, God?" Cricket reached under her pillow, retrieved the neatly folded hankie, and lovingly folded back the corners to reveal the treasured prize within. "See, God? Look! Aren't they beautiful? Sort of like the wings of Michael the archangel, don't you think? Dad gave them to me so I would always know he's forever with me wherever he might be posted, and I guess, if Dad can't be here with us, I'm glad he is posted with you. Good night, Dad." Cricket rewrapped the wings in the hankie with great care, placing them under her pillow. "And the same to you, God. I'll see you on the train tomorrow."

As the sun began to wake, spreading her early morning rays of pink and purple across the sky, Cricket, too, opened her eyes to meet this exciting new day. It was a typical summer morning in the San Joaquin Valley. The temperature soon rose with the sun, changing the pleasant morning air into the heat sent by a sun-bleached sky. She tiptoed down the stairs, crossed the garden, and went into the ranch house. There she found Grandpa George sitting at the kitchen table, reading the morning paper and sipping his usual mug of coffee. He slid his reading glasses down his nose and looked over them at Cricket.

"Want a cup, Tenderfoot?" he asked in his usual nonemotional manner.

"Sure, Grandpa, fill her up."

Although this was their usual morning ritual, it always made Cricket feel quite grown-up, even though it really wasn't an honest- to-God cup of coffee. More like a cup of milk with a coffee floater.

"You all ready for your trip?"

"I think so," said Cricket, sipping her coffee. "Mom helped me pack last night."

"We're going to miss you around here. I mean, who am I going to have my morning coffee with? No one around here gets up early enough to sit with me for coffee."

"I'll miss you too," said Cricket as she climbed up on Grandpa George's lap and put her tiny hand in his.

"Take care of Mom for me, will you? She's already so lonely without Dad. I hear her crying at night when she thinks I can't hear. She keeps his last letter under her pillow and reads it over and over. Maybe you can think of something that would make her feel better?"

"Not to worry, Button Nose. I'll take care of everything. You just have a good time and hurry home."

"What's up with you two?" said Makie, stepping through the screen door into the kitchen. "Hope you didn't drink all the coffee, Cricket." Makie gave them both a big hug and smile. "Finish up, Cricket, and go get yourself dressed while I fix breakfast. I've laid your clothes out on your bed. We don't want to miss the train."

"Don't forget what we were talking about," Cricket whispered in her grandfather's ear as she climbed off his lap. Grandpa George gave her a wink and a thumbs-up as she headed out the kitchen door.

A few steps onto the garden path, and she realized she had left her slippers under the kitchen table. Racing back to the ranch house, she hesitated for just a second at the sound of her mother's voice.

"I sure hope I've done the right thing sending Cricket north this year. It's just that . . . she had so much fun with my parents and . . . with losing Max and all . . . I just thought it might help her to have a change of scenery and—"

"She'll be just fine, Makie," said Grandpa George, reaching across the table to pat Makie's hand. "That little girl of ours is a lot stronger than we think she is. You did right getting her out of here for a while. A change will do her good. Gives an old fossil like me time to regroup too."

It made Cricket feel good to hear her grandfather compliment her for being strong, an attribute she wasn't so sure she really had. She quietly backed off the porch and ran home to get ready for her trip. They all piled into the front seat of Grandpa George's pickup truck and headed for the station, leaving the ranch behind. Halfway there, they came across a young man dressed in a Navy uniform hitchhiking along the side of the road. Grandpa George pulled to a stop, and the young man came running up to the driver's window. "Need a lift, young man?" said Grandpa George. "Sure could use one, sir," the young man answered. "Where you headed?" asked Grandpa George.

"The train station in Fresno, sir. My leave is up, and I'm shipping out. Got to get back to base."

"Hop in, young man," said Grandpa George. "That's where we're headed. I'd be honored to give you a lift."

"Thanks." The young man slung his duffel bag into the bed of the truck, and using the duffel as a seat, he settled in with his back to the cab of the truck, and the journey continued.

"Grandpa George, why did you say it was an honor to give the sailor a ride?" said Cricket.

"Because," he answered, "this young man and thousands like him, like your dad, are out there fighting for their country and our well-being, and they deserve any help we can give them. A ride to the station is the least we can do, don't you think so, Cricket?"

"Sure, Grandpa. Helping them is a great idea. I'll try to remember to do that too."

When they arrived at the station, the young man jumped down from the truck, grabbed his duffel, and said, "Thanks, folks. Sure appreciate the lift." Grandpa George gave him a hardy handshake, pressing a twenty-dollar bill into the young man's hand.

"Oh, no, sir, I can't take—"

"Take it, son. I hope someone would do the same for my boy." The two clasped hands again, exchanging a long, knowing look before the young sailor saluted Grandpa George and disappeared into the rush and crush of the crowd. Grandpa George placed Cricket's luggage on the platform and went into the office to collect her train ticket. She and Makie stood there in silence, both of them remembering the last time they had stood on that very spot, waving goodbye to Cricket's dad. She snuggled up to her mom, holding her hand. She closed her eyes and replayed in her heart the moment her dad disappeared into the distance as his train moved out of sight. Makie gave Cricket's hand an understanding squeeze as they waited for Grandpa George's return.

"The train's right on time." Grandpa George's voice jolted them both back into the present. "It should be here in a few minutes."

Finally, off in the distance came the train's whistle moaning its intended arrival, and then there it was, huffing and puffing its way into the station, billows of steam spreading everywhere on the station platform.

"Goodbye, Grandpa George," said Cricket, giving him a huge hug and kiss. "Remember what we talked about over coffee, okay?" "You bet. Now, don't you worry about a thing," he said, lifting

her up into the train's doorway along with her luggage. "I'll take care of everything, I promise."

Makie boarded with Cricket to help her find her seat and get her settled.

"Cricket, this is Mr. Washington." She looked up from her book to see her mom bringing a tall dark man with her. "He's the porter and will watch over you during your trip. If you have any questions, Mr. Washington is here to help you."

"How do you do, Mr. Washington?" Cricket said, noting her mother's approval. "I'm going to visit my grandparents. Will you be on the train during the whole trip?"

"Why, yes, Miss Cricket, I sure will."

Turning to Makie, he said, "Now, don't you worry one little bit, Mrs. Jordan, ma'am. Miss Cricket and I will do just fine, and I'll watch over her just like she's my own."

Mr. Washington looked very official in his neatly pressed uniform. His creamy, chocolate-colored skin framed a large bright smile. His eyes had a gentle twinkle, and his friendly laugh filled the room with warmth and reassurance. He had worked for the railroad since he was a young boy, as had his father before him, and took great pride in taking on the comfort and safety of every passenger in his charge. The train began to move as Cricket waved through the window to her family standing on the platform. Makie pulled a hankie from her purse to dab away the tears. Grandpa George put his arm around Makie's shoulders and gave her a comforting squeeze as they returned Cricket's wave.

Soon they disappeared out of sight, and Cricket settled back into her seat to watch the city, farms, and highways speed past her window. Well, she was in it now. Too late to change her mind. She missed Mom and Grandpa already. *Oh, well,* she thought, *I' ll see Grandma and Grandpa Bane tomorrow, and then everything will be all right.*

"Excuse me, Miss Cricket," said Mr. Washington. "It's almost lunchtime, and I'll be taking you to the dining car. I'm going to seat you with a real nice lady, Mrs. Parker. She's traveling to Seattle too. You two ladies will get along just fine."

"Thanks, Mr. Washington." Cricket leaned over and whispered in his ear, "You know, I've been on a train before, and I know how to do all this stuff."

"Oh, sure, Miss Cricket," he whispered back. "I know that. It's just that . . . well, you know I promised your ma I'd look after you, and you've got to let me do my job, okay?"

"Well . . . all right, Mr. Washington, but let me walk in front of you so nobody knows you're watching over me like I was a baby or something."

"That will do just fine, Miss Cricket. You go ahead of me, and I'll follow so no one will even know I'm with you." Mr. Washington said this with a wide grin and a soft chuckle.

With all the prim and proper attitude of what Cricket perceived a grown woman to have, she put back on her white gloves, brushed the wrinkles from the skirt of her dress, adjusted her hair ribbon, and picked up her small purse. With head held high, keeping in mind her posture, she proceeded down the moving hallway toward the dining car, with Mr. Washington a respectable distance behind. Next to sleeping overnight in her very own berth, having meals in the dining car was her most favorite part of the train travel. The tables were all set with spotless white table linen and glimmering silverware and glasses. Each table had a small vase of fresh flowers and a wonderful view of the moving landscape. To select and order your meal, the waiter would hand you a menu and a printed card and pencil to write down your selection. Cricket prayed that longhand wasn't required, since she only knew how to print. The train was very crowded, mostly with military personnel from all branches of the service scrambling to get home for their leave or return to base, like the young sailor who had ridden in the back of Grandpa George's truck.

Cricket seemed to get lost in the crush of so many people coming and going in such a narrow hallway. She was about to panic when she felt a gentle hand on her shoulder and looked up to see Mr. Washington smiling down on her. She reached for Mr. Washington's hand, returning his smile, and they proceeded to the dining car.

"Excuse me, Mrs. Parker, ma'am," said Mr. Washington. "This here is Miss Annie Elizabeth Jordan, and she's headed to Seattle to spend the summer with her grandfolks. I thought you two ladies might enjoy each other's company."

"Why, thank you, Mr. Washington," said Mrs. Parker, offering them both a friendly smile. "I'd be delighted to have the company of such a charming young lady. Please sit down, child." Mrs. Parker's voice was very pleasant. It was soft, refined, with a slight Southern accent.

Her well-groomed appearance gave her an air of comfort and old money. She had a plethora of black and silver-streaked hair that was combed into an attractive upsweep, topped by a charming little feathered hat that sat slightly tilted to one side. Her almond-shaped fingernails were well tended and painted a bright red, and although her age was somewhat betrayed by the wrinkles and darkspotted skin of her hands, they still held a reminiscence of youth and were an acceptable showcase for the large pale-blue stone, surrounded by diamonds, that she wore on her left-hand ring finger. "So, my dear, your name is Annie Elizabeth Jordan. That is a very lovely name."

"Thank you, ma'am, but my family and friends call me Cricket.

You could call me Cricket if you want to."

"Well, now, where on earth did you get such an unusual nickname?"

"My dad told me that on the night I was born, he stayed up all night waiting for me to arrive. When I finally did get born, he said I was so small and made such little sounds that I reminded him of a little cricket singing on a hearth, and except for my grandpa Bane, everyone has called me Cricket ever since."

"That's a wonderful story about your name. I think I shall call you Cricket too, if I may?"

"That would be nice," said Cricket, who was very pleased to find their new friendship getting off to such a grand start.

"I imagine your father is very proud of the charming young lady you have become," said Mrs. Parker as she gently brushed back some random curls that had fallen onto Cricket's forehead.

"Do you get your lovely blue eyes and sunny freckles from him?"

"Well . . . I'm not sure. I mean . . . well, maybe . . ." Cricket's composure began to fall apart. "His eyes were really, really blue, and he had a great smile that made me feel warm inside. I know that much, but I don't think he had freckles on his nose like I do. I can't remember," stuttered Cricket as her self-confidence started to unravel. "People tell me I look just like him," she said, attempting to gather her poise. "Mom says she can look into my eyes and see his soul shining through."

Cricket lowered her head and wrapped her arms around her body, attempting to hold back the tears she could feel were coming. "He was killed in the bombing of Pearl Harbor," she continued, "and I'm starting to forget things about him. But I know he was very talented. He could fly any plane ever built, play the clarinet, and dance like Fred Astaire . . . you know, Fred Astaire in the movies. I can't do all that stuff. I may have his eyes, but not his talents." Cricket realized for the past few minutes she had been speed- talking and not letting Mrs. Parker get a word in edgewise. She sat back in her seat and folded her hands in her lap.

"Nonsense, dear." Mrs. Parker reached over and took one of Cricket's hands. "You have plenty of time to learn to dance or play an instrument if you want to. You mustn't be so discouraged so young. Oh, this awful war, it has taken such a horrible toll on everyone. I'm so very sorry about your father, dear child. How old are you, my dear?"

"I'm almost eight years old, ma'am."

"Almost eight years old! My, my, that does make you quite the young lady, and traveling by yourself too."

"Yes, ma'am. I've traveled on trains since I was a baby, but this is my first trip alone. My mom and I usually make this trip together, but this year, we're expecting a new baby and Mom has to stay home until it arrives. We're hoping for a boy so we can name him after my dad."

Cricket was relieved that her freckles, lack of accomplishments, and speed-talking didn't seem to be a detractor in her budding friendship with Mrs. Parker, whom she liked very much.

"Oh, my dear, this is something very special," said Mrs. Parker. "There is nothing like a new baby in the family to heal wounds and sorrow. I hope you get your wish and it's a boy, but a little sister can be very special too. We should celebrate. Waiter, bring us some tea and cakes, please."

Cricket sat back into her seat, awaiting this new adventure of tea and cakes. Would it be somewhat like the Mad Hatter's tea party in *Alice in Wonderland*? Suddenly she heard a familiar laugh and caught the faint scent of Bay Rum aftershave. A group of servicemen pushed their way through the dining car toward an empty table at the far end. Cricket looked up and saw the back of the last young man passing her seat.

"It's him! He's not dead! It's really him!" Cricket cried out in pure joy. In a flash of a second, she was out of her seat and pushing herself through the crowd of uniformed adults. The young man who was the last to pass Cricket's seat was about to take his place at the table when she rushed toward him, threw her arms around his neck, and buried her face into his shoulder.

"Daddy, oh, Daddy! I prayed you were all right, that you would come home. Mom and I missed you so much!" Cricket could feel his arms tighten around her as he stood up, holding her close.

By this time, the dining car had become eerily quiet, as no one could resist watching this tender moment of reunion.

"Little miss, little miss, I think you have mistaken me for someone else," said the young man, still holding Cricket close.

She pulled back and looked into the face of a stranger. "Oh, you're not my dad . . . you're not my dad," said Cricket, almost in a whisper.

She threw her arms back around his neck, and all the weeks and months of sorrow she had held back came surging to the surface and spilled like a cloudburst of rain from her small body. Her sobs brought tears to the eyes of the most stoic of adults who witnessed her heart breaking before their eyes. The young man was at a total loss as to what to do.

Fortunately, Mr. Washington saw what had happened and rushed in.

"I'll take care of this, sir," said Mr. Washington as he took Cricket's sobbing body tenderly into his arms. Mr. Washington carried her through the car and back to her seat across from Mrs. Parker.

"I'll take her, Mr. Washington. Give her to me," said Mrs. Parker.

Mr. Washington gently placed Cricket into the waiting arms of Mrs. Parker, who rocked her back and forth, and this comforting motion began to calm Cricket's wretchedness. Mrs. Parker dried her tear-stained cheeks and eyes and patted her gently on the back. "It's all right, child. Everything will be all right," Mrs. Parker said as she continued to rock her back and forth.

"I was . . ." Cricket tried to get her sobs under control. "So sure he was my dad. He laughed like him, and he even smelled like him. I . . . miss him so much." Cricket's sobs began to subside.

"It's all right, dear. We're supposed to miss loved ones we've lost. It's a natural process to grieve and feel bad for a while, but then we must honor the ones we've lost by living the most wonderful life we can, in their honor. And that is what you must do for your father." "Thanks, Mrs. Parker. I'm okay now. Sorry to be so much trouble."

"No need to apologize, dear. I'm glad I was here to help you," said Mrs. Parker. "Now, let's get on with our celebration of your impending sibling. We'll even have an extra cup of tea in honor of your father. Waiter, you may bring our tea now."

The waiter scurried off to fill Mrs. Parker's request, moving in sync to the gentle swaying of the train. Cricket looked up to see the young man she had mistaken for her father heading in her direction. "Hello, little miss," said the young man as he squatted down to talk with Cricket eye to eye. "I recognize you. Your grandfather gave me a ride to the station this morning. That's why you thought you knew me. Are you okay?"

"Yes, sir. I'm sorry I bothered you, but you reminded me so much of my dad."

"That's all right, little miss. It's my honor. If I'm ever lucky enough to have a little girl of my own, I hope she will be just like you. Your dad was a lucky man. What's your name?" he asked.

"I'm Annie Elizabeth Jordan," she said, shaking the hand he had extended. "But you may call me Cricket."

"That's a great name. Pleased to meet you, little Miss Cricket. My name is Stack, Robert, seaman first-class. Well, I'll leave you ladies to your tea. You take care, little miss. You're a brave kid."

With that, the young sailor stood up straight, offered a salute, and disappeared into the crowd. "Well, now, Cricket, where do your grandparents live in Seattle?" asked Mrs. Parker.

"Oh, they don't live in Seattle. They live nearby in Everett." "What a coincidence! I have a married daughter that lives in Everett," said Mrs. Parker.

"Are you going there to visit her?"

"No, dear. Not exactly. Mr. Parker and I adamantly opposed Margaret's marriage. I find her husband to be a rather mean, nasty man who doesn't treat my daughter with the respect she deserves. I come to Seattle several times a year to stay for a month or two, and Margaret brings the children to see me in Seattle and we keep in touch by phone, naturally. But let's not talk of troubling things. Let's talk of happier days. Oh, look, here comes our tea, and we shall toast to the happy event of the arrival of your new sibling."

Mrs. Parker opened her purse to replace the lace hankie she had used to wipe Cricket's tears. She placed her purse on the table, and Cricket couldn't help but see its contents.

"Mrs. Parker, is . . . that a gun . . . I mean a real gun?"

"Oh, this old thing!" she said, removing the small single-shot pistol from her bag. "It was a gift from my husband for our first anniversary. Where I come from in Texas, everyone carries a gun. Lord, even our preacher carries a gun. It's become a habit for me to just stick it in my purse. I've never had to use it, and I hope I never have to."

It was really quite lovely for a gun, although it was the first one Cricket had seen up close, since Grandpa George kept all his guns locked in a cabinet and out of reach. The small barrel was carved into a beautiful design of a vine of roses. The handle was opalescent pearl, with the initial *V* in gold leaf.

"Excuse me, Mrs. Parker, but what does the *V* stand for?" "It stands for my first name, dear, *Vivian*. Shall I pour tea?"

Their lunch was a complete success as far as Cricket was concerned. Mrs. Parker made her feel so grown-up. Fortunately, printing was acceptable in making out the menu selections, and the tea service was quite amazing. It was delivered on a large silver tray occupied by a stately silver teapot, a small silver pitcher filled with cream, a silver bowl holding small square cubes of sugar, sugar tongs, and a china plate with slices of lemons arranged in a circle. The cakes arrived on a beautiful silver three-tiered server, small little works of art frosted and decorated to please a queen. Cricket beamed with delight as they ended their luncheon with her very first official serving of tea, which she filled rather amply with cream and sugar.

That night, Cricket lay in her upper berth, letting her thoughts review the day to the gentle rocking of the train and the clicking of the wheels on the track. After she brushed her teeth and changed into her PJs in the ladies' room, Mr. Washington helped her up the ladder to her bunk and buttoned the curtains to her snug little cave. *Imagine me,* she pondered, with a large yawn and heavy eyelids, *me, Annie Elizabeth Jordan, having lunch and tea with Mrs. Vivian Beaumont Parker from the state of Texas, where everyone carries a gun, even a preacher.* A very ostentatious start to her summer adventure. There was no doubt about it, in Cricket's mind, that extra special things happen once you are no longer considered a baby. Her turning eight years old was so much more exciting than the birthdays she had celebrated before. Kneeling by her window so she could see the moon and stars, she reached into her purse and took out her father's aviator wings, held them tight, and began her prayers.

"Hi, God, it's me, Cricket, speaking. Thanks for this special day. I really like my new friend, Mrs. Parker, and all that tea service stuff was really fun too. Thanks for sending her to take care of me and to keep me company. I'm not exactly home yet, so could you please just keep an eye on me for a little while longer? I sure would appreciate it. I know now, God, that my dad is never coming home, that he is going to stay in heaven with you. Would you please tell him for me that I will try my hardest to live the best life I possibly can? To honor him, like Mrs. Parker said. I'm not exactly sure just how to go about that, but I'm sure you will let me know along the way. Tell my dad I love him and I'll try not to feel so sad. Bless Mom and our new baby, Grandpa George, and Grandpa and Grandma Bane. Good night, God. Sleep tight, and I'll see you in the morning."

Morning arrived, and Cricket awoke to the soft rocking of the train. Peeking out of her upper bunk window, she could see the sun starting to rise as it changed the predawn shadows from opaque to the warm hues of pale gold. The rich red soil and glistening granite rocks raced by her window, and puffy white clouds floating lazily in the sky began turning pink on their tummies as the sun hurried to claim the day. Cricket slipped into the clean clothes she had laid out the night before, opened her curtains, quietly stepped down the ladder, and went into the ladies' room to wash her face, brush her teeth, and comb her hair. On her way back to her bunk, she came across Mr. Washington assisting an elderly gentleman.

"Good morning, Mr. Washington."

"Why, good morning, Miss. Cricket. How'd you sleep?"

"Just fine, thank you. It was sort of like sleeping in a rocking chair."

"Give me a second here with Mr. Reynolds, and I'll take you to the dining car, Miss Cricket."

She started to protest the need for Mr. Washington to escort her to the dining car and decided the better of it.

"I know, I've got to let you do your job. I remember. I'll wait for you in my bunk." Cricket gave Mr. Washington a big smile.

As Mr. Washington escorted Cricket to the dining car, she could smell the eye-opening aroma of freshly brewed coffee mixed with the odd scent of wheel lubrication that filled the corridors, and it reminded her somewhat of her morning ritual with Grandpa George, which she missed already. They arrived just as the dining car opened, and he seated her at a table near the entrance. The waiter arrived to give Cricket her menu to look over.

"You need any help with the menu, little lady?" asked the waiter. "No, thank you. I know how to do this," she said with a touch of pride.

The view from the dining car was quite spectacular. The landscape was lush with greenery, clear and sparkling streams, and tall towering trees. In the distance, Cricket could barely see Mt. Baker, and she knew she was getting close to her destination. She made out her menu to include orange juice, pancakes, sausage, and to top it all off, tea with plenty of cream and sugar. She had just finished her breakfast when Mr. Washington appeared on the scene.

"Are you finished, Miss. Cricket?" he asked. "Yes, thank you."

"Well, let's get you back to your seat, and I'll help you pack up and get ready. We're about forty minutes outside of Seattle."

Cricket could hardly wait to reach her destination and the grandparents she so adored. The undeniable promises of the season seemed endless. Life was sweet, and all things were possible. Mrs. Parker was right; to live to honor someone you have lost makes losing them less painful. But nothing in her young world could even begin to give a hint that this would be her last trip to visit her grandparents, her last summer of innocence, the last time she would ever believe in anything like fairies, magic, and particularly, a saying like "happily ever after."

CHAPTER 5

Vivian Beaumont Parker

VIVIAN HAD A HARD time releasing the sorrow she felt for the sobbing child she had held in her lap. So young to feel so much pain. And sadness always seems much bigger when you are very young and so small. She closed up her bag and placed it on the seat next to her. Gazing out the window at the passing landscape, she let her hand rest on the handbag beside her and the contents within. The sun felt warm, and the swaying of the train, mesmerizing. It seemed like another lifetime since she lived in Davenport, Texas, and was as young and vulnerable as Cricket. Davenport was a very small town tucked in an even smaller corner of the vast state of Texas. The only thing separating Davenport from Oklahoma was a wide marshy swale in the rambling, silt-filled Red River. Vivian's parents owned a homestead spread of approximately eight hundred acres and raised cattle for a living. It was a hard life, but certainly not an unusual one for folks trying to make their way by living on the land. Vivian was the only girl in a family of six boys. While her brothers worked side by side with their father, tilling the land and tending to the cattle, Vivian helped her mother with baking, cooking, doing the laundry, chopping wood for the stoves and fireplace, and feeding the pigs, chickens, and horses. In the summer, the mother and daughter put up canned goods from the garden they planted and filled the family pantry with many things berry—pie, jam, and preserves from the berries they searched out along the riverbanks.

School wasn't a top priority in the Beaumont family, but all seven children managed to get a basic education due to their mother's insistence and homeschooling. From an early age, Vivian knew that a rancher's life was not the dream she wanted to follow. It was a mean, ill-tempered life that had aged her mother far beyond her years, and she wanted nothing to do with it. Vivian's only respite from her dismal life and the constant torture and bullying of her brothers was a small nook next to the fireplace where she could escape her colorless existence by transporting herself away in books. There she could be a princess in a vast castle, travel to a strange land, be a mighty heroine or an elegant lady depicted in the magazines. One evening just before her eleventh birthday, Vivian looked up from her reading and found her eyes slowly traveling the corners and bleakness of the sparse living room. Her attention rested on her mother, who was rocking in a spindly old chair near the fire, attending to the mending. Vivian took note of her mother's dull, lifeless, premature gray hair, her weathered complexion, the frown lines that had etched into her face from utter disappointments in life, and her labor-worn hands, more like the hands of an old washerwoman than a woman of only forty-two. If she didn't do something to escape this hellhole, she told herself, that picture of her mother would be her someday. Before her twelfth birthday, Vivian had read every magazine and newspaper she could get her hands on, hoping she would come across something, anything to aid in her escape. There was no family budget for such frivolous things like newspapers or fashion magazines, so Vivian's drive for freedom drove her into a life of crime, where she stole newspapers and magazines from the alley trash bins behind the barbershop and beauty parlor. An article about the prestigious Brookshire Academy for Young Ladies had caught her eye, and she began to develop a calculated plan to escape the life of a rancher's daughter. With all the cunning and diligence of a master spy, Vivian got started on her campaign to convince her father that the best possible future for her lay in her attendance of Brookshire Academy for Young Ladies, which was located just outside Houston.

At first, she ran up against a huge wall of rejection. But little by little, her father softened in his opinion, due, she guessed, to a great deal of assistance from her mother, who saw this as Vivian's chance to have a better life. By the time she reached her sixteenth birthday, Vivian had finally worn away her father's objections, and since the cattle business had been fairly good over the past several years, Vivian got her wish and was allowed to make plans to attend Brookshire Academy starting that coming fall. Out of necessity, Vivian became an excellent seamstress. The summer before her long anticipated departure for Brookshire Academy, she perused every fashion magazine the local drugstore had to offer. The antique treadle sewing machine that had originally belonged to her grandmother hummed well into the night as she set about putting together a basic yet classic wardrobe to suit her new station in life. The first of September finally arrived. Vivian carefully packed her few but adequate belongings.

As her mother hugged her goodbye, she whispered in Vivian's ear, "Get as far away from here as you can. Never look back. Live the life I never had a chance to. I'll die happy if I can only know that you're free."

"Thanks, Mom. I knew you made this happen," Vivian whispered back. "I love you."

The two stood holding tight to their final hug. Suddenly, Vivian's mom held her at arm's length, looked deep into Vivian's eyes, and said in a rather stem voice, "Go!"

Riding beside her father in the old buckboard horse-drawn wagon down the rut-filled dirt road of Davenport, Texas, Vivian reached the train station, boarded the train headed to Houston, and as her mother requested, never looked back. Although Vivian felt at the start somewhat like a prairie bird without feathers, it wasn't long before she was watching and learning all that she needed to know to fit in perfectly with all the other young women, most of whom came from very wealthy families. Vivian also learned, almost immediately, that it was much better to be rich than poor, and the former was now her new goal in life. In no time at all, Vivian became best friends with five of the richest girls in the school. Soon, she was being invited to their homes on weekends to attend Texas cookouts, picnics, holiday events, and Christmas balls. Vivian was a fast learner, and before she finished her first year at Brookshire, it was impossible to discern any difference between the little country girl from Davenport and the top young debutantes from Houston. The evening before her first Christmas ball, Vivian found it impossible to sleep. She had borrowed a dress from her very best friend, Clarisse Parker, who had given Vivian permission to alter it in any way necessary to make it feel like her own. Vivian remade the gown until no one could possibly recognize its original appearance. She took in the bodice until it was figure forming, showing off her small waist, and lowered the neckline just a tad, just enough to show the proper cleavage. The color, pale sky blue, complimented Vivian's deep-brown eyes and her sultry black hair, which fell in a mass of natural curls almost to her waist. Vivian knew she wasn't an ugly girl, but she had no idea of the impact her exotic stature and features had on the male gender. She was truly stunning, with a one-of-a-kind look that stood out in a crowd of pastel-plumed blond schoolgirls like a scarlet feather on a white dove. Clarisse had made arrangements for her brother Wade to escort Vivian to the ball.

After hours of the most intense preparation, the two young ladies majestically descended the vast circular staircase of the Parkers' three-story replica of a Southern plantation mansion, and Vivian took the hand of the man that would one day soon become her husband, Wadsworth "Wade" Parker. The evening was pure magic. The ballroom and hallways were laden with huge pungent pine boughs and giant poinsettias, imported just for the occasion. Voluptuous red bows were tied to chandeliers of red and green lights, and ten-foot-tall Christmas trees were decorated with multicolored ornaments and delicate china angels with fairy wings. Packages of all shapes and sizes were stacked, in abundance, under each of the ten different trees, wrapped in a myriad of colored paper and vibrant holiday ribbons. In the center of the dining room stood a huge long table covered with an elegant handmade lace tablecloth from Ireland. Four large silver candelabras were placed at even intervals down the center of the table, giving the room a warm holiday glow. The food choices were beyond belief, a gourmet adventure Vivian had never seen or even dreamed possible.

Pheasants displayed with a plethora of feathers and brandy- soaked fruits. Pork, lamb, and beef crown roasts, whose centers were filled with chestnuts and cranberry dressing; a whole pig, wrapped in leaves and cooked over twenty- four hours in a deep pit dug in the backyard; trays of freshly caught trout; large ice-chilled china bowls filled to the top with crab legs, clams, and jumbo shrimp. Salads of all descriptions, tossed, and gelatin molds of everything from fruits, shredded vegetables, to exotic imported figs. Vivian had no idea that a potato could possibly be prepared in so many different forms— baked, slivered, creamed, au gratin, fried, twice-baked, and stuffed. Last but not the least, a copious amount of beans that were baked— pork and beans, Boston beans, lima beans, and of course, red beans and rice. On either side of the large fireplace stood massive ornate sideboards with round ornately hand-carved legs. Each sideboard had a huge beveled glass mirror hanging over the Italian marble countertop. These magnificent antique sideboards served as the dessert station for the banquet, another unbelievable feast for the body and the eye. Three-tiered cakes depicted Christmas scenes of carolers standing in a town square surrounded by trees, a miniature town with sidewalks, streetlamps, and one-horse open sleighs. Other cakes were designed to look like tall stacks of Christmas packages with matching bows. A large sheet cake depicted an ice pond with skaters, trees, and a snowman. There was a rumspiced fruit compote; intricately decorated little petit fours; trays of Christmas cookies decorated as ornaments; a two-foot-tall gingerbread house with a roof of tiny individual tiles, shutters of painted toothpicks, and glass-like windowpanes made of paper-thin sugar glaze; giant hothouse strawberries dipped in Belgium chocolate; puddings of all genders; latticework-covered pecan, berry, lemon, chocolate, and sweet potato pies; and Vivian's favorite, delicate little cream puffs filled with the most delightful-tasting creams.

The orchestra was located in a small alcove overlooking the ballroom. The exquisitely gowned ladies, along with their tuxedo- dressed gentlemen escorts, swirled across the dance floor to the waltzing rhythm of violins, cellos, piano, and flute. The whole tableau looked like a scene from a Currier and Ives painting. Wade and Vivian made an elegant couple. Vivian, with her striking stature and beauty, and Wade, who was tall, handsome, and a poster boy for Southern gentlemanliness and charm, waltzed the night away, since Wade had filled out Vivian's dance card entirely with his name, alleviating the chance that some other young man might catch her fancy. By the end of the evening, other couples vacated the dance floor just to watch in awe as the dazzling young couple swirled past to the lyrical notes of a waltz by Johann Strauss. This was a night of splendors for Vivian that would live in her heart for years, sustaining her during the blacker days to come.

Wade's courtship of Vivian was a marathon of elegant balls and parties, of dozens of flowers delivered almost daily. Their name appeared in the social column of the newspaper regularly, describing, in great detail, Vivian's wardrobe from hat to shoe. Vivian chuckled to herself. If they only knew she had designed and made her own clothing, what would the hoity-toity set think then? At the end of the annual winter sleigh ride and dance, in front of all those attending, Wade knelt down on one knee, placed a huge aquamarine ring surrounded by diamonds on the ring finger of her left hand, and asked Vivian to marry him. Vivian was left almost speechless, but she managed to whisper, "Yes," and fell willingly into Wade's arms. Vivian and Wade officially announced their engagement at the upcoming Christmas ball and were married in a lavish ceremony that spring.

They settled into an expected routine for a newly married couple living the big Texas life. She volunteered at the local hospital and arranged fund-raisers for the Saint Martha's Orphanage. Wade took over running the Parker Ranch, and when his father died, he converted several hundred acres of grazing land into oil- producing wells. The Wadsworth Avery Parkers also kept the social life of Houston in the forefront of the news with their lavish and resplendent dinner parties, cookouts, and balls. Their ability to put on the most outstanding events was unmatched anywhere in the entire county. When their daughter, Margaret, was born, Vivian was ecstatic. Her life took on a real meaning as a mother, and her interest in the social scene began to fade. She found the social life they had been living to be shallow, hollow, and unfulfilling, and she devoted herself to motherhood with great gusto. On the other hand, Wade had come to relish their social standing and resented Vivian's lack of interest in being Houston's premier hostess. In his frustration with Vivian's allconsuming role as a mother, Wade began to spend more and more time at his gentleman's club in town, playing cards with his buddies, drinking, and ladies of the night became one of his many new distractions. This was not what Vivian pictured her married life would look like. Whenever Wade arrived home late, when he managed to come home at all, his drunken advances disgusted her, and she was repulsed by his rough grasp and stale whiskey breath. It became so unbearable that she began bolting her door at night.

One morning, around two thirty, Wade came staggering in from a night of his usual debauchery and reached for the doorknob of Vivian's bedroom door. He tried the knob several times, shaking it and pounding on her door. When he finally realized it was locked, he went wild. He beat on the door, bellowing for her to unlock it immediately. He made threats about breaking the door down, and when Vivian refused to answer or unlock the door, break it down he did. Vivian sat up in bed terrified as Wade burst through the door, leaving it hanging ajar on its split hinges. His eyes were bloodshot and wild, his usual tidy appearance unkempt, unshaven. Reaching down with his huge hands, he jerked Vivian out of bed and held her, trembling, in front of him. "No wife of mine will ever lock me out of a bedroom I have the right to be in! Do you hear me?" he shouted, glaring at her through his red-rimmed eyes.

"Wade, please, you're hurting me," cried Vivian as the pressure of his grip increased along with his anger. Ignoring her pleas, Wade continued his rant as if he hadn't heard a thing she was saying. He ranted and sneered about her unsophisticated background, which she now wished she had never disclosed to him, how she wormed her way into the family, how she was nothing but poor white trash, how she had shut him out of her life just to raise a child, a child who probably wasn't even his. He came up with every hurtful accusation he could think of and a few that really had nothing to do with her. "You can start acting like the wife of a Parker, or I'll take that kid away from you so fast you won't know what happened. And don't you think I can't," Wade hissed between gritted teeth. "She'll spend the rest of her life in boarding schools, and you'll never see her again, and you can bet on it."

Then, like the quiet in the eye of a storm, Wade's ranting suddenly stopped, and he just glowered down at his small terrified wife. Vivian's heart pounded, and her throat became desert dry, as she feared what was about to come. With one swift move of his hand, he slammed her, stomach down, onto the bed.

"No, Wade, no!" cried Vivian. "You're hurting me. Wade, please stop . . . stop!" Vivian could hear the ripping of her nightgown and then a horrifying silence. She felt his rough huge hands crawl over her body, probing and searching for his pleasure with sweaty palms. Next, she heard the click of his belt buckle, the sound of a zipper running down its track as he unceremoniously mounted her from behind, grabbing her hair like the reins on a horse. The pain was excruciating, and the shame and degradation even worse. Wade muffled Vivian's screams and pleading by shoving her face into the pillows. Vivian gasped for air and fought helplessly under the weight of her husband's large frame. He sodomized her at his leisure for what seemed like hours; his drunken state allowed him to extend the duration of his attack. His breath smelled of liqueur and cigars as he muttered obscenities into her ear, describing the unimaginable, twisted things he still had in store for her. Abruptly Wade abandoned his brutal attack, released Vivian from his grip, and sauntered over to the glass-top bar table in the corner of the room. He poured himself a drink and sat down in the armchair by the fireplace. Vivian slowly sat up on the edge of the bed, wrapping the sheet around her shaking body. Could he be finished? Her heartbeat and breathing began to return to normal. She was about to reach for her robe when Wade turned toward her.

"Crawl over here like the bitch you are," he demanded. "Crawl?" repeated Vivian.

"Yes, crawl on your hands and knees . . . without the robe." Vivian knew better than to disobey or argue with Wade when he was in this condition. Any opposition to his desires could bring on another rage with who knew what consequences. So she dropped to the floor and began her crawl until she reached the other side of the room and Wade's feet.

"Turn around, I want to see your ass. Turn around, bitch!" said Wade. "Face on the floor, ass in the air. Do it . . . do it now!" Wade's voice became insistent, and his breathing sounded like a panting dog.

"Oh god, what now?" She began to tremble and shake all over.

Vivian heard the clanking of the fireplace tools and suddenly felt the ice-cold steel of the handle of the poker thrust inside of her. Wade was laughing and asked how she liked that? Maybe she would like the other end of the poker better. Vivian began to plead with Wade to stop. She was bleeding, and the pain was unbearable as Wade continued to rape her with the poker. Again, Wade abruptly stopped his torture, and the room fell quiet. Vivian was terrified to move or look to see what was happening. Suddenly, the poker was removed, and Wade mounted her from behind, continuing his rape, applying each thrust with such force that it rattled Vivian's teeth and made her gasp for air. He finally reached his climax and fell breathlessly on top of her until she thought she would be crushed. When his breathing took on the sound of a deep sleep, Vivian carefully struggled out from under him, slipped into her robe, and silently tiptoed out of the room. Vivian was enraged, defiant, bruised, and bleeding. A strength she had never felt before encompassed her entire traumatized body, and she was determined that something like this would never happen to her again.

The next morning, Vivian arrived at the breakfast table, seated herself, and began to sip her coffee as though nothing had happened. Only a slight bruise on her right cheekbone was visible from her night of terror. When Wade joined the table, he looked hungover and sheepish. He grumbled a terse "Good morning" and proceeded to engross himself in the morning paper. Soon, Margaret and her nurse arrived at the table, and the child's cheery nature brightened up one corner of the bleak atmosphere. Last to arrive at the breakfast table was Clarisse, Wade's sister and still Vivian's best friend, and Clarisse's husband, Walter. They were an amicable couple and frequent visitors since moving to Austin, where Walter's family owned a tannery. Clarisse was one of the few people Vivian truly enjoyed spending time with, but with her being Wade's sister, Vivian didn't feel she could confide in Clarisse when it came to her brother's beyond-shameful behavior and her crumbling marriage. Over the passing of breakfast, Wade requested that Vivian pass him the salt. Vivian smiled, daintily pressed her napkin to her lips, picked up the saltshaker, stood up, and walked over to Wade's side. She bent over to whisper in Wade's ear, placing the salt firmly on the table in front of his plate. She embedded her fingernails firmly into his shoulder, out of sight of the other breakfast guests.

In her finest Southern drawl, Vivian quietly said, "Good morning, darling. Did you have a good night's sleep?" She whispered. "Now," still smiling, "I want you to pay very close attention to what I have to say. It's important to the state of your well- being that you know, if you ever—and I mean *ever*—enter my bedroom again under any circumstances, even if your hair is on fire, I'm going to take that cute little old pistol you gave me for our first anniversary and change you from a stallion to a gelding, even if it means blowing your manhood all over my new imported flocked French wallpaper." Vivian placed her other hand on his arm, increasing the pressure as she spoke.

"Now, you do understand me, don't you, darling? I mean *really* understand me?" Vivian stared Wade directly in the eye and held that gaze with a stare as cold as black ice until Wade blinked and turned his eyes away. "Here's your salt. Enjoy your eggs," said Vivian as she gracefully floated from the room, leaving her husband to reflect upon her unusual strength and unexpected stance.

A kind of silent, unspoken agreement took place that morning between Vivian and Wade Parker. Although Wade continued his drinking and philandering outside the home, he did so with much greater discretion, and he never again entered Vivian's bedroom, drunk or sober, and their life took on a public appearance of mutual complacency. Vivian devoted her days and nights to raising her child. Wade's business savvy and his longstanding membership in the Good Old Boys' Club with those who controlled the state and its vast holdings surrounded Vivian with all the financial and material existence that allowed her to contribute generously to many charities through the community and gave her daughter every advantage. Vivian accepted her role in this peculiar lifestyle. Over the years, it almost seemed tolerable and normal—at least that was what she told herself. She derived a tremendous enjoyment from the self-confidence she had acquired in developing a spine. An inner peace became her daily companion. The train jolted. Vivian was brought quickly back from the past. She glanced around the dining car and realized she had been daydreaming and most of the passengers had left. She felt herself releasing the tight grip she had unknowingly placed on her handbag and its contents.

"Excuse me, ma'am," said the waiter. "Can I get you anything else? More tea perhaps?"

"No, thank you, waiter. I'm fine," said Vivian as she shook the cobwebs of the past from her head. She saw Mr. Washington approaching.

"Oh, Mr. Washington, what time do we arrive in Seattle tomorrow morning?" said Mrs. Parker. "About nine thirty, ma'am." "Could you please wake me at 8:00 a.m.? I'll take my tea in my compartment."

"Yes, ma'am, I certainly will," said Mr. Washington.

Vivian returned to her compartment and sat by the window, enjoying the view, and reminisced over her recent thoughts. She prided herself in wearing her secret knowledge of the triumph over her abusive husband so many years ago, like the set of an invisible armor that gave her a special strength. An armor that would one day, unexpectedly, save her life and the life of Annie Elizabeth Jordan as well.

CHAPTER 6

The Arrival

AS THE TRAIN PULLED into the Seattle station, Cricket's heart raced with anticipation. The conductor had barely placed the step in front of the stairs when Cricket leaped onto the platform, her eyes searching the moving crowd.

"Miss Annie, Miss. Annie," cautioned Mr. Washington, who was staying close behind her. "You stay here now with me till your grandfolks come. Don't want you getting lost now."

Mr. Washington turned to see Mrs. Parker arriving at the stair's edge.

"Here now, Mrs. Parker, you let me take that suitcase for you.

And watch your step, please, ma'am."

Cricket heard her grandfather's voice calling, "Annie, Annie!" As the crowd parted, she saw him, his tall, lean frame and graceful stride coming into view. There was no mistaking those twinkling emerald-green eyes and handsome, rugged features, even though he was much grayer than Cricket remembered.

"Grandma, Grandpa!" Cricket responded, receiving a warm hug and kiss from her grandmother just before being encircled in her grandfather's strong, loving arms. In the midst of Cricket's excitement, she suddenly realized Mrs. Parker's presence.

"Grandma, Grandpa, I'd like you to meet a new friend of mine, Mrs. Parker." "Thaddeus and Arvilla Bane," said Cricket's grandfather, extending his hand to Mrs. Parker.

"So nice to finally meet you," said Mrs. Parker. "Cricket has told me so much about you both and how much she loves her visits with you."

"Oh," Cricket added, "this is Mr. Washington, Grandpa and Grandma. He looked after me on the train."

"Thank you so much," said Grandfather, shaking Mr.

Washington's hand. "We are much obliged."

"It was my pleasure, sir, my pleasure indeed," said Mr.

Washington as they waved goodbye to him and Mrs. Parker. "Goodbye and thanks, Mrs. Parker," Cricket hollered as they went their separate ways and disappeared out of sight.

Everett was located in a large cove on Puget Sound, a huge bay almost completely enclosed by land. In the 1940s, it was a small sleepy lumber town plucked directly out of a Norman Rockwell painting, where the air was filled with the fragrant scent of freshly milled wood that reminded Cricket of the smell of newly sharpened pencils at the start of school. While some of the surrounding regions were bustling with the expansion of wartime production and activity, Everett was still surrounded by rich green fields of strawberries and orchards of cherries and apples. The orchards led up to the edge of a magnificent forest of tall stately Douglas fir trees that spread into the majestic Cascade Mountains. Cricket and her grandfather spent entire days hiking and searching for wild blackcaps in those mountains full of wonder, wildlife, and beauty. The mornings were crisp and dew laden, and the warm afternoons smelled of fir, bark, and moss. The forest floor was thick with layer upon layer of twigs and long-forgotten carpets of leaves. The filtered light created beautiful, lacy shadows that mixed with small patches of fragile mists that were suspended over the rocks and swaying ferns. Breathtaking beams of sunlight streamed down through the cathedral-like canopy of trees that reminded Cricket of sunbeams through stained glass windows in a dusty old church. No city sounds intruded upon the woodlands' immense quiet, only the distant chirp of birds, the creaking of the trees as a soft breeze gently flowed over its canopy, and the scampering of small creatures leaving behind a whisper of crushed leaves and snapping twigs. It was here in this arena that Cricket and her grandfather explored nature at its best. They spied a mother bear teaching her cubs to hunt berries, crawled under the manzanita bushes to search out mushrooms, watched a beaver colony repair their dam. Cricket thought her grandfather was the most wonderful man in the world. As Cricket and her grandfather were hiking back to the park's parking lot, she stopped to tie her shoe.

Looking up at him, she said, "Grandpa, can we talk?"

"Why, sure. Here's a nice, shady spot. Let's rest for a while, and you can tell me what's on your mind."

They removed their shoes and dangled their feet in the cool mountain stream and rested their backs against a moss-covered log. "All right, now, what do you need to talk about?" said Grandpa. "Okay, here goes," began Cricket, and then all her worries and fears just poured out of her. She told her grandfather about how this thing called a war was really scary, about how awful she thought it was that so many people that didn't ask to be involved were bring killed, like her dad, just because they got in the way. And the Ten Commandments said, "Thou shalt not kill," so if it was wrong to kill most of the time, how come it was okay during a war? How much love did moms and dads have to give their children? Could a new baby use it all up so there wouldn't be enough to go around to the other kids?

Grandfather gently picked Cricket up and sat her snuggly in his lap, giving her a warm, loving hug.

"Go on, sweetheart," he said.

"All the tears and the pain you have in your heart after someone you love dies . . . does that ever go away? And do you ever feel normal again? Even if you honor their life by living your own life well, like Mrs. Parker told me, will I ever feel happy again? Inside, I mean?"

"Well, little lady, you sure do have a few things on your mind, don't you?" said Grandpa. "Let's start from the top. Yes, war is an awful thing and innocent people who never asked to be involved, like your dad, do get hurt, and although the Ten Commandments do say 'Thou shalt not kill,' there are some things in life that are worth fighting and dying for."

"And what things are those, Grandpa?"

"Evil would be one of the most important things that good men have always had to fight against. Evil corrupts the heart of a man and steals his soul for all eternity. It fills the world with iniquity and vileness wherever it tries to plant its immoral roots. It's an affliction that good men can't ignore or tolerate. Another would be a man's right to protect his home, family, or country. You have the right to protect these things that mean so much to you, and although we always hope to resolve the issues that threaten our well-being without violence, sometimes we aren't given any other choice. This is why we have laws and courts in place to help guide us through such situations. But there are always a few that see only violence as a method to resolve a matter. So your answer is no, war is not a good thing, but there are times that it's the only path we are given. It's a difficult subject to comprehend as an adult, let alone as a child. Perhaps you will understand better as you grow older.

"Now, to your question about a parent's love. There is no such thing as a limit to how much you love your child, no matter how many children are in the family. Your mom and dad could have a dozen children, and they would love each and every one of them equally. A parent, especially a mom, has a heart filled with love that is endless for each of her children.

Someday, when you're a mother, you will understand just what I mean, but in the meantime, you have nothing to worry about.

"Will you ever feel happy inside again? I think the answer is yes. One day soon, life will feel normal, and although you'll never forget your dad and how it felt to lose him, God gives us the ability to heal our wounded souls and move on, and this will happen for you. I promise."

"Oh, thank you, Grandpa," said Cricket, throwing her arms around his neck. "I knew God would give you the answers for me. I always feel so much better after a talk with you. You always know just what to say."

"Here, let me dry your feet. We'll stop by the creamery for an ice cream cone before we head for home. It's probably not a good idea that your grandmother knows I'm eating ice cream, with my diabetes and all. That will remain our little secret. Deal?"

"Deal, Grandpa," she said as she proceeded to pick a large bouquet of wildflowers just in case the "ice cream caper" was discovered.

"Flowers are always a good thing, huh, Grandpa?"

"Always. And wildflowers are your grandmother's favorites." Grandpa smiled, and the two explorers and ice cream lovers headed for town.

Every other week, Cricket would accompany her grandmother on the bus to town. For a very brief time, Grandpa tried to teach Grandma to drive. Grandma's idea of approaching and passing through an intersection was to ask the passenger, "Is it clear?" If the answer was yes, and without looking in either direction, Grandma would put the pedal to the metal, launching her vehicle through the intersection with rocket speed, her philosophy being that the faster one got through an intersection, the less likely one would be hit.

Needless to say, Grandpa suggested public transportation was a wiser choice for Grandma, and to tell the truth, Grandma was much relieved. The first stop upon arriving in town was always the bank. There Grandma would deposit Grandpa's paycheck, and a designated sum went into savings. They would then proceed on to the phone company or the electric company, paying the bills in full and in person. "What does *credit* mean, Grandma?" Cricket asked on one of their downtown outings.

"It's a boil on the nose of personal integrity," she said. "Buying what you can't afford is a map to personal disaster."

I' ll have to remember that, thought Cricket.

On this summer's first trip to town, Cricket and her grandmother had just passed by the newsstand when Grandma stopped to briefly visit with her friend Mrs. Landry, with whom she had been friends for many years, ever since Grandpa and Grandma first moved to Everett. Sara Louise Landry was one of those people who was actually born right in Everett. She graduated high school there, married her high school sweetheart, Martin Landry, there, and became an interested and active member of the community, teaching Sunday school, volunteering at the Red Cross, acting as president of the Garden Club, and founding the Safe Harbor organization, which provided clothing and food baskets for the poor. Mrs. Landry and Cricket's grandmother also volunteered as civilian defense air observers. Every Wednesday from noon to 4:00 p.m., the two of them would go to an observation room on the roof of the tallest building in Everett, the J. C. Penny building, watching for enemy aircraft. On the wall next to the window was a silhouette chart of all military aircraft, foreign and domestic. When a plane was spotted, the observer identified the appropriate silhouette and called in the type of plane and its location. Cricket loved going with her grandmother to the observation room, high above the city. They allowed her to give her opinion about the observed plane, and that made her feel very grown-up and important. Grandma said we must all do our part, and she counted this as her part in the war effort. Martin Landry was a much-loved man in the community. He had been the local pharmacist for almost twenty-five years and knew everyone in town. People confided in him just as they did with Doc Miller. It was a sad situation for the entire community the day Martin was taken ill, and it was discovered he had liver cancer. He lingered for only six months and died one night in his sleep. "Good morning, ladies," said Mrs. Landry. "My, my, Cricket, you have really grown since last summer! Are you having a good time here on your visit?"

"Yes, ma'am, I'm having a great time. How is your dog, Scooter?" "Oh, she's just fine. You'll have to come over and play with her one day soon. She loves being around children." "Arvilla," said Mrs. Landry, "do you have a minute?" "Certainly, Sara. What is it?" said Grandma.

"I've been hearing some rather unsettling things about Adder Toomey and this bone he has to pick with Thad," said Mrs. Landry. "Martha Richard's daughter, Evelyn, works at Murphy's Pub on weekends, and she said, after Adder had a snoot full, he made all kinds of threats concerning Thad. He just can't seem to get past Thad's involvement in saving the Eto farm, which ruined Adder's plans for converting that land into a housing development. He said Thad cheated him out of a deal that would have set him up for life." "Not to worry, Sara," said Grandma. "Thad's heard all that a hundred times and feels it's just the whiskey speaking. Adder's just a jerk when he's drinking."

Cricket was listening intently to the conversation once she heard that Adder Toomey had made threats directed at her grandfather. She was happy to hear Grandma state it was nothing but a drunk speaking, but still, the thought of anyone hurting her grandfather made her feel very uneasy. *It's strange,* Cricket thought, *as many times as I have been in the Toomey house, I've never seen Mr. Toomey acting mean or threatening. Maybe that only happens at Murphy's Pub!* "Grandma, is it okay if I go over and look at the magazines while you talk to Mrs. Landry?"

"Certainly, dear, I'll be just a few minutes," said Grandma, continuing her conversation with her friend.

While Cricket was looking over all the different magazine covers, she spotted one that showed a captured Japanese film footage of a large group of Marines and other soldiers marching with their hands held on top of their heads. The headlines read, "BATAAN DEATH MARCH." She tugged at Grandma's sleeve.

"Excuse me, Grandma. Look at the picture on the cover of the magazine. Isn't that Uncle Kenny?" Grandma took the magazine from her hands and looked very carefully at the picture of the weary, battle-worn soldiers marching in a long line, then suddenly, her face turned an ashen white as she gasped, "Oh my Lord!" placing her hand to her lip. Then her legs gave out from under her, and she slumped to the ground.

"Arvilla . . . Arvilla!" called Mrs. Landry. "What is it?"

"Sara, look at this picture. Look here. It's my boy Ken. He's alive! After months of not knowing . . . he's alive." Grandma began to sob with tears of relief and joy.

The men from the nearby barbershop ran toward them to assist. Cricket dropped to her knees and grabbed her grandmother's hand.

"Grandma, Grandma, what's wrong?" she said.

Cricket's mother's youngest brother, Ken, had been missing in action for months. The family had no idea if he was alive or killed in action. Now Grandma was staring at her son's picture, thin and gaunt, but alive. The picture was one of many of the forty thousand prisoners captured at the fall of Bataan and Corregidor in the Philippines. The prisoners were force-marched fifty-five miles from Mariveles, Bataan, to San Fernando under conditions no one believed possible. Of these forty thousand, over half died of starvation or maltreatment. Just lagging behind in line was a shooting offense.

"Someone call Thad Bane!" pleaded Mrs. Landry.

"Arvilla has had a terrible shock." Grandpa arrived to find the chaos had drawn a large crowd. The magazine disappeared off the shelves as worried citizens scanned the pictures for any sign of their sons, brothers, or husbands. Grandpa and Cricket helped Grandma into the car, and they headed for home. Grandma was still crying as she said, "Thank God, Thad! Our boy is still alive! Ken is alive."

Everyone knew everyone in this small town, which could sometimes be a curse as well as a blessing. All the merchants called their customers by name. Mr. Hansen, the milkman, would leave a small gift for any newborn on his route. Doc Miller still made house calls and often stayed for supper. In some cases, that supper was the only fee the family could afford. For the past two years, Everett had been on a marathon fund-raiser for a new fire engine. There had been bake sales, community dances, scrap drives, raffles, donations, craft fairs, and auctions until finally, before New Year's, the needed monies were raised. The firehouse threw a big open house celebration, and at least half the town showed up to see the brand-new, state-of-the- art bright-red fire engine, the volunteer fire department's pride and joy. The telephone company ran on a local switchboard where all calls were hand-transferred and connected by operators, the Barstow sisters, Millie and Edith, being two of the company's finest. They assumed the role of the community's information hub, 911, *On Star*, *People Magazine*, and "Dear Abby" all spun into one.

Dressed in their dark flowered dresses and sensible shoes, wearing their hair in tidy buns, they could be seen at community events gathering what might possibly become an ultimate source of some very juicy gossip. But when it really mattered, when some disaster struck, the Barstow sisters were the first to step forward with assistance. Like the Saturday morning when Cricket and her grandparents were at the weekly farmers market, held on the front lawn of the high school in the middle of town on Main Street. An eerie quiet fell on the crowd that just minutes before had been laughing or conversing with neighbors and friends over stacks of sweet corn, berries of all colors, freshly baked goods, and bins of every variety of vegetable you could imagine. All the adults stood transfixed, like everything was in slow motion. They seemed to be holding their breath as they all watched the green car with the military insignia on the side drive slowly through town past the once-cheerful shoppers. This car meant only one thing. Its occupants were there to officially notify someone that their husband, son, or brother had been killed in action. There were so many families with young men serving in the military that the sight of that car sent a collective shiver through the crowd like an arctic freeze in the middle of summer.

Cricket's grandparents were among those whose hearts sank at this ominous sight, having three sons in the service. Before the sun set, Miss Edith and Miss Millie had rallied the town, who wrapped their hearts around Jean and Bob Hannon, who had just been notified that both their sons had been killed, James, in the sinking of the *Yorktown* during the Battle of Midway, and Robert, shot down during the US-carrier-based bombing of Tokyo, possibly one of the young pilots Cricket's father had trained before the Pearl Harbor bombing. Their loss soon became the pain and sorrow of the entire community. Everett, like so many small towns of that era, was a wonderful place to raise a family. There hadn't been a violent crime in the town for almost twenty years, and even that one paled in comparison to today's standards. It seemed that an amateur threesome of moonshiners tried to set up a still in the nearby mountains. When their ineptitude caused their enterprise to blow up, it took half the timber stand with it, and much of the town's livelihood went up in smoke. This, needless to say, didn't sit well with the residents. This spawned town meetings and a great deal of chatter in all kinds of gathering spots—Murphy's Pub, the barbershop, Elks lodge, the firehouse, and Sue Sue's Café. Several days after the big event, a log raft floated down the river into the main harbor. Tied to the raft were the moonshiners, stripped naked, tarred, and feathered, with a sign around their necks that read, NOT IN OUR TOWN! No one was willing to take credit for this misadventure, but there were mumblings down at Murphy's Pub, talk of doing much worse to these misguided entrepreneurs. Miss Millie, just a girl at that time, was browsing at the yarn shop that morning and witnessed the raft's arrival. She fainted dead away and took to her bed for a week. It was more than likely her first, and possibly her last, encounter with the sight of a naked man. After Cricket was tucked snuggly into bed, she began to give her prayers for that evening a lot of thought. With so many things of importance to discuss, she didn't want to forget anything. Once she was certain she had covered all her bases, she slipped from bed onto her knees and began.

"Hi, God, Cricket here. How is everything going for you? I guess with so many bad things happening around the world, you must be pretty busy. Thanks for giving Grandpa the answers to my questions. He explained so many things to me. We started with this war thing, and I guess there are a lot of things that I'll just have to wait until I'm more grown-up to understand. I was happy to know that new babies don't use up all of a parent's love, that there is always plenty to go around. This is a big relief and a big worry off my mind. Speaking of being relieved, Grandma and Grandpa were so relieved to find out Uncle Kenny is alive, but he looked pretty worn-out, and now they have been notified that Uncle Kenny is officially a prisoner of war, probably somewhere in Japan. Please, if you have a minute, look in on him. It would mean a lot to Grandma and Grandpa. "Grandpa and I took a long walk in the woods last week, and you sure did a wonderful job on the forests around here, and the ocean, rocks, and cliffs . . . not bad either. Very impressive. Is Mother Nature a relative? I hear people talking about her while talking about you at the same time. Moms are pretty special, aren't they? Well, anyway, you both have a real knack for building things that are pretty spectacular. Thanks! Say hi to my dad. Bless Mom, the baby, and Grandpa George. See you in the morning! Good night." Cricket held on to her wings just a little longer than usual. She felt an opaque sense of disquiet, uneasiness. "Oh, one more thing, God, I overheard a conversation between my grandma and Mrs. Landry that mentioned Mr. Toomey being very angry with my grandfather and something about a threat. Please don't let anything bad happen to Grandpa. He's sort of like a dad to me now. Mom and I really need him. Can you look into this, please? Again, good night!"

Cricket wrapped her treasured wings back into her dad's hankie and placed it under her pillow. She couldn't help but let her thoughts drift to this situation between Grandpa and Mr. Toomey, and what exactly did this all mean to her world? She fell asleep with visions of Mr. Toomey chasing Grandfather and her through a dark hall. Grandpa seemed anxious and they tried to run faster, but Mr. Toomey was catching up with them. The hall narrowed and came to an end against a huge locked door. They couldn't go any farther. Mr. Toomey was almost upon them, his eyes wide and savage, like that of a wild animal, and his hands had turned into long sharp knives, stabbing and slashing at Grandpa. Cricket pounded on the locked door, screaming,

"Help us! Please open the door! Help us!"

"Annie, Annie dear, wake up. You're having a bad dream," said Grandpa. "It's okay, sweetheart, everything is okay."

"Oh, Grandpa!" she said in relief.

He picked her up in his arms and held her tight. Her body was damp with perspiration, and the moisture of her tears left her hair stuck to her cheeks. Her breathing was forced and rapid.

"Grandpa, are you okay?"

"Yes, Annie, I'm fine. It was just a bad dream, not something real. Want to sleep with Grandma and me tonight?"

"Oh, yes, please! It was very scary. Grandpa, it seemed so real."

That night, Cricket snuggled safe and warm in between her grandparents in their bed, where everything felt secure and unassailable. No nightmares could enter here, Cricket told herself, but she couldn't see around the corner of the future where a nightmare might foretell the ominous things to come and just how close this bad dream might be to reality and the evil Adder Toomey of her dreams.

CHAPTER 7

Addergoole Toomey

LIKE EVERY TOWN, BIG or small, Everett had its distinctive characters—Doc Miller, Mr. Hansen, Sheriff Jim Davis, and the Barstow sisters being just a few who peppered the township of Everett with spice and charisma. Most citizens would say that the sheriff, who took his guardianship of the community's safety very seriously, probably was the one person who touched the most lives in many ways. He knew every family personally, and all their trials and tribulations as well. To the great chagrin of the town's youth, he also knew every child by sight and name. Just to keep the potential troublemakers in check and on their toes, Sheriff Davis would make an unannounced pass through the halls of the school, swing in and out of a few classrooms, and make a point to call the usual suspects by name. "How you doing, Dickie Solter? Keeping your grades up?" Or "Hey, there, Bobby Kelly, when's the last time you mowed the lawn for your mom? Things are looking a little shabby in your front yard. Best you get to it this weekend." Or perhaps "Frankie Barker, where are you? Ah, there you are. Why are you hiding in the cloakroom? Afraid I might see that black eye you got in that fight at the park last week? If I catch you at it again, we're going to have a talk down at the jail."

The youth of Everett began to believe the sheriff had eyes in the back of his head. This personal approach was applied to the troublesome adults of the community as well. Take Adder Toomey, for example. When sober, Adder seemed to be an ordinary citizen, father and husband, but when he became a customer of Murphy's Pub, a dual personality seemed to rear its ugly head. Alcohol was not Adder's best friend, although he seemed to think so. This side to Adder's nature had caused him nothing but trouble and embarrassment to his family. The sheriff had hauled Adder in for an overnight in jail more often and for more infractions than he cared to remember. Drunk in public, disturbing the peace, assault, bar brawls, and worst of all, domestic violence. On the latter, Sheriff Davis did his best to keep this from becoming public fodder out of respect for Adder's wife, Maggie, and their four children. But despite the sheriff's best efforts, there were whispers about town of Maggie's surreptitious visits to Doc Miller, the unexplained bruises and cuts, a trip to the hospital for a broken arm and, later, a broken wrist.

Adder's disappointments in life, imagined or real, began when he was just a boy and multiplied into his adulthood. His father, Fagan Toomey, was a harsh, ill-tempered man who unleashed his personal misery upon his eldest son like an unexpected cyclone. Nothing Adder could do ever pleased the man. For reasons Adder could never understand, his siblings, four brothers and six sisters, never reaped Fagan's whirlwind of cruelty like that heaped upon him. Adder's long list of abuses began as early as four years of age, when his father would expect him to perform chores that were beyond his physical abilities.

"Boy," his father shouted one time, "fetch wood for the fire!

And be quick about it!"

He ran to the woodshed to fulfill his father's request only to find all the logs that had been split were huge and heavy. He struggled and strained but couldn't lift the logs, let alone carry them the long distance to the house. He finally found five logs of a smaller nature, and he raced back and forth from the shed to the house, carrying one log at a time, but couldn't find enough smaller logs to completely fill the woodbin. Adder prayed his father wouldn't notice, but to no avail. Fagan noticed immediately the sparse number of logs and began his rant and rage at Adder's failure.

"You call this a finished job, you lazy, good-for-nothing whelp? There's not enough wood here to even start a fire, let alone heat the room."

"But, Father, the logs are too big for me. I can't pick them up!" said Adder, already cringing at his father's tone of voice.

"Well, maybe you need an incentive to try harder!" barked Fagan as he slowly and deliberately sorted through the bin that contained the kindling pieces of twigs and small branches.

Finally, Fagan pulled out a long thin branch of willow and snapped it in the air like he was appraising its ability to sting. Finally, he turned to Adder and sternly demanded he drop his pants and bend over the arm of the sofa. As Adder reached down to unbutton his pants, he realized, to his horror, that he had wet himself and was standing in a puddle on the living room rug.

"I'm sorry, Father! Please don't switch me! I'll do better next time, I promise . . . please!" Adder began to cry in fear, and the more he cried, the angrier Fagan became.

"Look what you've done, peed on the carpet like a little girl! Are you a little girl, boy? Are *you*?" said Fagan as he grabbed Adder by his shirt collar and threw him toward the sofa.

"Over the arm, boy, and make it fast!" Adder was too small to reach the arm without help, so he shoved the footstool up to the sofa, climbed up, and bent over.

He waited in total dread, waiting, waiting, and finally the switching began. The first blow, he would discover later, cut a bright-red swath across his buttocks, the next two slashed open a bloody ribbon of skin across his small thighs, then another, and another, until Adder lost count.

"Fagan!" screamed Adder's mother, grabbing Fagan's arm. "Stop or you'll kill the boy. Stop!" Fagan threw Adder's mother to the floor and poured the remainder of his wrath on her, whipping her back, her arms, and one ugly blow across her face. Then, like the eye of the storm, he stopped and observed his destruction. Adder and his mother held their breaths while waiting to see if the storm had passed. Fagan looked down at his terrified wife and sobbing child.

"Maybe you should have killed the bastard before he was born . . . whore."

With that, Fagan broke the switch across his knee and tossed it into the fireplace, leaving his wife and child cringing on the floor of the darkened room. Adder's main goal in the youth of his life was totally directed at reaching some form of approval from his father. He was sure that if that could be accomplished, it would end the years of brutal abuse and perhaps open a door for the kind of love and respect Adder had witnessed between other boys his age and their fathers. He tried impressing his father with school grades, but he was only an average student and found the task beyond his reach. Those times during the school year when he was required to bring home his report card for his parents to see and his father to sign were excruciating.

"Stand up, boy!" his father demanded of Adder as he looked at each child present at the dinner table. "Let's see what wonderful scholarly endeavors your brilliant brother has accomplished this time."

Fagan examined the card and read the teacher's statements. The room grew silent, and Adder's knees began to shake in fear and apprehension. Fagan took his time going over the contents of the card. Finally, he finished and placed the card on the table, looking at Adder over the top of his glasses.

"I see there is a C in reading. Does that stand for *clown* or *creep*? And another C in spelling. Hmmm . . . perhaps that C stands for *curse*, like you are to this family. Ah, what's this? Another fantastic C in math. That C must stand for can't, like you can't do anything well? Last by far from the least, another incredible effort on your behalf . . . a C minus in, of all things, penmanship. You can't even get a decent grade in writing! Take a good look at your brother, children. He's the perfect example of a failure, a good-for-nothing bum, an incompetent loser, and he always will be. I don't think we need to be exposed to that kind of incompetence, so from today forward, Adder will eat his meals from a bowl on the back porch with the dogs, which is better company than he deserves."

Adder took his plate and retired to the back porch. Little did Fagan realize how relieved Adder was to be freed from the nightly torture of sitting at the dinner table and listening to the berating of everything he did or said. He spent the rest of his younger childhood eating on the back porch with the dogs, secretly delighted with his father's decision and totally happy with his nonabusive and loving meal companions. Next, he tried sports. Swimming, track, basketball. When Adder happened upon football and excelled, he thought that would finally be his path to acceptance. Fagan actually attended several of Adder's games and complimented his athletic abilities. After Adder's mishap with the Bane brothers concerning his insulting treatment of their little sister (a mishap that ended his budding football career), Fagan reverted to, and even intensified, his former disposition for cruelty and indifference.

"Stand up, boy!" said Fagan in his usual tone of contempt. "Let me look at you." Adder struggled to stand on his painful leg with a very swollen knee. "Well, aren't you a pitiful sight? Black eye, scratched face, split lip, bum knee. No more football for you, boy. You truly are the world's biggest fuck up. You can't even get laid without screwing it up! That little 105-pound Bane girl whipped your sorry ass, or did her brothers show you what real men look like? What's that surprised look on your face? You didn't think I knew, along with everybody else in town, that the Bane boys beat the crap out of you for manhandling their little sister? I know everything about you, boy, and you are one sorry example of a walking, talking piece of horseshit, I can tell you that!" Fagan glowered at Adder, and Adder stood there speechless. He had no acceptable excuse for his miserable condition, certainly not one that would suffice with Fagan. These continual verbal beatings gave Adder a fertile field in which to plant and nurture his seeds of hatred toward the Bane brothers, their haughty sister, Thaddeus Bane, or anything Bane, even including any Bane grandchildren. He dug the roots of his loathing deep and watered and fertilized them generously until these acres of disdain grew in number and flourished. After Adder could no longer play football, the only thing that seemed to arouse any kind of attention from his father was his boastful reputation for drinking and debauchery and the vastly exaggerated chronicles of his exploits with the many girls he dated. Adder Toomey had finally found a persona that pleased his father; the more tawdry and lurid the tale, the greater his father's interest. Having discovered a path to what he thought was his father's affection, Adder honed his promiscuous and wanton behavior with the enthusiasm of a stealthy leopard pursuing a gazelle.

One night, the grandfather clock in the foyer struck 3:00 a.m. as Adder stumbled through the hall and headed for the stairs. The light went on in the study, and his father's voice called his name.

"Adder? Come in, boy."

It was a command, not a request. He entered his father's study, a place that was always by invitation only.

"How was your evening?" asked Fagan. "Great. Just great."

Adder knew the routine, a blow-by-blow description, drink by drink, dirty joke by dirty joke, and finally every obscene thing that took place between Adder and any girl he had for company. Since many of Adder's evenings ended with his female companion slapping his face and leaving him standing speechless, he learned early on to make up an Academy Award–worthy story, making himself sound like a real rounder and ladies' man when the truth was, the only companions to put up with his disgusting behavior were well-paid hookers. He needed the worst possible stories; otherwise, his father would lose interest, and he would be dismissed. As Fagan aged, he seemed to gain more and more pleasure at the thought of Adder invading the innocence and virtue of Everett's finest families, like a poisonous snake slithering through the halls of all the sanctimonious, hypocritical pillars of the community that had looked down their noses at the Toomey family for years. The more attention Adder received from him, the more he was driven to make up his exploits to include every virgin within the town's limits, none of whom ever realized they had been added to Adder's list of young women painted with the scarlet brush of shame.

Fagan Toomey finally drank himself into the grave, dying just two days before Adder's twenty-first birthday. When the will was read, Adder sat in total disbelief in discovering that his father, Fagan Toomey, truly did not believe he was Adder's biological father and that he, Fagan Toomey, took great joy in Adder's vile reputation only as a way to seek revenge against Adder's mother and whoever her lover had been. Adder begged his mother for the truth, but she refused to talk about her past. She took the name of Adder's real father with her to her grave. There were speculations and rumors after the conditions of Fagan's will circulated through town, but no one knew for sure. Fagan condemned Adder as a bastard—in fact, if not in law—and wrote him out of his will. Adder was humiliated and devastated. He felt betrayed beyond measure and never spoke to his mother again, which brought about a large breach between himself and his siblings. All those years of feeding Fagan those counterfeit, lecherous stories, only to find that the man he had thought was his father had encouraged him to build and intensify his fictitious, disgusting reputation, one that would follow him as actuality through his life, only to reap revenge upon a wife he believed had betrayed him. Adder died inside on the day Fagan Toomey's will was read.

There was no funeral or memorial service for the tortured, angry soul of Adder's youth, but what grew out of the ashes of his disappointments would one day jolt the whole town and the Bane household in particular. Adder saw himself as the town joke, a disinherited bastard, the subject of whispers, of snickers, and the town's main source of back-fence gossip. In truth, as time passed, his plight was hardly mentioned. Well, perhaps over a beer or two at Murphy's Pub now and then, but over the years, the details were mostly forgotten. The misconception of the town's interest in his circumstances led Adder on a lifelong challenge to make something of himself in spite of his father's opinion of him or the town's skeptics.

It became a distorted obsession that consumed him in an attempt to prove the town's detractors wrong, and this tunnel vision lured him into one failed venture after another: Shares in a silver mine that turned out to have been salted and contained nothing but slate shale and nuggets of silver melted down from old flatware. Toomey's Dungarees, the manufacturer of a strong denim material for long-wearing work pants, a patent that was already owned by a company in San Francisco by the name of Levi's. A drive-in restaurant that would serve people meals in their cars. This one almost got him laughed out of town. Who in their right mind would want to eat a meal in their car? Adder's many failed attempts to succeed, to succeed at anything, also included selling shares in a six-hundred-acre piece of property in the Black Hills of South Dakota for gold speculation. The land turned out to be on an Indian reservation and was unavailable for prospecting. Next came Toomey's Bees, the raising and renting of bees to local farmers. Why on earth would anyone want to pay for something Mother Nature did for free? An unexpected hard freeze took care of this scheme by killing off all his stock of bees. The sad list went on and on, and as Adder's failures mounted, his dreams began to taste bitter and dry as they died and turned to ash and dust. He was just about to give up on ever doing something special, something outstanding in his life, when one long boring afternoon, while sifting through his endless paperwork as a file clerk for a mortgage company, Adder overheard a conversation taking place in the next office. The US government had decided to send all those of Japanese descent inland, away from the coast, for the duration of the war. This was being done under the assumption that any number of the Japanese living in these areas could be possible spies and in collusion with Japan to invade the United States. I mean, after all, look what they did to Pearl Harbor! They could be planning the same horrific invasion here on the West Coast. All their land and most of their personal belongings were to be confiscated, making a great deal of prime farmland available for bargain prices. This could be Adder's big break, his chance to finally make it big. He saw himself as a real estate mogul, finally making the town eat crow. His star was about to rise. He'd show everyone who had ever laughed at all his past endeavors that he was a force to be dealt with. He'd make them sorry. He'd finally show them, and that applied to the snooty Banes in particular. Hatred, as Adder Toomey and the quiet community of Everett was about to discover, can be a thirsty master whose desire for revenge is never quenched.

CHAPTER 8

Thaddeus Duncan Bane

CRICKET'S ADORATION FOR HER grandparents was infinite, and for her grandfather in particular. He stepped in as a surrogate father after her father was killed and helped Cricket and her mother through the roughest and saddest time in their lives. Cricket was the first grandchild and absolutely wallowed in her grandparents' and uncles' (the Brothers) overt attention and affection. With her mom expecting a new baby, she could definitely feel a possible demotion in the wind. The once "everybody's princess" was about to become "child ordinaire," but here, in her grandparents' home, she still reigned omnipotent, for now, and loved every minute of it. Thaddeus Duncan Bane grew up in a poor farming family. His passion for defending the underdog and fighting injustice wherever he found it was apparent even in his youth. It was the driving force behind his financial struggle to obtain a law degree. Lulled by the hypnotizing motion of the backyard swing, Cricket spent hours during lazy, warm afternoons listening to her grandmother tell stories of her grandfather's brave and heroic efforts to right wrongs and bring justice to an unjust world and their life together as a young couple. Cricket was an avid reader even at an early age and a born romantic. With her magnifying her grandmother's stories, her grandfather became her King Arthur, Robin Hood and Count of Monte Cristo all rolled into one. She wanted to marry someone just like him when she grew up.

"Tell me again, Grandma, about you and Grandpa and how you fell in love with him when you were only my age," Cricket said, knowing full well the story she had already heard many times.

"Well, yes, it's true," Grandma began. "I did fall in love with your grandfather when I was only six years old. I saw him at a church social one Easter Sunday. He was tall, handsome, with a wonderful smile. It was love at first sight, at least for me, but being seven years younger than he was, he didn't know I existed, but I knew, even then, we would marry one day."

"When did Grandpa fall in love with you?" Cricket asked, already knowing that answer too.

"Well, when I was about ten years old, your grandfather left our small farming town and went to the city. He worked three jobs to put himself through law school. It took him almost six years, but he finally graduated and returned home. By then, I was sixteen. Then he asked me to the church Autumn Barn Dance—"

"Then you were married, came out west, and raised your family. First came Uncle Donald, then Uncle Franklyn, my mom, and Uncle Ken, right?"

"That's right, my little Cricket. Finally a girl, your mom, your grandfather's pride and joy." Cricket liked the idea of being someone's pride and joy. It sounded important and very permanent. But she wasn't sure if you obtained this prominent status by way of birth or personal effort. Was it, perhaps, a gift one received for, let's say, your birthday or Christmas? She decided to research the question and bring it up in her prayers that night.

"Grandpa fought for liberty and justices, just like the Pledge of Allegiance to the flag, right?" said Cricket without stopping to take a breath.

"And you lived happily ever after just like Cinderella and the prince, or King Arthur and Guinevere, didn't you, Grandma?" "Yes, sweet girl," said Grandma as she leaned down to give Cricket a warm hug and a quick kiss on the tip of her nose.

"We lived happily ever after." Cricket's childhood fantasy was a far cry from the real truth, but in her mind's eye, it was indisputable. The facts, unfortunately, weren't covered with fairy dust.

Thaddeus Bane's six-year struggle to obtain his degree was just that, a struggle. Many times, Thaddeus thought of giving up and just returning to the farm, but there was something deep inside him that kept him going. Once he finally graduated, the facts didn't get much brighter. The only position he could find was that of a lowly clerk in the back dungeons of some obscure law office that reminded him of a scene from *A Christmas Carol.* Returning home, Thaddeus felt despondent. All those years of studies and hard times, and still he had no job with any possibilities of a future. Finally, tales of the West caught his imagination, tales of a new frontier, new cities, and new industries, new opportunities for anyone willing to put in the hard work. Surely, there were possibilities for a hardworking young attorney in such a place. Thaddeus had been courting Arvilla Kimber for almost a year. She had been his greatest supporter to follow his dream, and he couldn't imagine a life without her in it. They married in the spring of 1907, Arvilla just short of her seventeenth birthday, and Thad a few weeks short of his twenty- fourth. Like pioneers of old, they packed up their few belongings and headed out west. Their hopes were high, their love was new and strong, and the world lay in front of them like a rich field just waiting to be harvested. The harshness of the new West wasn't much different from the harshness of scraping out a living as a dairy farmer. Although the train trip was arduous, the excitement of a new life kept their spirits high; with a deep faith in God, each other, and the hubris of youth, they forged ahead and never looked back. These two young dreamers were taken with the vast green forests, the crystal blue lakes and rivers, and the tall statuesque mountains of their new home in the Northwest, in the state of Washington. It was more than obvious why it was called the Evergreen State and very much in contrast to the relatively low lands of Wisconsin, where they both had spent most of their lives. They arrived in Seattle on a late spring morning. The sky was cloud-covered and filled with rain. They settled into a small boardinghouse in a modest part of town, only a short trolley car ride to the center of town, where Thad spent his days searching out the possibilities for employment. When opportunities to practice law seemed few and far between, Thad began to look into the booming forest industry. The lumber mills to the north were hiring logging crews and were taking those with little or no experience and a willingness to learn. Running out of money and options, Thad hired on at Jamison's Lumber Mill in Edmonds, just a little north of Seattle, and thus began the new married life of Arvilla and Thad Bane in a series of lumber camps over the next few years. They raised their young family in rough-cut logging cabins with no electricity, no indoor plumbing or running water. Arvilla used a wood-burning stove for cooking and warming the kitchen, a washboard to do the laundry, and gave birth to her children at home with the assistance of a midwife.

"Arvilla, dear, here's a nice cup of ginger tea, to help relax you," said Thad as he adjusted the pillows behind her back and stroked her hair. "I've called Mary. She's on her way. Looks like we'll be new parents again soon. I've told the boys, and they are really excited. They're next door with the Hudsons. You're not to worry." Thad pulled up a chair next to the bed and grasped Arvilla's hand. "I love you more than life itself, and never more than just now, this very minute. Your beauty takes my breath away."

"Oh, Thad, you're such a silver-tongued devil. Here I am, as big as a house, hair a mess, hanging down all over the place, and you call me beautiful. Go on now," said Arvilla, giving his hand a loving pat just as the next labor pain struck.

"Never more than now, my dear. And these gifts, these glorious children you give to me and the world, your generosity humbles me and—ah, someone's knocking on the door. It must be Mary. I'll be right back." The night seemed endless, and Thad flinched with every moan and gasp that Arvilla let escape as the process of childbirth progressed toward morning. As the sun rose, Thad saw the fatigue that etched its lines of exhaustion and pain across Arvilla's sweet face.

"How's she doing?" asked Thad, searching the midwife's face for a sign.

"She's doing just fine, Mr. Bane, but I don't see the child arriving for some time yet. Perhaps it's best if you go to the mill and busy yourself, and I'll send one of the boys when you're needed back here."

"Well . . . okay. But I want to know just as soon as anything happens." Thad gently kissed his sleeping wife on the forehead.

"She'll be just fine and a lot less nervous without you pacing the floor. Now you scoot and let me do my job." Mary gave Thad a broad smile of assurance and all but pushed him out the door as he, reluctantly, headed for the mill. Hours passed till it was almost midday. Mary gently washed Arvilla's sweat-stained face with a cool, damp cloth, helped her slip into a dry nightgown, and fluffed up the pillows for her back.

"Stay strong, Arvilla. The baby is almost here. Just a few more pushes should do," said Mary.

Arvilla took a deep breath, grasped the rope that had been tied to the bedposts, and with one mighty push and the last of her strength . . .

"Bear down," she heard Mary coaching her. "Just one more push, Arvilla. Here it comes."

Then Arvilla heard what she had been waiting for, her newborn's first sound: a healthy, boisterous cry that said, "Here I am, world, here I am."

"It's a girl, Arvilla," said Mary O'Malley. "It's a beautiful, healthy baby girl."

"Oh, Mary, I know Thad was praying for a little girl! He loves his boys so, but he'll be so happy to have a little daughter." She looked down at her new daughter as Mary settled the little infant in Arvilla's arms.

"She really is beautiful. Look at those long eyelashes. I can't wait for Thad to see his new baby girl. Did you send one of the boys down to the mill to tell their father the baby has arrived?"

"Yes, Arvilla. I'm sure Thad will be here any minute. You rest now."

The last twelve hours of labor had been tough, and Arvilla was exhausted. She held her new infant close as she gave way to the fatigue and allowed her heavy eyelids to close just for a minute. *Until Thad gets here,* she told herself. The relief from pain, the warmth of the soft blanket, the joy of the birth of a healthy baby coaxed Arvilla to drift off into some much-needed sleep.

"Hello," said Franklyn Bane to the receptionist at the Jamison Lumber Mills Edmonds office. "My mom sent me to fetch my father, Thad Bane. The baby has been born, and I have a new little sister." He grinned with great pride.

"What wonderful news!" exclaimed the receptionist. "Let's see where your dad is working today." She searched through some papers on a clipboard. "He's in building number 2, trying to get one of the saws working. That's down the stairs and the first building on your right."

"Thanks," said Franklyn, and he hurried down the stairs. As he reached the bottom of the stairs, there seemed to be a flurry of activity, with shingle weavers and mill workers scurrying in all directions.

"Hey, Big Dan," said Franklyn, "what's going on?"

"What you doing here, boy?" said Big Dan, a bear of a man and one of Thad Bane's closest friends at the mill.

"Mom sent me to get Dad. Our new baby has been born, and—"

"Listen to me, Franklyn. There's been an accident. I need you to run back to the office and have them call Doc Miller. Tell him to get ready for a bad cut. Your dad had a saw blade jump a knot and cut him pretty bad. Tell him I'm bringing Thad. I'll be right behind you. Now, hurry!"

Franklyn's heart seemed to drop to his knees as he turned on his heels. He raced back up the stairs and dashed into the mill office.

"Big Dan said to have you call Doc Miller's office and tell him they're bringing my dad in with a bad cut," said Franklyn, choking back his fear.

"Hurry, Big Dan said, hurry!"

"Hang on, Thad," said Big Dan as he worked with the skill of a nurse to stop Thad's profuse bleeding with a tourniquet.

"I'm going to get you to Doc Miller's. Your boy has gone ahead to let him know what to expect."

"Is my hand gone, Dan? Did I lose it? Tell me the truth," said Thad.

His voice grew weaker as he started to go into shock.

"I don't know, but it's pretty bad. The doc will know what to do." Big Dan hoisted Thad up over his shoulder like he was a bag of feathers and carried him up the stairs, through the office, and toward a waiting car.

Thad could feel himself going in and out of consciousness. What would happen now? What if he lost his hand? Who would hire a one-handed man? How could he take care of his family with a new baby to be born any minute? The pain was excruciating. The scenery out the window passed the moving car as if in slow motion. Big Dan released the pressure of the tourniquet for a few seconds, and the bleeding poured out through the bandage. The tourniquet was reapplied. The trip down the hill to Everett seemed to take forever.

"We're here, Thad," said Big Dan. "We're here at Doc Miller's. Hang in there, Thad." Thad felt Big Dan haul him from the car onto his brawny shoulders again.

He tried to say "Thanks," but nothing came out of his mouth. He was cold, very cold. His hearing faded until his world went silent and he started to fall, faster and faster, swirling through a dark hole. Everything went black . . . black, cold, and quiet.

"Thad, Thad, darling, can you hear me?" Thad opened his eyes to see his wife's worried face smiling down at him. "You've been unconscious for three days, and you've lost so much blood we thought we were going to lose you. But Doc Miller said he thinks you are going to be all right now, dear." Arvilla bent over to give him a hug, and Thad recoiled in pain from the slightest pressure.

"I'm so sorry, dear," said Arvilla. "Look, sweetheart, look what I've brought you."

She reached behind her and took a small bundle from the nurse, unwrapping the blanket, and Thad Bane met his daughter for the very first time. Thad forced his somewhat-blurry vision to focus on the small entity being presented to him. Did he hear correctly? Was this tiny being his daughter? Arvilla moved closer, and Thad gazed in disbelief at the daughter he had so prayed for. He reached up to touch her little hand, and immediately she grasped Thad's finger. That was the beginning of a bond that would last a lifetime. Thad's injuries were serious. He didn't lose his hand, but Doc Miller couldn't save the last three fingers of his injured left hand. Thad was out of the hospital within a week and under the care of his loving family. But his concerns about providing for them grew daily, and he felt his future looked bleak. One evening, at the end of his first week of home care recovery, there came a knock on the door. Arvilla opened it to find Mr. Henry Jamison, owner of the mill where Thad worked, standing with hat in hand on their doorstep.

"Why, Mr. Jamison," she said.

"Good evening, Mrs. Bane. I came to pay my respects to Thad.

Is he up to a visitor?"

"Please, Mr. Jamison, do come in. Thad, dear, you have a visitor," said Arvilla. Thad swiveled his chair around to greet Mr. Jamison with a hearty smile. He started to rise.

"Please, Thad, don't get up," said Mr. Jamison. "I'll just sit here next to you. How are you feeling?" "Much better, thanks." Thad cradled his heavily bandaged hand.

"Good . . . that's good news. If there is anything you need, please let me know."

"That's very kind, but we're fine. But I don't know when I'll be able to come back to work."

"That's what I came to talk to you about, Thad. Your ability to negotiate contracts between the workers, organized labor, and the mill owners has not gone unnoticed over these past few years. We could use a man with your talents and knowledge of the law upstairs in the office. Would that kind of job be of interest to you? With a considerable raise in pay, naturally."

Thad couldn't believe his ears; one minute he was worried about how he was going to support his family, and the next he was given the kind of job he had always wanted. God does work in mysterious ways. Who could have guessed that almost losing his hand could turn into such a blessing?

"Why, yes," said Thad, still somewhat in shock at the splendid offer. "I mean, certainly. Getting back into the field of law has always been my goal."

"Good," said Mr. Jamison. "I had hoped you would find the job change offer appealing." Mr. Jamison stood and reached his hand out to Thad, and the two men shook hands. "I'll have my secretary draw up our agreement, and there will be an office waiting for you when you feel up to returning to work." Thad walked Mr. Jamison to the door and once more shook his hand. "Thank you again, Mr. Jamison. I can't tell you how grateful I am for your faith in me. I won't let you down, sir."

"I know you won't, Thad. That's why I made you the offer. Now take your time healing, and I'll see you at the office when you've made a full recovery." Mr. Jamison patted Thad on his shoulder, tipped his hat to Arvilla, and disappeared into his waiting car dutifully attended to by his chauffer, who stood at the curb, holding the back door open. Thad was so elated he hardly felt the pain in his healing hand, and Arvilla was delighted at the thought of living back in Everett, out of the mountains, in her own home, with all the amenities of lights, water, indoor plumbing, paved sidewalks and streets, and everything she might need for her growing family only minutes away instead of hours. Within the year, they were settled in a lovely little three-bedroom home on Norton Street located on a small hill overlooking downtown Everett. It had a front porch with a swing, living room, dining room, large kitchen, and screened-in back porch.

The yard was ample and filled with fruit trees, the perfect spot for the importance of tree forts for the boys. Its location was within walking distance to shopping and schools—pure perfection in Arvilla's eyes. Thad was finally in his element, and his long-derailed legal career was, at last, on the move. After the United States entered World War I in 1917, there was an upsurge in the shipyards of Puget Sound and the lumber industry. The western part of the state had given up its cattle ranges and replaced them with thousands of acres of wheat. The temperate areas between the mountains and the coast became the fruit basket of the States, growing a large range of fruit orchards and berries. Along with the end of the war came sharp cutbacks in production, and much unemployment resulted. Organized labor protested with large strikes, including the Seattle Revolution of 1919, in which about sixty thousand workers walked off their jobs. Thad was in a prime position to step in and help resolve many of the main issues.

At the end of the story that Cricket knew so well, she asked, "Then did you and Grandpa become rich and famous?"

"Well, not exactly, sweetheart. We had a comfortable home and we got by, but rich and famous? No. As a matter of fact, when your grandfather finally struck out on his own as a hardworking, up-and-coming attorney, he was absolutely impossible. He did so much work for people that couldn't afford to pay much. If anything, we were as poor as church mice for years." Grandma said this with a look of deep love and great pride on her face. Closing her eyes and allowing the warm summer moments to transport her imagination, Cricket tried to picture her grandparents' meager circumstances. All she could conjure up was a Disney version of Minnie and Mickey Mouse, huddled together in the doorway of an arch in the baseboard of some run-down old country church, eating stale bread crumbs from the floor. Along with "Poor as a church mouse," Cricket would always recall with tenderness a few of her grandmother's other sayings, like "A wolf in sheep's clothing," "The whole kit and caboodle" (What is a *caboodle*, anyway?), "Stiff as Job's turkey" (Who is Job, and how come his turkey is so stiff, and how did it get that way?), "Heavens to Betsy," and last but far from the least, Cricket's favorite, "As mad as a wet hen."

As Cricket's afternoon of revisiting her grandfather's history came to an end and she and her grandmother went about their preparation for dinner and the return of Thaddeus Duncan Bane to his hearth and home, Cricket was totally unaware that before the summer drew to an end, she would have an opportunity to see her grandfather, as a lawyer and retired judge, perform at his finest in an event that would unnerve this small community and close the door forever on her fairy-tale world.

CHAPTER 9

Summer Friends

THE NEIGHBORHOOD IN EVERETT where Cricket's grandparents lived was a precursor to the suburban housing developments that would spring up across the nation at the end of the war. It consisted of about four blocks of Lombard Street, which culminated at the north city limits. The houses were all the same floor plan with a slight variance in the facade. Five steps up to a small porch, some houses with the living room to the left, while others with the living room to the right. Each had a living room, small dining room, bathroom, bedroom, and kitchen with an eating area, and a staircase going down to a very large basement and upstairs to a loft and one bedroom. The back porch led to an elongated backyard and a one-car garage that was accessible from the alley in the back that divided the block in half. This neighborhood was peopled with hardworking, blue-collar families and a plethora of children about Cricket's age, six of whom became her best friends for a month each summer. This small assemblage included Tommy and Chris Wilson, eleven-year-old twins who lived directly across the street from Cricket's grandparents. They were lean, blond, all-American boys with luminous smiles freely given to all who approached. They were more than just identical twins; they were more like mirrored images of each other. As they headed toward their teens, it became easier to detect their individual personality differences.

Tommy, the more serious of the two, worried about grades, being on time, finishing homework, and the like, while Chris was very easygoing, laid-back, and not overly concerned about everything in general. Tommy was a by-the-book type of boy and loved working part-time at his dad's hardware store, learning the name and purpose of every tool in the place. Chris, on the other hand, was very close with his uncle Rocco, his dad's brother, who owned a cattle ranch a few miles out of town. Chris spent all his spare time on the ranch riding horses and learning how to brand, herd, and care for cattle and the general running of a ranch. It wasn't long before the twins' different interests began to show in their dress and attitudes. Tommy dressed in beige cords and an appropriate shirt, and Chris's choice was head-to-toe cowboy— jeans, plain shirt, and boots. The local school wasn't pleased that Chris's attire varied to such a degree from their idea of an unspoken dress code, but his mom stood her ground, insisting that it was of great importance that twins be allowed to express their own individuality to become healthy adults. The school acquiesced to her demands, and Chris was allowed to be himself. Two doors down from the Wilsons lived the Toomey family. Maggie, wife to the sometimes nice and sometimes-ornery Adder Toomey, was a pillar in the community. She not only had her hands full raising her four young children, but she also found the time to help every neighbor for blocks around at one time or another during a time of illness or crisis.

She was everyone's angel and a living reminder of the true meaning of neighbor and friend. The oldest of the Toomey children, twelve-year-old Mike, had his Irish heritage written all over his freckled face, which was topped by a bushel of curly red hair. Unlike his rather dark and moody father, Mike had a sunny disposition and cheery nature, accented by deep dimples on either side of his warm, quirky smile. Directly across the street from the Toomeys lived Myrna Fisher. Myrna was the epitome of an old soul in a young body and a real piece of work in the bargain. She was petite in stature, with enormous brown eyes that were framed by thick, horn- rimmed glasses and a small pointed face draped by straight dark- brown hair. Reading was her passion, and leveling judgments on others, her hobby. Myrna was a walking, talking tablet of the Ten Commandments, the contents of the Constitution of the United States, a complete list of the Bill of Rights and its amendments, not to mention all things moral in the Judaic-Christian world. There was no doubt in anyone's mind that one day Myrna would assume the role of the first female Supreme Court justice, a dean of some prestigious university, the president of a large international conglomerate, or possibly the first woman president of the United States. At the very end of the block lived Katrina and Marvin Waters. Kat was a rather shy ten-year-old, and *pale* was the one word that best described her. Her light golden hair tumbled in a profusion of curls almost to her waist and framed her amazing crystal blue eyes and porcelainlike skin.

Marvin, Kat's fourteen-year-old brother, was rather dark and brooding in comparison. A few years prior, Marvin had sustained a severe head injury in a motorcycle accident, which left him prone to sullen mood swings. He had sudden fits of anger and was somewhat mentally slower than others his age. Even though he was the eldest of the group, he seemed to enjoy his friendship with all the kids on the block. Cricket and Kat were best friends, and she didn't seem to mind that Cricket was two years her junior. That made Cricket feel great, and that truly cemented their friendship. Kat could sing like an angel, and she and Cricket loved to put on a musical show in Cricket's grandparents' backyard, with her grandmother as their sole audience. Cricket wasn't too sure she had any talent worth displaying, so she would provide the costumes and narrate the show. Grandma would clap and proclaim the whole production a raging success. After the applause had died, they celebrated their successful opening with milk and cookies at Grandma's kitchen table. No wonder everyone loved Grandma, Cricket thought to herself as she closed her eyes and let Grandma's praise and love wash over her like a warm breeze, for she certainly was a one-woman band of support for everyone she knew.

One Sunday, Mr. and Mrs. Waters took Kat and Cricket to Seattle to see a matinee performance of *Swan Lake*, put on by the junior class of the Seattle Ballet Academy, the very same ballet academy where Cricket's mother had studied dance for over a year. It was a magical event that she would always remember. The theater was large and high-domed, with row upon row of soft red velvet seats and special box seats that hung over the main floor like private little balconies. Hanging in the center of the theater were two enormous crystal chandeliers that rose, disappearing up into the auditorium's domed ceiling just as the performance was about to begin. As the chandeliers dimmed, the stage lights began to highlight the stage. The music of the orchestra slowly filled the auditorium as the curtains swung open to disclose a fairyland setting, and the corps de ballet filled the stage with snowy-white tutus. By the final curtain, when the swan had fluttered her final gasp of life, Kat and Cricket were in tears of both sorrow and delight. It had been an enchanting experience from the first arabesque to the last pirouette. No wonder her mom loved dancing so much, Cricket thought. Nothing in the world could possibly be more graceful or beautiful. There was one more fantastic surprise to their splendid afternoon: La Glaciere, a shop that specialized in everything ice cream. Any flavor, size, combination of ice cream that anyone could imagine. It was any child's dream. La Glaciere was one of the first ice cream specialty stores on the West Coast to offer more than just flavored syrup to top off its ice cream. It had as many different kinds of toppings as it had ice cream flavor selections.

Cricket thought long and hard to find the perfect combination and finally settled for chocolate raspberry ribbon with fresh raspberries, almonds, and mocha-flavored whipping cream. Kat went pretty much straight strawberry. Strawberry ice cream, fresh strawberries, and custard-flavored whipping cream. Mr. and Mrs. Waters were extremely conservative in their choice of just one scoop each of vanilla and no toppings. What a wasted opportunity, thought Cricket. Just plain vanilla when there were so many other exotic choices? Maybe, when you were as old as they were, Cricket decided, you had already tried all the flavors there were and nothing was very interesting anymore. Cricket promised herself as she felt her delicious concoction bring her taste buds to a standing ovation that she would never settle for just plain vanilla, no matter how advanced her age.

Cricket and Kat chattered and laughed incessantly, reliving the day's events all the way home to Everett, intensified by a slight sugar high from La Glaciere. Just as they were almost home and turned on to Lombard Street, Mr. Waters jammed on the brakes and brought the car to a sudden stop.

"What the devil are you doing in the middle of the street at twilight?" said Mr. Waters. "I could have run right over you!"

"Well, you don't own the goddamn, fucking street, do you?" stuttered Adder as he stumbled his way to the car.

"Please, Adder, I've got my wife and kids with me. Watch your language," said Mr. Waters.

"Excuse me all to hell," mocked Adder, hanging on to the driver's door for support as he shoved his head into the open window. "Well, well, well . . . heard that Makie's little princess was back in town." Adder glared at Cricket, who sat snugly against Kat in the back seat. "How the hell is your fucking stuck-up mother, anyway?" he said with a twisted grin.

"That's enough, Adder. Go home and sleep it off," said Mr. Waters. He put the car in gear and drove off down the street toward the Bane home.

"Was that Mr. Toomey, Mike's dad?" asked Cricket. "Yes, dear," answered Mrs. Waters.

"He's just had a little too much to drink. He'll be fine with a little sleep." Cricket kissed her grandparents good-night, and as they closed her bedroom door, she replayed the highlights of her wonderful day. She slipped the handkerchief from under her pillow, unwrapped the treasured wings, held them tightly in her hands, and began her prayers.

"Hello, God, Cricket here. How is everything going? Thanks for the great day . . . the ballet, the ice cream. It was all just wonderful! I'm so glad you made such lovely music and dance for us to enjoy. Good job! As you know, my mom was a dancer, and I bet she was splendid onstage. Did Dad ever see her dance? Ask him when you have a minute. Please bless Mom, our new baby-to-be, Grandpa George, Grandma and Grandpa Bane. Tell Dad I love him, and thanks again for today. One more thing, God. You know my friend Mike Toomey, who lives down the street? Well, there is something about his dad that made me very uncomfortable, sort of scared. I don't know . . . it's just a bad feeling, like tonight, when he stared at me in the car. Maybe it's nothing, but I just thought I'd mention it in case I needed a special blessing or something. Thanks again, God. Talk to you tomorrow night."

Cricket rewrapped the wings and tucked them under her pillow. As hard as she tried to concentrate only on the wonders of the day, the image of Mr. Toomey's contorted features kept overshadowing her thoughts. Why was he so angry? And the villainous look he gave her made goose bumps ripple all over her arms and tummy. Cricket would see that look again before the summer turned to fall. She would feel the impact of Adder Toomey's loathing and animosity toward the Banes. She would come face-to-face with the evil of immorality. She would learn the meaning of the word *fear*.

CHAPTER 10

Marvin

THE WATERS FAMILY HAD lived in Cricket's grandparents' neighborhood almost as long as her grandparents and the Toomey family. Jonathan Waters, Marvin's father, was originally from Utah, where he lived a traditional Mormon life with his parents and his five brothers and three sisters. His inquisitive mind stretched and strained at the confines of the conservative structure and expatiations of the Mormon philosophy. He wanted more. He wanted what was contemporary. He wanted to expand the boundaries of his narrow world and its predictability. Jonathan's hunger for a different life caused a wide rift with his father, and soon it became obvious that to find his bliss in this world, he would have to leave everything he knew and strike out on his own. Jonathan pursued his interest in the West, where stories of possibilities, riches, and adventure were everywhere you turned. It wasn't long before the reality of the bone-cracking, backbreaking work available to a young man with few skills pulled his fantasies up short. He wasn't a young man to be easily discouraged, though. While working as a laborer for a pipe-laying company just south of Seattle, he met Melanie, a golden-haired beauty who tended the front counter of her father's livery and leather shop. Within a year, Melanie and Jonathan were married, and being a fast learner, Jonathan soon became manager of the business, and eventually the owner, when Melanie's father passed away two years later at the early age of forty-six. Jonathan Waters was also intuitive, and he could foresee the popularity of the automobile. When he had the opportunity to move away from the livery end of the business and open his own dealership in the small up-and-coming community of Everett, Washington, he jumped at the chance, and thus the Waters Kaiser- Frasier Automobile Dealership was born.

Marvin was born just three months after their move to the Everett area. It was obvious from a very early age that the boy had an adventurous spirit. Before he had even started school, he had already broken an arm falling from a tree while pretending to be a topper and chipped a front tooth attempting to fly from the roof with his handmade wings of old sheets glued to a balsa wood frame. He was tossed out of Sunday school for questioning the church's theory of Adam and Eve versus evolution and had to be rescued at the age of five by local fishermen while attempting to sail a washtub across the mouth of the harbor. And who was the number one suspect for an unexplained use of fireworks in the local park that set a fifty-foot spruce on fire? Marvin. Nothing was really out-and-out criminal, but certainly enough to give his parents pause to consider making Marvin an only child. Marvin was a bit of an enigma. Since the motorcycle accident, his personality had developed periods of now-and-then dark moods. He was riding behind a much older friend, the two boys joy-riding down a country road when, out of nowhere, a buck jumped in front of them. The driver swerved, crashed through an abandoned fruit stand, and hit a tree. The young driver was killed, and Marvin spent almost two months in a coma. His recovery was slow, but he made much better progress than the doctors expected, given Marvin's serious head injuries. He lost a whole year of school, with his short-term memory loss making learning difficult for him, and his mood changes made his personality unpredictable and scattered. Although no one else thought anything of it, Marvin felt clumsy and awkward about being a year behind his classmates, which inhibited his enjoyment of school and his ability to progress. With these circumstances in mind, many of his teachers overlooked his lack of enthusiasm for studying and passed him on to the next grade even though he was unprepared for the new challenges. But even with his mood swings, Marvin was great fun. Being considerably bigger, stronger, taller, and older than Cricket and any of the other children on the block, Marvin would lead in the construction of the fort that was built each summer. Mr. Waters allowed the neighborhood kids to scavenge through his workshop for scrap wood and borrow the necessary tools for their construction project.

Marvin shared his knowledge and the whereabouts of his favorite fishing holes, knotted long ropes for them to climb trees, showed them where to find wild berry patches in the nearby forest, took them hiking and day camping, and told the very best scary, hair-teeth-and-eyeballs stories in the evening as they all sat in someone's front yard, awaiting the call to come home for the night. "Once upon a dark and stormy night, two hobos were sitting huddled around their campfire when, suddenly, a scream was heard from out of the darkness, and . . .," his story would begin. Granted, that's a cliché in today's world, but back then, that was pretty scary stuff. Kat and Cricket would sit transfixed, snuggling close together in anticipation of the horrible event to come, their hands clasped and eyes open wide, searching the fringe of the twilight around them.

Myrna, on the other hand, would roll her eyes and mutter some derogatory remark, like, "Balderdash, what foolishness!"

Inevitably, one of the Wilson twins would sneak up behind Myrna and give an awful shriek, scaring her half to death, causing everyone to roll on the ground in laughter until their sides hurt. Myrna, who saw nothing humorous in the event, would usually shake her head in disgust at what she perceived as childish behavior, excuse herself, and with a flip of her hair, head for home.

"When will you guys ever grow up?" were her last remarks as she climbed the stairs to her front door. Cricket was very fond of Marvin. He had amazingly good looks, a mature, well-developed, lean physique, a mop of dark curly hair that was always tousled and spilled down his forehead, and a devilish sense of humor. This was Cricket's very first crush on any boy. Marvin was always there to hoist her over a fence or give her a boost up when they were climbing trees or playing hide-and-go-seek.

"Here, Cricket, give me your hand," he'd whisper, and up she would fly into the tree.

They hid among the branches, out of sight of everyone on the ground, while whoever was "it" scoured the area looking for them in vain. If kick-the-can was the game of the evening, Marvin concealed Cricket behind a fence, waited until the coast was clear, then dropped her on the other side and sent her scurrying toward the can and victory. Cricket only saw Marvin's dark side once; that was the day Frankie Barker, the bully who lived between Cricket's neighborhood and the park, knocked Cricket off her bike. She was on her way to deliver some of her grandmother's freshly jarred jam to Mrs. Landry when Frankie jumped out from behind a bush. He rammed a stick into the spokes of her bike, sending her head over heels to the ground and shattering the jam in all directions. Cricket landed with a thud and tumbled into a wooden bench.

She began to cry as Frankie and his friends laughed and pointed, calling her names. "Cry baby!" "'Fraidy cat!"

She was scraped from head to toe, which stung like crazy, covered in dust, and humiliated in the bargain. Every time she attempted to get up, Frankie accelerated his barrage of insults and shoved her back to her knees. His friends chimed in until Cricket began to feel she might be in some sort of danger instead of just being harassed by a group of jerky, toad-faced boys. Then, out of the blue, just like Superman in the comics, Marvin appeared. Cricket sat pressed against the wooden bench and watched, wide- eyed, as Marvin grabbed Frankie by his collar. There was a horrible scuffle. Frankie was about Marvin's size and put up a good defense, until Marvin's superior strength took over and Frankie was soundly trounced. Marvin forced Frankie to crawl on his hands and knees to beg Cricket's forgiveness. "Say it, shit-for-brains! Say it, or I'll beat it out of you!" shouted Marvin. "Say 'I'm sorry, Cricket. Please forgive me!' Say it, Frankie!" Frankie spit out the required words between whines and crying.

Then Marvin dragged Frankie, kicking and screaming, over to Cricket's bike and forced him to take off his shirt and pants, dip them into the fountain, and wipe her bike clean of all the rocks and dirt. Next, Marvin held Frankie in a chokehold until he almost turned blue as Frankie's supposed friends looked on from a safe distance.

"Listen, you big ugly piece of whale shit," Marvin muttered into Frankie's ear. He rubbed Frankie's face into the dirt. "Don't you know that it hurts to be dumped off a bike?" he said.

"Did you hear me, you little puss pocket? Answer me! Did you hear me?"

Frankie whimpered. "Yes, I hear you." "Yes, I hear you, sir!" commanded Marvin.

"Yes, I hear you, sir," repeated Frankie. Marvin yanked Frankie to his feet and held his face just inches from his. Frankie had lost all his loudmouthed bravado as Marvin continued to berate him.

"You're twice the size of little Cricket. Haven't you heard the saying 'Pick on someone your own size,' you fat-bellied, stinky-breathed asshole?" Marvin yanked him upright again so hard his feet left the ground, and Frankie began to cry and snivel as Marvin kept him hanging in the air.

"What's this?" said Marvin, breaking into a laugh, looking down at the front of Frankie's pants. "You peed your pants, Frankie, just like a little baby. You peed your pants! What do you guys think of your bigmouth friend now? Hey, Sam, Barney, Walt," Marvin hollered, "what do you think of your brave leader now, standing here in wet underpants?" Marvin finally dropped Frankie, who sat on the ground shaking.

"If I ever see you or any of your nitwit friends anywhere near Cricket again, I'll beat all four of you to a pulp. Do you understand me, butt wad?" "Yes, yes!" squealed Frankie.

Marvin let Frankie go, and he grabbed his clothes and fled in tears.

"I'll get even with you, Marvin Waters, you just wait and see!

I'll get you!" screamed Frankie once he was at a safe distance.

Frankie's true and stalwart friends had decided discretion was indeed the better part of valor and had taken flight, leaving Frankie to face his plight on his own. Marvin stood, fist clenched, watching as Frankie faded from view. Cricket sat mesmerized by what had just happened and had long since stopped crying in amazement when Marvin made his appearance. His command of the scene was unbelievable and totally heroic. She felt like a damsel in distress being rescued by the handsome prince. She thought that perhaps, under certain circumstances, there was more truth than fiction to fairy tales and took into consideration the fact they might offer more value than she had originally imagined. I mean, after all, when they play out right in front of your eyes, it's hard to relegate them back into the only-a-fairy-tale category.

Marvin came over to Cricket and helped her up, saying, "Are you okay, Cricket?"

"I think so," Cricket said, but she wasn't totally sure. She was covered with dust and dirt.

When she attempted to stand, she winced at the sting and pain of the scrapes and bruises. Blood ran down her leg and elbow.

"Here, let me take a look at you," said Marvin as he tried to observe the damage through her dusty exterior.

Marvin picked Cricket up in his arms and carried her over to the park fountain and washed off her badly scraped knee and elbow. "It's okay, Cricket. I don't think Frankie and his goons will bother you again. He's just a jerk. Pay him no mind."

His face was expressionless, and his eyes seem veiled as he looked past Cricket into the water. She felt gratitude, adoration, and a strange sense of foreboding all at the same time. During the high season of the strawberry harvest, Marvin talked the entire group of neighborhood kids into being field-workers and picking strawberries; after all, they would be paid twenty-five cents a flat, and that meant extra money for movies or rides at the coming county fair. The first day of their employment arrived. The pickup route had assigned them to be collected on the corner of Lombard Street at 4:00 a.m. Their form of transportation was in the backs of large trucks. The tableau that they presented looked more like a scene out of the movie *The Grapes of Wrath* than it did a gathering of soon- to-be-rich, strawberry-picking moguls. Nonetheless, there they all were, joggling down the road, bouncing around the back of a truck like farm animals. When they arrived at their destination, everyone was assigned a row in the field to pick and given instructions on acceptable size and color. Everyone except Cricket. The straw boss judged her too young to be seen picking in the fields, so her job became chief in charge of passing out empty flats to be filled and stacking filled flats to be transported. For her endeavors, she was to be paid an undecided amount at the end of the day, which probably came out of the straw boss's own pocket. As it turned out, this was a backbreaking job even for youngsters, let alone adults of all ages. Cricket managed to pick two rows of strawberries before her size and age were discovered, and that was more than enough of an education in the agriculture business for her. Being bent over for hours at a time, a straw boss snapping at your heels for every berry left behind or picked too soon, was not a career Cricket intended to pursue. Nope, she definitely intended to keep getting As in her subjects, and a college degree became her top educational priority. At the end of the day, everyone was dead tired. Naturally, Marvin scored the best with a grand total of$5.00. Tommy and Chris came in with $4.00 each, while Mike made $3.75, Kat $2.00, and Myrna $1.75. The straw boss gave Cricket $1.00 for her efforts. A grand total of $21.50 for their day as farmworkers. The Lombard Strawberry Cartel only lasted three more days. By unanimous opinion, it was decided that a change in their career course was in order. But the summer's spendable income account was plush, and at a nickel a cone, their favorite indulgence, ice cream, was pretty well guaranteed for the rest of the season. At the end of their short venture into the business world, Cricket was exhausted. Her clothes were stained from handling all those strawberries, her back ached, and she had sunburned the part in her hair since she didn't wear a hat. She was so tired she could barely gather enough energy to say her prayers.

"Hi, God, Cricket here. I'm sorry I missed a few nights of my prayers. I had my very first job, and it really wore me out. Have you ever worked as a field hand picking fruit or vegetables or stacking filled crates? Well, it's no dream occupation, let me tell you. I'm going to study extra hard when I get back to school, because I sure would hate to have to do strawberry picking for a living. "I got into a scary situation the other day when Frankie Barker and his idiot friends jumped me in the park on my way to Mrs. Landry's house, just in case you weren't looking. Marvin came along and saved me by beating the pajesus out of him. I was so happy to see Marvin, and I cheered him on as he tormented Frankie. "Was that an awful thing to do? Is there somewhere in the Ten Commandments that says that's a sin? I just couldn't help myself, because that Frankie is such a stinker. He really deserved it, God, honest. But if I was wrong, I apologize. I'll try not to gloat if that ever happens again. "Bless Mom, our almost-baby, my grandparents, and my dad, and let's add Marvin to the list. Good night, God! Hope you had a great day."

The camaraderie and laughter of those days rang clear and pure and came from the heart, hearts filled with the guileless naïveté of unsullied youth. A smile was an everyday accessory that multiplied with the waning of the day. Bonds were built with the unquestioning expectation their shelf life would last *forever*. How cruel the days just ahead would seem when the mirror of righteousness shattered, sending the painful shards of disbelief deep into their young and innocent souls.

CHAPTER 11

Mary Frances

FOR SEVERAL WEEKS OUT of each summer, Mike Toomey's cousin Mary Frances would join Cricket and the neighborhood children. As the only daughter of Adder Toomey's older brother—the one and only sibling out of ten that Adder had any contact with—Mary Frances was spoiled beyond imagination by her adoring father. One day, Cricket overheard Mr. Toomey complaining to his wife that Mary Frances was "spoiled rotten," so she asked Mary Frances about it.

"I heard Mr. Toomey tell Mrs. Toomey that you were *spoiled rotten.* What is that supposed to mean?"

"Not to worry," said Mary Frances. "All that means is that I get what I want when I want it, and what's wrong with that?"

Cricket had to agree; that was a pretty sweet deal. Perhaps she should discuss this new classification with her mother to see if she could arrange something similar for herself. Mary Frances was a twelve-year-old champion jump roper, and she could spit watermelon seeds farther than any of the boys. Her dark, flashing eyes signaled an impish nature. Her shiny black braids woven with bright-colored ribbons flew into the air when she jumped rope and hung past her waist when she stood. Cricket thought Mary Frances was marvelous. She could run faster, climb higher, and swim farther than any of the other kids. She was also the instigator of several unanimous group actions that caused them to get grounded a time or two, but Cricket didn't care. She was the first free spirit that Cricket had ever met and more fun than anyone she knew. She wanted to be just like her.

"Hi, guys. What you been up to while you were waiting for me to arrive?" said Mary Frances with a devilish wink. Cricket chimed right in to bring Mary Frances up-to-date.

"We play games in the evening, we worked the strawberry fields for three days and made over twenty dollars the very first day," she claimed with pride, "and we are just about ready to start building our fort now that you're here."

"Booooooring," said Mary Frances. "Now, let's get this summer going!"

Boring, thought Cricket. *Hmmm, I wonder what Mary Frances has in mind.* They all packed a lunch and headed for a picnic at the edge of a nearby strawberry field, where a juicy, fresh dessert was theirs for the picking. A small grove of eucalyptus trees on the field's edge offered the perfect shade and setting. After lunch and gorging themselves on fresh strawberries (which were a lot more fun to eat than pick), Myrna gave an obligatory sermon on what she deemed to be a possible infringement of the law by helping themselves to someone else's strawberries, but after a brief discussion, the matter was deemed a minor infraction at best, and Myrna was voted down. Mary Frances stood, pulled a cigarette from her pocket, and lit it.

"Anyone want a drag?"

Cricket decided this was the perfect time to begin embracing the life of a free spirit and immediately raised her hand to volunteer, but Marvin intervened, dictating that Kat and Cricket were much too young to take up the habit of tobacco. Myrna jumped to her feet and gave a lecture on the wickedness of such a habit, going into great detail of its physical and social evils. She made it sound like tobacco was the gateway drug to total damnation, and she also described the function of the lungs and how the tars and nicotine affected the human body and the lungs' health. "How are you going to like that cigarette when your lungs can no longer do your breathing for you guys?" lectured Myrna.

"Myrna," said Mary Frances, "you're such a little prude. Don't you know that the word *evil* is just *live* spelled backward?"

Myrna rolled her eyes and crossed her arms as Mary Frances, Tommy, Chris, Mike, and Marvin passed the cigarette around. By the amount of coughing that took place, those who were forced to abstain determined that no one in their group was the smoking pro they pretended to be. A victorious Myrna stated, "I told you so."

"Well, what's on the menu for this summer?" asked Mary Frances.

Everyone chimed in with suggestions, mainly the same things they had done for years: build a fort that worked as a clubhouse, play games, spend time in the woods, get ready for the Fourth of July parade.

"Is that it?" said Mary Frances with a shrug. "The same old stuff?"

"Well, yes," answered Marvin. "What did you have in mind?" "Hmmm . . . I was thinking more like . . . more like something different for a change," said Mary Frances with a look of contemplation. "Maybe a party without parental supervision?" "Fat chance of that happening," said Tommy.

"Yeah," agreed Chris.

"What difference does it make if there's parental supervision or not?" Cricket asked.

Marvin and Mary Frances began to laugh, and Myrna, Kat, and Cricket looked at one another, puzzled, but still mulling over the idea. The idea was very intriguing to Cricket. What if this was her last chance to launch her new persona as a free spirit?

"What kind of a party will it be?" she asked.

"Well, maybe one with music and some cold beer," said Mary Frances, looking over the group for possible approval.

"No way!" insisted Myrna. "We'd get in so much trouble it would be winter before we got off being grounded." "Yeah," agreed Tommy and Chris, "our dad would kill us if he caught us drinking."

Mike thought for a minute and added, "My dad drinks so much I doubt if he'd even notice if I had a drink. He'd probably want to join us, but it sure would upset my mom, and you know, Mary Frances, she sure would call your folks if we got caught."

"*Caught* is the operative word here," said Mary Frances with a twinkle in her eye. "If we're smart about it, no one needs to know. I promise you, you'll have more fun than you've ever had."

"My grandpa gives me a sip or two of his beer sometimes, and to tell you the truth, it's pretty nasty-tasting stuff." Cricket made a face. "Couldn't we have something else to drink that tastes better? Like lemonade?"

"Yeah, if we add a little gin to it!" Mary Frances added a brief jitterbug demonstration to the conversation.

"Maybe it's not such a good idea, guys," said Marvin. "I'm sure we can think of something that won't get us in so much trouble."

"Okay, you chickens, you don't know what you're missing," said Mary Frances with a giggle. "I don't give up easily. I'll get you guys to loosen up yet."

"Hey, Cricket, I'm sorry to hear about your dad," said Mary Frances as she walked over to Cricket and gave her a big, long hug. "It must be awful to lose one of your parents. How's your mom doing?"

"Thanks. We're doing all right," said Cricket, somewhat taken aback by Mary Frances's tender consolation. "I really miss him."

Her remarks took Cricket by surprise, since no one else had mentioned her dad's death, and she really appreciated her thoughtfulness. There was something different about Mary Frances this summer. Not only had she exchanged childhood ideas for adult behavior, but she also even walked differently, with a certain sway of her hips and a smile that seemed to be saying something other than happiness. Her eyes had taken on a look of implied secrets. Her once straight-up-and-down, childish figure had begun to bloom with a hint of the young woman to come with a budding bustline. Tomboy actions had given way to coquettishness, and all these changes had most definitely caught Marvin's attentions. Marvin had begun to show up in a neatly ironed cotton shirt instead of his usual well-worn Tshirt. Suddenly, his hair was always combed, and the scent of aftershave could be detected. Wherever they went as a group, Marvin and Mary Frances were always side by side, talking and laughing together. Cricket found this change in Marvin's behavior very strange and unsettling, a feeling she could only describe as uncomfortable. The first weekend after Mary Frances's arrival was her thirteenth birthday. Everyone was invited to a family picnic followed by a girls-only sleepover in the Toomeys' backyard. Kat, Myrna, Mary Frances, and Cricket helped Mrs. Toomey decorate the house while the boys set up makeshift tents for the girls' sleepover and decorated the yard, trees, fence with a million little fairy lights. The girls and Mrs. Toomey made cookies, husked corn, and fried chicken. Cricket's grandmother baked the birthday cake as a surprise for Mary Frances, and Tommy and Chris's mom made homemade ice cream. The picnic table was decorated with a "Happy Birthday" paper tablecloth. Napkins and party hats and brightly colored balloons were tied to every bush, branch, chair, and porch rail. At the end of the day, everyone hurried home to get cleaned up and put on their Sunday best. When they returned, which was just after sunset, the entire backyard had taken on a magical, fairyland appearance, with twinkling lights, streamers, and balloons dancing in a gentle evening breeze. "Oh,

Aunt Maggie, it's just beautiful!" said Mary Frances as she swirled around slowly to take in every corner of the yard and its captivating enchantment. Cricket's grandparents, the Wilsons, the Fishers, and the Waters all arrived carrying gaily wrapped packages for Mary Frances. Mrs. Toomey served wine for the adults and berry punch for the children. Mary Frances was the perfect hostess. She opened each package with care, read each card, and thanked each person giving her the gift. She received a large assortment of hair ribbons from the Wilsons, a Nancy Drew book from the Fishers, a beautiful pink glass-bead bracelet from the Waters, and a small stained glass picture frame from Cricket's grandparents, who had placed a picture of all the neighborhood children in the frame.

"Here, dear," said Mrs. Toomey to Mary Frances. "This is a gift that your parents sent along as a surprise instead of making you wait until they come to pick you up in a few weeks. Open it." The expression on Mary Frances's face changed from teenage indifference to childish glee and honest excitement as she removed the paper and ribbon.

"Oh, look!" she exclaimed. "A gold locket with a diamond in the center. And it has my name on the back, 'To Mary Frances, with love, Mom and Dad.'"

Mary Frances opened the locket and, to her delight, saw a picture of her mother and father inside. Mary Frances showed her new locket to everyone there, and it was obvious she was more than pleased that her parents had sent it with both their names on it. In her heart of hearts, she was praying that her parents would reconcile, dropping the divorce, and that her family would be whole again. She immediately put it on.

"I'll keep this forever and never take it off," said Mary Frances, clasping it around her neck. Mrs. Toomey helped Mary Frances pick up all the paper, ribbons, and scattered remains of the gift wrappings, took the empty glasses into the kitchen, and returned to the guests.

"It looks like Adder is going to be a little late tonight. Something to do with work. So we'll start dinner without him," said Mrs. Toomey, seeming embarrassed. "Please, everyone sit down. Dinner is on the way."

The meal was scrumptious. Crunchy fried chicken, corn on the cob with melted butter, potato salad, homemade biscuits, and raspberry jam—an absolute flavor party. Finishing off the feast were Cricket's grandmother's birthday cake of white chocolate and pink roses and Mrs. Wilson's delicious, hand-churned vanilla ice cream. They all sang "Happy Birthday" to Mary Frances as she enthusiastically blew out her thirteen candles. They had eaten like little pigs, laughed until their sides hurt, and hailed Mary Frances's entrance into her teenage years. With great gusto and innocent revelry, they cheered as the party poppers sent a flurry of confetti and streamers into the air that returned to earth in a slow, graceful shower of a million multicolored pieces of paper. Finally, it was time for the adults to head for home. Mrs. Toomey and Mary Frances thanked everyone for all their help and lovely gifts. Mike, Tommy, Chris, and Marvin gathered up their sleeping bags, said "Good night," and headed for the Waters backyard to settle in for the boys' sleepover, and Mary Frances, Kat, Myrna, and Cricket snuggled down in their tents at the Toomeys'. It must have been well after midnight, and the girls were still giggling and chatting in their tent. Mary Frances kept them in stitches with tales of her exploits and life in the big city. She had figured out that making her parents feel guilty about their pending divorce afforded her the opportunity to pretty much get and do anything she pleased. Neither parent wanted to be made the "bad guy," so they tried to outdo each other by saying yes to just about anything.

"If my mom says no to me wearing lipstick to school, my dad will say it's okay. If my dad says no to Saturday-afternoon matinee dates with a boy, my mom will say yes. So for now, I do what I want. You can't believe just how great it is not to have your parents running your life, not making every decision about your life. It's really great being able to do what you want when you want to," said Mary Frances, not doing a very good job of hiding her real feelings of pain and sorrow. "I tell my parents I'm going to a friend's house for a sleepover, and instead, I meet some kids and we hang out as late as we want. They never check up on me. I hang out with kids from high school, and they really know how to have fun. We drink, dance, you know, just party. Some of them have parents who travel a lot and never seem to be at home, so we always have a place to go. You guys don't know what you're missing." "But don't you feel bad lying to your parents like that?" asked Cricket.

"Why should I?" snapped Mary Frances. "They lie to me all the time. 'Everything's fine, dear.' 'Not to worry, sweetheart, Dad and I will work everything out.' And all the time, they're planning a divorce. I don't have a vote on whether my family stays together or falls to pieces. They just don't care how I feel."

Cricket's envy of Mary Frances's freedom and latitude began to turn into sadness and pity as she watched Mary Frances struggle to justify her status and behavior. Maybe being a free spirit wasn't such a great life after all. Cricket vowed to rethink her decision of a lifestyle change at some later date. The big secret girlie news of the summer was the fact that Mary Frances had started her period. The rest of the girls were in awe of having a friend that was actually going through this passage into womanhood and was willing to talk about it. Mary Frances described in great detail the entire process from menstrual pads to monthly cramps. She told them stories of the embarrassment of bloodstains showing on her clothing when she was unprepared for her periods to start, being excused from gym activities, and how awful boys could be with their teasing once they got word of the event. Cricket didn't find any of this humorous; as a matter of fact, she was appalled. Once she knew all the intimate details, the very thought of going through this every month completely reversed her wish to be much older than she really was. She hoped that by the time she reached Mary Frances's age, modern science would come up with a much better system. Finally, the girls had laughed themselves into exhaustion and cuddled down into their blankets, falling soundly asleep. Sometime into the early morning hours, out of the darkness of their dream-laden sleep came a loud, startling sound that shattered the silence of the warm summer night.

"What was that?" whispered Kat as Cricket sat up with a start, trying to adjust her eyes to her surroundings, lit only by the stars and a huge full moon. "I don't know," said Cricket, puzzled.

"Mary Frances, Myrna, wake up," said Kat, gently shaking their shoulders.

"Cricket and I heard a loud noise. It woke us up. Listen."

One by one, each of them shook off the fuzziness of sleep. The four of them sat stonelike, straining their ears for whatever it was that had awakened them. Just as they were about to chalk it all up to a bad dream or some cat challenging a nearby garbage can, there came a crash and the sound of breaking glass from the kitchen in the house, followed by loud, angry voices. They sat there barely breathing, until another crash shattered the night. Footsteps were heard outside the tent. The girls clung to one another in fear, then without warning, the tent flap door was flung open, and there stood Mike.

"You girls okay?" he whispered. "I could hear the noise over here all the way to the Waters backyard."

Mike and Mary Frances were attempting to excuse the situation as nothing to be alarmed about when a bottle came flying through the kitchen window. They all looked at each other for a second and then began to cross the yard, hunched over low to the ground as if in combat mode, tiptoed up onto the porch, avoiding the shattered glass, and peered into the kitchen window. There, framed in the lighted window, stood Mr. Toomey, shirtless, with his face twisted into a strange, wild expression. A film of sweat covered his skin like the condensation on a windowpane. His eyes were narrow and glaring; his usual tidy appearance was ruffled and disheveled.

Mike said, "Come on, you don't want to see this."

Mary Frances agreed and suggested a quiet exodus from the porch, but Cricket, Myrna, and Kat were frozen in place and couldn't seem to make their feet move. Mrs. Toomey, dressed only in a light nightgown, stood trembling while Mr. Toomey held her firmly by her arms as his six-foot-plus frame towered over the small woman. "How can you do this to our family?" said Mrs. Toomey, with tears streaming down her cheeks. "You're nothing but a womanizing drunk and a bully!" she continued as she struggled to free herself. "Everyone in town knows all about you and your other women . . . the drinking and bar brawls. You're an embarrassment to your children. My father was right about you. I should have listened to him, because it takes a bastard to know a bastard. He was the king of bastards! I never should have married you."

"I'm going in and break this up before it gets any worse," whispered Mike.

"No," said Mary Frances. "He'll beat the shit out of both of you just like he did last time you tried to stop him. You can't help her, Mike."

Mike stood there in anguish, with tears streaming down his face as he watched his father continue his rage against his mother. Mr. Toomey jerked his terrified wife closer. "Maybe if I weren't married to the ice bitch, I wouldn't have to look outside my home for companionship," he hissed, bringing his face close to hers as he increased his grip on Mrs. Toomey's arms.

"What makes you think your whores would have anything to do with you if you didn't pay them?" shouted Mrs. Toomey. "Your breath stinks of whiskey, you smell like a horse, you're perverted and enjoy hurting people, so just what do you think is so appealing about you that would make a woman want to make love to you unless she gets paid? Now, let me go!"

Mr. Toomey seemed taken aback by her outspoken tirade. As he looked down at her, slowly a strange smile came over his face. Mike couldn't take any more. "I'd like to kill him when he's this way," he whispered. Mary Frances put her arms around him as a sign of understanding.

"Go back to the Waters," said Mary Frances. "You can't do anything here. None of us can."

Mike darted off the porch and disappeared from sight just as Mr. Toomey renewed his attack. "Why don't I show you what my other women like about me?" he said, releasing one of her arms to free his hand to caress her breast. "Come on, baby, you know you want it. Relax."

"I said, *let me go*!" Mrs. Toomey shoved herself away from her aggressive husband. Pulling her free arm back as far as she could, she slapped Mr. Toomey sharply and directly across the face. The reaction of the audience on the porch was a collective gasp and an involuntary, lightning-fast step back from the window. Mr. Toomey's response was swift and violent. He lifted her off her feet, smashed her onto the top of the kitchen table, and struck her with such force that her head jerked to one side and her mouth began to bleed. Without pause, he ripped the nightgown from her body and stood glaring down at her nude, struggling form. Cricket heard her breath escape her mouth and another uncontrollable gasp. She instantly clasped her hand over her mouth in fear that Mr. Toomey would hear, discover their presence on the porch, and unleash his wrath on them. They were all transfixed to the spot and unable to move or look away. They pressed their shaking bodies against the porch handrail and backed away from this terrifying spectacle. The scene before them took on a sensation of slow motion as they waited, in panic, for the next horrific moment. The kitchen became eerily quiet. Mr. Toomey continued to hold his wife firmly pinned on the kitchen table before him. He appeared transfixed by her struggling, naked body. His eyes seemed to hungrily savor every curvature and hollow of her small, voluptuous frame. Then, with studied determination, Mr. Toomey held her hostage with one hand while the other hand began to explore and roughly caress his unwilling subject. Soon he replaced his roving hands with his mouth, and he began to cover her body with his tongue, like a famished child licking an ice cream cone.

"Kat, Cricket, Myrna, let's get out of here before it's too late. Come on," whispered Mary Frances, snapping them out of their hypnotic state, grabbing their hands and pulling them from the porch. They all huddled together in their tent, still shaken. Not saying a word, they strained their ears for what seemed an inevitable disastrous conclusion. But just as suddenly as it all started, it ended. No more shouting, angry voices. Just ended, as the lights went out and all was quiet in the Toomey house.

"I've never in my life seen anything like that before," whispered Myrna, breaking the silence.

"Me neither," said Kat. "That was awful! Poor Mrs. Toomey.

And what an awful thing for Mike to have to watch."

"Listen, you guys," said Mary Frances. "Please," she pleaded, looking intently at each of them, "please promise me you won't say a word about this to anyone, and I mean *anyone*. Something awful, and I mean *awful*, will happen if you say anything. Promise, cross your heart and hope to die?"

"Okay, if it means that much to you," said Myrna, "but couldn't the sheriff do something if he knew?"

"No." Mary Frances shook her head. "Nobody can help, that's the problem, so just promise, okay?" The cocky, self-assured Mary Frances had disappeared, and the young girl of thirteen sat in front of them, pleading her case. "They fight like this all the time. It doesn't mean anything. They'll be just fine in the morning, just wait and see."

"Gosh, Mary Frances," said Kat, "does this kind of thing really go on all the time?"

"Yeah, they fight all the time, and everything is always okay in the morning. It's just when he drinks too much he gets like this. Otherwise, he's a pretty nice guy, honest."

"See, didn't I tell you that drinking was a bad idea?" said Myrna in her usual I-told-you-so attitude.

"Anyway, I need you guys to promise," pleaded Mary Frances, and they all held hands and promised. "Cross your heart," she said. "None of you will tell, no matter what. And that goes double for Myrna. Not a living soul, do you understand?"

"Okay, okay," said Myrna, "I double-promise." That next morning, Mr. and Mrs. Toomey appeared in the kitchen as if nothing had happened. Of course, they didn't have a clue that anybody had witnessed the argument. They fixed all the children a nice breakfast in an atmosphere filled with warmth and smiles. The only sign of the violence from the night before was a small cut on Mrs. Toomey's lip. Other than that, Mary Frances was right; everyone acted as if nothing had ever happened. The breakfast was as delicious as the meal of the preceding evening. Mrs. Toomey was undoubtedly a wonderful cook whose talents extended to more than just dinner. She served fresh-squeezed orange juice, fluffy scrambled eggs with tiny little pieces of bacon blended in, muffins filled to overflowing with fresh blueberries, and tiny little demitasse cups filled with a few tablespoons of real coffee diluted with lots of cream and sugar. The conversation was light and cheery, and the Mr. Toomey of the night before held absolutely no resemblance to the man sitting directly across from Cricket, smiling and participating in this morning feast. He seemed gentle, kind to his children, loving and considerate to his wife. The perfect father and husband. Cricket found the whole situation a deep mystery. Adults were strange and extremely complicated people. They changed like a chameleon, and no one seemed to care or take notice. While children, on the other hand, were expected to remain constant, striving for perfection in school and in their social lives. It was all very confusing. *Maybe,* thought Cricket, *it's another one of those "you'll understand when you get older" things. Could there be a separate set of rules for adults and another set for children? No wonder it takes so many years to learn how to become an adult.* As Cricket was enjoying her breakfast and pondering the confusing issue of the adult world, there came a knock on the door, which was closest to Cricket.

"Cricket, dear," said Mrs. Toomey, "would you please answer the door while I attend to more muffins?"

"Sure, Mrs. Toomey." Cricket opened the door to find Sheriff Davis standing on the stoop. He stepped through the doorway, removed his hat, and addressed Mr. and Mrs. Toomey. "Maggie, Adder, I'm on my way to check on Miss Perkins. She says Rooster Darby's dog ate her newly planted gladiolas, and she had the poor thing locked in her garage, awaiting some form of execution, I guess. Since I was passing your house, I thought I'd check and see if everything is okay. Got a call last night reporting some strange noises in your neighborhood. You folks heard anything?"

Mary Frances flashed a serious look at Myrna, Kat, and Cricket, a quick warning of silence and the promise they had made the night before. Mike looked up with a slight smile on his face, then everyone busied themselves, passing dishes around the table.

"Last night we celebrated Mary Frances's thirteenth birthday," said Mr. Toomey. "The girls camped in the backyard and stayed up to the wee hours of the morning giggling and telling ghost stories. I don't imagine the boys, who camped at the Waterses', were any quieter. I hope they didn't keep too many people up with their noise."

"Care for a cup of coffee and some breakfast, Jim?" said Mrs.

Toomey. "No, thanks, Maggie. I best get on over to Miss Perkins's before I have a neighborhood war on my hands. If you're sure everything is okay, I'll be on my way." He paused in the doorway and gave Mrs.

Toomey a long, thorough look, like a man reading a road map. It felt like everyone at the table was holding their breath. Then he said, "Happy birthday, Mary Frances," and walked out the door. Not a word was said, not a gesture made, and all went on with breakfast like the night before had never happened.

That night, safe and sound in her bed in her grandparents' home, Cricket started her prayers, which, for some reason, seemed to come hard on this occasion.

"Dear God," she began, "I'm a little confused tonight. I saw something awful last night that I'm not allowed to tell anyone, but I don't think telling you would break my promise, since you know everything anyway. I have a funny feeling about Mr. Toomey. He really scares me, even before I saw him hurt his nice wife, Mrs. Toomey. I feel like I should tell someone to help Mrs. Toomey, but I can't break a promise, can I? Please think this over and help me know what to do. Bless Mom, our baby, all my grandparents, and a little extra for me. Good night!"

Cricket couldn't get the picture of Mr. Toomey and the night before out of her mind. His violence, the wild look on his face, the evil look in his eyes. No matter how nice he was over breakfast, she could still see the monster of the night before lurking behind the smile and cheery exterior. Before summer was over, she would see his violence rise up again, and this time the object of his twisted rage would come closer to Cricket than she could ever imagine.

CHAPTER 12

Sheriff Jim Davis

As THE BARSTOW SISTERS represented the social and emergency communications of the community, Sheriff Jim Davis represented the stability and security that sheltered the small town of Everett and covered it with a reassurance of peace, safety, and a sound night's sleep. Jim wasn't a native of Everett, but pretty close to it. He was born on the East Coast, and his parents came west, as did so many others during the twenties, looking for a kinder climate and more opportunities to make a decent living. The Davises, along with their four children, settled in the small town of Marysville, just a few miles outside of Everett. Jim's dad was a giant of a man, six eight if he were a foot, and over three hundred pounds. It was said that he had a heart to match his immense size. As good-natured as they came, he made friends everywhere he went. Although his birth name was James, his large size, even as a small child, garnered him the nickname of Bear, which followed him well into his adult life. Upon migrating to the West, Bear Davis found a job befitting his size and extraordinary strength; he became a feller for the Jamison Lumber Company. The job of a feller is to make the undercut (a wedge-shaped piece) on the side of the tree that he wanted to fall toward the ground. Gravity and the weight of the tree did the rest. By making the cut close to the ground, wasting valuable wood by leaving a high stump was avoided. The cut was made with a two-man crosscut saw known as a misery whip. It was a backbreaking job since some tree trunks were several tons and measured two hundred feet or more in length. Bear Davis soon became an expert feller, able to drop a tree of any size on a pinhead as easy as the sandman rocking a baby to sleep. He soon had another nickname pinned on to the first, Sandman, Sandy for short, and that was how James Byron Davis became Sandy Bear Davis. By the time Jim was a young man, he had become a crew chief under his dad's watchful eye. After he married, he moved his family into the town of Everett, got a job working in the sheriff's office, and went from there to deputy and then was elected to the office of sheriff, a job he held for years. Like his father before him, Jim Davis was a formidable figure. Tall, husky, and all muscle. It was impossible to miss him in a crowd. Over the years, he made it his business to know every single person in town, all their children, even the family pets. This was a great comfort to all the parents and a curse that had to be carried by their children, particularly their teenage children. Jim loved his community and all the people in it, and he took his job as their guardian very seriously. Over the years, he turned domestic disturbances into marriage counseling, a barroom brawl into volunteers for the building of the new school gym, teenage angst into free gardening for the elderly, and neighborhood arguments into fund-raising block parties to support different charities. He was ahead of his time, exchanging jail time for community service. Jenny Davis was one of her husband's strongest supporters, and her adoration of the man was blatantly obvious: no apologies, no excuses, just out there for all to see. When Jenny died of cancer just before the start of WWII, Jim became a shattered man that the town thought would never heal. He stood at her grave site stonelike and silent until her coffin was lowered into the grave, and then, as if the chambers of hell slowly opened, a sound of pain beyond grief came from the bottom of his soul and traveled past eternity. With time, Jim did seem to return to being himself, but there was always a piece, a small part of his being, that was never quite the same. He threw himself into his work, modernized the entire sheriff's office with a switchboard, hired a deputy, and talked the town council into purchasing two new squad cars with radios. During the war, Sheriff Davis helped organize many of the war efforts in the community, like air raid shelters, air raid wardens, emergency medical stations through the Red Cross, and he helped teenagers organize scrap drives. The sheriff and Thad Bane, Cricket's grandfather, became very close friends over the years. Before Thad retired from the bench, their jobs brought them into close contact almost daily. Arvilla, Cricket's grandmother, was very close friends with Jenny Davis, and before she became sick, the four of them saw one another socially as well. During the worst part of Jenny's illness, Arvilla was in their home almost every day, cooking meals, cleaning and caring for Jenny when she finally became bedridden. It was a kindness Jim never forgot, and it brought a special kind of closeness between the Bane and the Davis families that lasted a lifetime. During the winter of 1940, the weather was unrelenting. The rainfall broke all records, and it was the coldest winter in twenty years. The snowfall, which was usually fairly light, wreaked havoc on the community, causing every imaginable problem, from four-foot snowdrifts to downed power lines. There were so many emergency calls that the sheriff practically lived and slept in his car. An elderly couple who lived directly behind the Bane residence was awakened one night when a huge elm tree in their front yard, overloaded with ice and snow, came crashing down onto their roof. The Banes heard the crash, and Thad rushed to see what had happened while Arvilla called the sheriff. The tree had fallen right through the front of the house, blocking the entire front entrance. Hearing cries for help, Thad worked his way through the rubble that once was their living room and began to search for the elderly couple. He finally located them huddled in the hallway to their bedroom. Thad was about to pick up the lady of the house and carry her to safety when another loud snap was heard and the tree that was held up by some attic rafters gave way and came smashing through the rest of the house, trapping Thad's legs under the large branch. Just then, the sheriff arrived with two volunteers, and without missing a beat, he located Thad. Before anyone could decide what move was next, the sheriff placed his back under the huge branch and lifted it off Thad's legs. No sooner had the two elderly inhabitants evacuated and Thad carried to safety by the sheriff than the rest of the tree crashed through the remainder of the house, turning the entire structure into rubble. The sheriff and Thad stood speechless, watching the remainder of the house collapse, tossing dirt, debris, and tree parts into the air, twirling and mixing with the wind and falling snowflakes. Thad reached over and clasped Jim's hand. No words were spoken, but the silent "Thank God you're safe" and the "Thank you" resounded louder than the wailing storm. It seemed that Sheriff Davis was everywhere you looked. Everyone in town had a story of how he had helped or assisted them in a time of need or during inclement weather. Jim Davis also had a gracious sense of humor and never minded poking a little fun at himself or being the subject of a friendly joke. During the Strawberry Festival, he volunteered in the dunk tank of the sheriff's booth, which raised a good deal of change for all sorts of charities. He would yell and taunt the ball thrower, daring him to hit the bull's-eye and dunk him in the water. This drew a very large crowd of youthful exuberance with a legal means to gain revenge on the sheriff without any repercussions. He actually enjoyed egging his challengers on and never complained about spending most of the day in the water. At all times of the day and many times in the early hours of the morning, when the town was asleep, the sheriff's patrol car could be seen making its rounds around town: the park, where he looked to send teenage lovebirds home, the downtown area for patrol, businesses to check, and a now-and-then door check were just a few of his stops. He knew who was having domestic problems, and he would make sure these homes knew he was there by running his car's floodlight across the front of the house. Even Miss Perkins was on his nightly rounds just in case her phantom Peeping Tom turned out to be real. Jim's dedication was the one constant that let the whole town sleep a little sounder, as his caring presence spread a veil of reassurance, like a warm blanket, over the entire community. Without a complaint, he shouldered the responsibility for each and every member of this township, from those who painted the town with pride and courage to those who fell on the sidewalks outside Murphy's Pub, or the relatively small number of those, like Adder Toomey, whom he locked up from time to time to give their browbeaten wives a safe night of sleep. Would the fortitude and vigilance of this one dedicated man be enough to hold together the town he loved during the calamity that was about to befall this small community, a wound from which it might never recover? Did any one person have shoulders that broad and strength that great to carry a whole town in anguish? Jim Davis certainly had the heart and compassion to attempt such a monumental task that would hand him one of the biggest challenges of his career.

CHAPTER 13

The Curmudgeon

A SMALL TOWN'S VENUE OFFERS a bright spotlight, like an old vaudeville headliner act, on its one-of-a- kind, unforgettable characters, like its heroes, its angels of mercy, its town drunk, or its shady lady. But what town would be complete without its very own in-your-face, know-everybody's business busybody known as the curmudgeon? This unchallenged title fell entirely to Miss Bertha Perkins. She lived on the corner directly across from the city park. When it came to gathering information, either actual or nonfactual, her hearing and eyesight were equal in quality to that of a hungry hawk. Nothing in this world or the next pleased her. She had a bone to pick with every living thing in town. She swore that every dog within the city limits came to relieve themselves on her lawn, there wasn't a child born that was not intent on destroying her rose garden, and then there were her consistent and constant calls to Sheriff Davis about the local Peeping Tom, a phantom prowler who seemed to target the home of Ms. Perkins and her home alone. The location of Miss Perkins's home offered her a broad picture of the town's activities and indiscretions. She considered it her bond and duty to inform the sheriff, in great detail, of the most insignificant minutia of everything that took place within her view. It was the bane of Sheriff Davis's existence, but being the kindhearted, considerate man that he was, he made his token house call weekly to Miss Perkins, listened for half an hour to her complaints, and then handed off all her other observations and complaints to his deputy. Not only was Miss Perkins the hawker of all things bleak, but she also considered it her profession of choice to spend her days meticulously collecting every juicy little tidbit of gossip. Two of her abundant sources and main partners in gossip fodder were the Barstow sisters, who had the ear of the community via their positions at the phone company. Miss Perkins visited Miss Millie and Miss Edith regularly and gleaned whatever she could from the most innocent of conversations. Miss Perkins's other sources were Madge's Beauty Parlor, a particular fertile ground for information since, for some unknown reason, women tend to tell their hairdresser things they wouldn't even think to discuss with their best friend, and then there was the yarn shop down by the harbor, Mr. Yankin's Butcher Shop, the Pine Hill Quilting Society, and the local post office, which completed Miss Perkins's circle of sources. A good example of her mischief began one December just a few weeks before Christmas. She was shopping downtown when she just happened to see the mayor's unmarried daughter coming out of the Bide-a-Wee Baby Shop carrying several packages. Before the door shut behind the unsuspecting young lady, Miss Perkins's art of the innuendo was set in motion. Miss Perkins mentioned what she had seen to the checker at Wilson's Market, who in turn enhanced the tale and passed it on to Mrs. Grail, the butcher's wife, who added her own personal touch to the story and passed it on to her husband, who then told Sam the plumber that the mayor's daughter was pregnant and planning to marry the child's father, who was the son of the local pharmacist, who related this news to Mrs. Stanton as he repaired her clogged kitchen sink, who in turn phoned her husband, the local banker, to tell him that the mayor's daughter was not only pregnant but also that the child's father, the pharmacist's son, was under threat of bodily harm by the mayor if the young man didn't make an honest woman of his daughter. The banker, who was a close friend of the mayor, called to ask him if there was anything he could do to help with this crisis. The mayor came unglued at the news and called his wife to demand an explanation as to why he hadn't been told about his daughter's dilemma, and she, upon hearing of the disgraceful state of their daughter's reputation, fainted in a heap and whose maid immediately called Doc Miller, who in turn called the pharmacist, offering his condolences concerning the news about his son and the mayor's daughter, and requested a prescription for a sedative be sent out to the mayor's wife. In the meantime, the mayor's daughter, oblivious to the maelstrom of the rumors and chaos spreading around town, arrived for her hair appointment at Madge's Beauty Parlor, where Madge had just finished relating the expanded story of the mayor's daughter to Miss Perkins, who was getting a manicure. Upon entering the beauty parlor, the mayor's daughter was all bubbly with excitement over her purchases, which she removed from the shopping bags to show all the ladies.

"Look, are these not the cutest little things you have ever seen?" The mayor's daughter smiled as she laid out four tiny little sweaters, one for each season of the year. "And look at this teddy bear! Isn't it the softest little thing you've ever felt? I can hardly wait for next weekend, when I'm going to Seattle for my best friend's baby shower. I've never been to a baby shower before. I'm so excited!"

Miss Perkins, feigning complete innocence concerning the outrageous rumors flying about town, complimented the mayor's daughter for the appropriateness of her gift selection and left the beauty parlor without saying a word. It took almost two weeks to trace the culprit of the rumors, but when it came to rumors, Miss Perkins was always number one on the usual suspect list. It wasn't only that Miss Perkins was a rumormonger, but the destruction she sometimes left in her path of verbal hurricanes couldn't always be rebuilt. In the case of the mayor's daughter, the ridiculousness of the situation soon became apparent, and eventually the source of many laughs, but some of her meddling in the personal affairs of others left lasting scars and resentment. When it came to domestic violence or deeply personal matters, Doc Miller and the sheriff made every effort to handle these situations quietly and behind the scenes, sparing the families involved the embarrassment and humiliation of public knowledge. Take the case of Hannah Summers, who helped her family's meager existence by cleaning the houses of the well- to-do people in town. Hannah, a widow with three girls to raise on her own, married Charlie Summers, a ne'er-do-well, unemployed janitor and consummate drunk. Alcohol brought out Charlie's dark side, and Doc Miller, on too many occasions, attended to Hannah and the results of Charlie's rants and beatings. The sheriff had spoken to Charlie often about changing his ways, giving up drinking, and caring for his family. With each lecture, Charlie was very contrite and promised to change, but he never did. As time passed, the situation in the Summers household continued to deteriorate, with beatings becoming more violent and more frequent. Where once the signs of Charlie's abuse were hidden under Hannah's clothing and out of sight, now they were everywhere on her body, in the open for all to see. While making a purchase at the drugstore, Miss Perkins overheard a phone conversation between the pharmacist and Doc Miller concerning the treatment and care of Hannah Summers's injuries. Standing discreetly out of view of the pharmacist, Miss Perkins took in every detail of the sordid mess in the Summers household. She launched herself out the door and started her rounds with the news, which traveled through town like lightning, sparking all sorts of responses, from indignation to bewilderment. The secret was out, and Hannah was humiliated that her family matters were now a topic of town discussion. Her eldest daughter, fifteen-year-old Rachel, eventually became the target of Charlie's abuse and confessed to Doc Miller, while being treated for a few broken ribs, that the abuse was much more than just physical—it was sexual as well. Doc Miller called the sheriff, who immediately contacted his deputy to pick up Charlie Summers and bring him in. The sheriff was determined to put the fear of God in Charlie or lock him up on any trumped-up charge he could justify to keep him away from Hannah and her daughters. Unfortunately, the deputy took the phone call in his car just outside Miss Perkins's house, as he was finishing a check on her third complaint of an intruder in her yard that week. Even before the deputy had located Charlie, Miss Perkins's rumor mill had begun to churn out her malicious suppositions of this horrific situation. "You wouldn't believe what is going on right under Hannah Summers's nose, her daughter Rachel and Charlie carrying on right in her own home," the gossip began. When the gossip came back to Hannah, she was just finishing up her cleaning chores in the mayor's house. The mayor's wife, thinking she was being caring, offered Hannah her help and sympathy, totally blindsiding poor Hannah with what was going on between her daughter and Charlie. Hannah became despondent and in total despair. It shook her to the very core of her being. She was devastated and found this information beyond comprehension. How could this be happening in her own home without her knowing or at least suspecting? At first, Hannah thought of digging out her father's old pistol from its hiding place in an old suitcase in the back of the garage and tracking Charlie down, shooting him between the eyes, maybe poisoning him—a long, painful death would be something he deserved. Or perhaps stabbing him in his sleep? These were just flash fantasies and not realistic solutions. Hannah spent days and nights trying to cope with this nightmare. Each night after Charlie drank himself into a stupor, Hannah would take a blanket and sleep on the floor of her daughter's bedroom, with her body pressed tightly against the closed door. Hannah spent all her waking hours and into her nights trying to cope with this sordid situation. As time passed, she became more and more depressed. The disgrace, helplessness, and guilt began to consume her. She couldn't protect her children, not in that house, so she sent her three girls to stay with her sister in Tacoma. The following week, on her scheduled day to clean the mayor's house, Hannah arrived late, which was very unusual. Her demeanor was withdrawn, quiet, distracted. Her appearance, which was usually neat as a pin, appeared to be slovenly and unkempt, and she barely spoke a word. The mayor's wife was very concerned and tried to bring up the subject with Hannah, but she was unresponsive. Later that day, Hannah Summers was found in the basement of the mayor's home hanging from a beam. No note, but everyone knew what drove her to such a desperate act. The town also knew who had circulated the rumors and who, aside from Charlie Summers, was equally responsible for Hannah's sad and tragic death. This time, Bertha Perkins had gone too far. The results of her meddling ways, her malicious gossip, and the tragedy that ensued turned a spotlight on the true ugliness of her sordid pastime. Perhaps it was the well-founded reputation of using others' unfortunate circumstances to pursue her ill-gotten occupation that caused the sheriff to turn a deaf ear when she finally had something factual and important to say. For the first time in her long career as the ultimate curmudgeon, she had something to say that might reveal part of the mystery that would have the whole town locking doors that were once always open, but would anyone listen?

CHAPTER 14

The Big Day Arrives

CRICKET'S FAVORITE HOLIDAY NEXT to Christmas had finally arrived, the Fourth of July, with its Main Street parade and the Shingle Weavers Picnic, which was hosted by the many lumber mills in town that manufactured shingles and were the town's main source of employment. The weather was perfect, with no summer rains predicted for the weekend. Cricket and her friends' excitement factor was off the charts. Even Cricket's grandparents seemed exceptionally upbeat since hearing from the war department that their son, Cricket's uncle Ken, was indeed alive and being held captive as prisoner of war somewhere in Japan. For weeks, Cricket and her friends had been very busy making red, white, and blue crepe paper costumes. They sewed and fit their costumes in anticipation of their team's appearance in the parade. This year, they were all dressed as Uncle Sam, pulling a decorated red wagon with Mike's little brother, Pat, on it, wearing a firecracker costume. As they marched, they all waved the American flag to the beat of the high school band playing "God Bless America" and "It's a Grand Old Flag." Main Street was lined for blocks with enthusiastic supporters that cheered and applauded each team as they passed. The high school had assembled an elaborately decorated float, festooned in the school colors, that carried the football team and cheerleaders. The Elks Club's float depicted a scene of neighbors helping neighbors, and the fire department trotted out its bright, new red fire engine that carried Miss Firecracker, wearing her crown and robe, sitting atop the cab. Following the floats were the Shriners in their red tasseled hats and jackets, riding tiny childsize bicycles. The Boy Scout troops formed a snappy unit marching in unison like boy soldiers. The ladies' auxiliary, wearing light-blue sashes across their chests, represented women working hours and hours of volunteer time spent at the hospital, as airplane observers, air raid wardens, and fund-raisers for a plethora of charities. Cricket's grandmother was president and a very active member. The Garden Club, bowling team, Men's Choral Group, Moose Lodge, and the Barber Shoppers in their straw hats, fake mustaches, and red-striped jackets, harmonizing to "My Gal Sal," were all followed by the beribboned cars that carried the local dignitaries and mill owners who hosted the event. After the parade, the town assembled on the picnic grounds by Lake Stevens. This was where the majority of holiday events took place. There were boisterous logrolling contests, treetoppling events, baseball games, sack races, horseshoe competitions, swimming races, and best of all, free ice cream for all the children. The picnic tables were a masterpiece of outdoor culinary delights, all dressed and spread with a sumptuous variety of lovingly made sandwiches, fried chicken, sweet corn on the cob, corned beef, deviled eggs, homemade pies, cakes, cookies, and anything and everything strawberry, made by the ladies who hoped their endeavors would garner them a prize at the soon-to-be-held county fair. The women gathered on the benches near the lake's edge to keep an eye on the children. They could be heard comparing recipes, child-rearing practices, and talking of the challenges of running a household on ration stamps, which were required for everything from sugar to shoes. Also being discussed were the benefits and problems of growing a victory garden, how many meals could be made from one chicken, the pros and cons of oleomargarine versus the rationed real butter, and the very hot topic of women entering the job market, filling jobs in the factories that had been vacated by young men serving in the war. The war was a constant topic, and the fears of the daily news reports were shared by all. One of the hottest subjects of the day was the latest in state-of-the-art household appliances, the automatic washing machine, and rumors of other amazing appliances, like, of all things, dishwashers and an automatic percolator coffeepot. The men enthusiastically entered the competitions, cheering one another's accomplishments and having large belly laughs over any athletic misfortune of the opposing team. Late in the afternoon, they could be heard discussing the changes the war had made in our society, their sadness and frustration that they weren't younger or more fit to enlist in military service, and the male opinion of the absurdity of even thinking women were capable of working in a man's job— in a factory, of all places. *Please!* Many in this group of men acted as air raid wardens during blackouts. The western states were very sensitive and fearful of a possible Japanese attack along the coast. Others took first aid courses and training on fire control so they could act in a volunteer capacity if an attack ever came. But they were also filled with hope and the anticipation of the future prediction of a building boom after the war, of this new concept of affordable housing for all returning servicemen in developments that would later be called the suburbs. Cricket and her friends were allowed to run free all day until dusk, with their youthful exuberance propelling them throughout the day. The first thing they did was watch Marvin try his luck in the logrolling competition. This was an old logger's game of two opponents standing upon a large log in the water and attempting to make the other one fall off by rolling the log around and around until one contestant lost his balance and fell into the lake. "Come on, Marvin!" they all hollered in a chorus while he maneuvered the log with his feet, spinning first in one direction and then in the opposite to catch his opponent off guard. After several tries, his opponent was overcome by gravity, and he took a nosedive into the lake. Marvin did very well, and on the third round, his exceptional balance and strength gave him second place in his age group. Next, they gathered around to watch Tommy and Chris in the sack race. This competition was great fun to watch. A team of two, each one placing a leg into an old burlap gunnysack, gathered at the starting line to await the starting signal. With the bang of the gun, the teams all leaped forward in an attempt to maneuver the designated course to the finish line without falling. It was a lot harder than it looked. They cheered and jumped in anticipation as the race moved through a variety of obstacles. Tommy and Chris were in the lead at the halfway mark, and Cricket and her friends' excitement caught fire. With just two obstacles to go, Tommy and Chris were still in the lead, with one other team hot on their heels. "Go! Go!" they all screamed. Then finally, just by a nose, Tommy and Chris crossed the finish line—winners! The next event that was a must to see was the greased-pig race. Mike had decided that this would be a snap and well worth entering. After all, how hard could it be to capture a small piglet? Well, Mike was about to find out. The rules were simple: Each contestant was given a gunnysack and two minutes to capture as many piglets as he could. The one with the most piglets at the end of the competition would be the winner. One small thing they forgot to mention was that each little pig would be rubbed down with lard just before being turned loose into the pen, adding just a little advantage in the piglet's favor. Mike stood ready at the starting gate, awaiting the start signal. He had a slight smug smirk on his face as the whistle blew. Off Mike went, and off went the piglets scattering in every direction with great speed and a torrent of squeals. Mike followed suit, grabbing and snatching as one piglet after another slipped from his grasp. To add just a little more challenge to the chase, the pen had a large mud puddle in the righthand corner. Before the halfway whistle was blown, Mike had fallen into the middle of the puddle twice and was covered from head to toe. His friends were laughing so hard they could barely stand. Finally, and just in the nick of time, Mike captured two equally muddy piglets as the final whistle signaled the end of the match. They wouldn't know until the end of the day if anyone did better than Mike. After Marvin, Tommy, and Chris had collected their trophies, they came running toward the group, grinning victoriously. Mary Frances threw her arms around Marvin's neck and kissed him soundly on the lips.

"Oh, Marvin, you're just fantastic!" she said with delight. "And you guys, our heroes . . . our heroes."

She gave Tommy and Chris a big hug as she sang and danced around them, twirling as she went. Marvin picked her up, and the two of them began to spin and dance down the lake's edge toward the boat docks. This was Cricket's first experience with jealousy, and it stopped her in her tracks. Why did she find this friendly sight of two people exchanging mutual joy so upsetting? She had no idea what these feelings were, but she knew she didn't like them. Sheriff Davis strolled past and stopped to congratulate the winners.

"Say, Mike Toomey, is that you under all that mud? Good job, son! I think you are one of the top four winners. Better check back at the piglet ring."

"Yes, sir," said Mike. "Thanks, Sheriff."

The sheriff patted Mike on the top of his head and then continued his vigil, strolling through the picnic grounds, stopping to talk with this person and that person, keeping his eyes open for the usual troublemakers.

"Did you guys notice? The sheriff seems to know everything," puzzled Mike said.

"Yes, indeed", everyone agreed.

"My grandma said he has eyes in the back of his head," said Cricket. "I imagine that makes it a little difficult to comb your hair, wouldn't you think?"

Marvin and Mary Frances laughed and shook their heads, and they all moved on to celebrate all the victories by eating as much ice cream as they could hold. The cool water of the lake lapped at their ankles as they sat on the boat dock, splashing, enjoying their freedom, skipping stones. They reminisced about all the funny events of the day, made fun of Mike's encounter with the two piglets, and talked about how they were looking forward to the main event that would take place just as soon as it turned dark: the fireworks! Mary Frances decided to teach each of them the latest dance she had learned from her high school friends: the boogie-woogie. She grabbed each of them one by one and began her gyrations. Since most of them could barely get by with a slow dance, this jitterbug stuff was really confusing. To everyone's great surprise, Marvin took to this new dance like Fred Astaire of movie fame. Marvin and Mary Frances began to dance, and they really got into the groove, as Mary Frances put it. The rest of the group sat on the dock and clapped out a beat for the aspiring Fred Astaire– Ginger Rogers team as the two swung and swayed to the speedy beat. Marvin tossed Mary Frances over his head and between his legs, twirling one way and then another. They were fantastic together, and everyone applauded and screamed at their finale. Marvin and Mary Frances bowed in response to the applause and pleasure in their performance. Marvin picked her up and ran to the end of the dock, where he dropped her into the lake. He followed, and soon so did they all. Exhausted from all the laughing and the swimming, they all crawled out of the lake onto the dock and laid their tired, wet bodies on the warm wooden planks. The day had been simply perfect. Glorious weather, a feast fit for a king, good friends, and unforgettable memories. They were oblivious to the beauty and how unencumbered this special moment of time would become, and they were, as they might never be again, living in the moment, in the present, in their innocence. Like the ever-increasing circles and ripples made by the stones they tossed into the lake, they were blind to the fact that their righteous world of absolutes was about to dissipate, that tomorrow would no longer be recognizable, and that all they had believed in before would vanish forever.

The Fireworks

AS TWILIGHT ARRIVED, THE music of the Elks Lodge band began to play tunes of Glenn Miller, Tommy Dorsey, and Benny Goodman. Teenagers gathered in groups, eyeing one another with youthful exuberance, and the dance floor was filled with couples leaving behind their troubles, worries, and fears for at least this one beautiful holiday eve. Fireflies decorated the forest's edge, adding to the celebration, and paper Chinese lanterns strung up all around the bandstand gave the area a magical glow. Cricket's grandparents stepped onto the dance floor and began to dance to the music of "Embraceable You." Cricket loved to watch them dance; they seemed so lost in each other's private circle, gliding across the floor like two entwined columns of wispy smoke caught in a gentle breeze. They flawlessly floated across the floor with such grace that other dancers paused on the sidelines just to watch them pass. Then, finally, it was Cricket's turn.

"May I have this dance, Miss Annie?" her grandfather asked. Then, just like they had done a hundred times before at home,

Cricket's grandfather placed her feet atop his, and away they twirled, dancing and spinning to the music. She looked up into his gentle eyes and traced the lines of his handsome, smiling face with her eyes, and there seemed to be no one else on the dance floor, no one else on the planet, and the music was for them and them alone. Through the years, this instant in time would flash across Cricket's mind every time she heard the tune "I'll Be Seeing You," and she would close her eyes and see the face of her grandfather, the fireflies, and feel the magic of this special memory as if it were just yesterday. The air had picked up a touch of coolness as the sun proclaimed its departure in radiant hues of orange and purple. Soon the stars were seen trying to emerge, one by one, into the pristine twilight sky, and the night began its capture of this glorious day.

"Cricket," said Grandmother, "run and get your sweater, dear. I don't want you catching a cold. It's under the blankets at the end of our picnic table. And, Cricket, bring one of the blankets too, dear."

"Okay, Grandma," Cricket answered.

She dashed between tables, benches, and people until she reached the thinning edge of the picnic grounds and their table. She gathered up her sweater and a blanket, then she noticed a small stack of cut wood about fifty feet beyond the picnic grounds. Thinking that the small slender sections of wood would be perfect for their campfire, Cricket set down her sweater and blanket and hurried to collect some. Out of the twilight, a tall phantomlike figure abruptly appeared in front of her. She came to a startling halt, causing her to tumble unceremoniously to the ground. Stumbling to her feet, Cricket looked up to see a familiar face.

"Well, well," he said with a sinister sneer. "What do we have here? Our very own little Miss Shirley-fuckin'-Temple, a little lost lamb far away from her fuckin' flock, I think."

He took a long drink from the bottle he was carrying in a brown paper bag. "Where are all your little asshole buddies, may I ask?"

"Everyone's getting ready for the fireworks," she said, and her voice began to quiver.

"What you doing out here so far from the crowd? Ain't you afraid of the Big Bad Wolf or the Boogeyman?"

His face twisted into horrific contortions as he tossed his now- empty bottle into the darkness. "I don't believe in the Boogeyman or the Big Bad Wolf," said Cricket. "I'm way too old for that stuff."

But even her attempted bravado failed to keep her voice from cracking with the building fear as he stumbled toward her.

"Too old, are ya?" he said mockingly. "You remind me of your goddamn, snooty mother, who thinks her pussy is better than everyone else's, thinks she's too good for the likes of me."

"Do you know my mom?" Cricket asked with surprise.

"You bet I do . . . and her three motherfuckin' brothers too. The whole nasty bunch of you Banes and your highfalutin attitudes . . . I know you all," said Adder Toomey as he swayed back and forth.

He had the same disheveled demeanor and distorted features Cricket had seen the night of the birthday party sleepover, the same unkempt appearance, blurry red eyes, slurred speech, loud voice, and threatening posture.

"I'm just gathering a few pieces of wood for our campfire," said Cricket.

Feeling a deep sense of foreboding, she added, "I best be going.

My grandparents will be looking for me. Bye, Mr. Toomey."

And she turned to walk away. Adder lunged forward, roughly grabbing Cricket by her arm, yanking her almost off her feet. He leaned down, holding his face close to hers. His breath was rancid, and his eyes were large and wild-looking.

"Just gathering wood, huh?" he said tauntingly. "And just where is that little prick-teasing tramp, Mary Frances?"

His voice picked up volume, and his grip on Cricket's arm became tighter. "Off in the woods, screwing some young stud? Is that where she is, huh?"

Cricket struggled to free herself, and her fears grew stronger. "Mr. Toomey, you're hurting me . . . let go . . . let go. She's not in the woods, I swear. I don't think Mary Frances even knows how to use nails or screws. She did an awful job on our fort. She and Marvin went back to the boat dock to look for Marvin's lost pocketknife. Honest . . . that's all." Adder grabbed Cricket's other arm as well and held her even tighter. Cricket reached panic mode when she realized his expression was the same as the look he had while holding Mrs. Toomey on the kitchen table that awful night after Mary Frances's party. Adder began to grin an evil smirk as he dragged Cricket toward the wooded area near the edge of the beach. She kicked and screamed and finally ripped herself free of his grip. He staggered and lost his balance, falling facedown into the sand. Everything inside Cricket told her to run, but she stayed frozen. Stumbling to his feet, Adder began to rant.

"Just you wait until I find that little whore. She'll be sorry. I'm not taking that crap from any thirteen-year-old slut! I'm not taking any more crap from anybody, and that includes your-holierthan- thou, cocksucker grandfather, who always sticks his fuckin' nose where it doesn't belong! I'm through, do you hear me? Through with all you Banes and your bullshit! Through with marriage bullshit! And through with Mary Frances's prick-teasing bullshit. Through with everything!" Adder seemed to be howling at the moon, which had just risen over the surrounding forest.

As he bellowed about his angst against the world, he shook his fist in the air. He reached down and grabbed Cricket's wrist while he continued his raving and bluster against Mary Frances and the town's treatment of him. "I'll get even with you all . . . every goddamn one of you. Just you wait and see." His grip tightened as his voice became louder with every complaint.

Cricket's heart thumped against her chest. Her breathing started to come in gulps and gasps, and her whole body was shaking. She was terrified and could feel the tears starting to flood her eyes when, out of the deepening darkness, she heard Kat and Myrna calling her name.

"Cricket, Cricket, where are you?" they called. "Kat, Myrna, here I am!" Cricket yelled.

Adder lifted Cricket off the ground and held her face-to-face. "You believe in the Boogeyman now, don't ya, now that you're looking at him right in the eye?" Adder unexpectedly released his grip. Cricket fell to the ground as he staggered into the darkness and out of sight. Without looking back, Cricket ran toward the picnic grounds and her friends.

"Kat, Myrna, here I am. Let's go, let's go," said Cricket emphatically, picking up her sweater and blanket, and they didn't stop running or look back until they were well within the picnic grounds, surrounded by familiar people.

"Holy cow, Cricket, what's the rush?" panted Kat as they arrived at the campfire.

"Mr. Toomey was out there looking for Mary Frances, and boy, was he mad." Cricket bent over with a painful stitch in her side.

"Wow, after seeing his temper at Mary Frances's party, I sure wouldn't want him mad at me," said Myrna, "and I sure wouldn't want to be in Mary Frances's shoes when he catches up with her either."

"I think everything will be okay," said Cricket with total false confidence.

"Remember how mad he was at the party and how nice he was the next morning? Well, I guess he just gets extra grumpy at night. Everything will be okay tomorrow." Cricket wasn't sure if she was trying to convince Kat and Myrna or herself. She rubbed the arm and wrist Mr. Toomey had so roughly gripped and continued her pretense of bravery and wisdom, all the while shaking inside. But Mr. Toomey was right about one thing—there was such a thing as the Boogeyman, and Cricket looked him right in the eye and had her first glimpse of evil. With the setting of the sun, they covered their sunburned bodies with something warm and sat around the campfire, waiting for Mary Frances and Marvin to join them. They told stories of witches and ghosts while awaiting the most anticipated event of the day, the fireworks, which would be launched from a big barge out on the lake. Mike told a story of a rogue bear that roamed the woods, looking for little children to eat for supper. The huge bear was ten feet tall when standing on his hind feet and stalked the forest during a full moon, like this night. Chris related the tale of a ghost of an old man who haunted the lake's edge, searching for his lost dog that drowned in a heavy storm. Tommy's contribution was the story of a giant that lived deep in the mountains and came down every Halloween to steal children, whom he took back to his cave and became his slaves. All pretty scary, top-notch tales back in the forties told around a roaring campfire.

In the midst of their storytelling, confusion began to stir among the adults at the rear of the picnic tables. Cricket looked up to see what the fuss was all about, and she heard her grandmother gasp, "Oh my Lord!" as her eyes frantically searched around the campfire edges for sight of Cricket and her friends. She seemed immensely relieved at seeing Cricket and turned back to give her attention to the adult situation. Mrs. Fisher showed up at the campfire with a rather frantic look on her face replacing her normal calm demeanor. "Myrna, come with me, *now*," she said, grasping Myrna's hand and dragging her away and out of sight. "I can't believe it . . . it's just too horrible," said Mrs. Anderson, Tommy and Chris's mom. "Has anyone called the police?"

Soon the police arrived, and Sheriff Davis was trying to calm all the men who were talking in loud voices. Mrs. Waters, Kat and Marvin's mom, cried hysterically as the women gathered to console her. Tommy rushed into the crowd and returned to tell all of them that Marvin was in some sort of horrible trouble.

"What's going on? What's this all about?" they all asked. "I don't know exactly," said Tommy.

"It's hard to tell with everyone talking at the same time." "Didn't you hear anything about what Marvin is supposed to have done?" asked Chris.

"Well," Tommy went on, "I heard the sheriff talking to Mrs. Toomey, and he was telling her Marvin looked responsible for this. Then Mrs. Waters was crying, and pretty soon they were too upset for either of them to talk. Next, Mr. Waters arrived and took Mrs. Waters to the car. Deputy Dan helped Mrs. Toomey into the police car."

"What does this all mean?" Cricket asked. "What happened to who?"

"I don't know," said Mike. "It's pretty confusing, but I think Marvin is in big trouble for something everyone thinks he's done, and now Marvin has disappeared. The sheriff said if Marvin isn't found soon, he's bringing out the dogs to assist in the search, and you guys know how scared Marvin is of dogs. In fact, I think dogs are the only things Marvin is afraid of."

Kat came running toward the campfire and pulled them all together, whispering that she had seen Marvin leave the picnic grounds about sunset, headed for the fort at the edge of the strawberry fields. She begged them to think of something to help him. Then Kat rushed back to her mother, and it was agreed that they would slip away to find Marvin and bring him back to explain this awful misunderstanding. Guided by the full moonlight, the four of them raced down the dirt road, through the hedgerows, and across the strawberry field to their fort. There they found Marvin, curled into a ball like a small child, sobbing uncontrollably.

"Marvin, Marvin, where've you been?" said Mike. "The sheriff is looking all over for you."

"Yeah," said Tommy, "everyone is pretty excited down at the lake. What's going on? What happened?"

Marvin continued to sob and mumble something about being sorry, about not meaning to do it, about being scared he was in trouble.

"Being in trouble isn't even a description of what's happening.

What did you do?" said Chris.

"Marvin, I'm sure you didn't mean to do anything bad," said Cricket, taking his hand to get his attention. "But everyone thinks you did, so you've got to come back with us so you can explain this awful mistake."

"Can't you tell us, Marvin, what happened?" said Chris. "Marvin, can you hear me?"

"I give up," said Mike. "Cricket, you try to get him to talk."

The long-awaited fireworks display began. It filled the sky with huge balls of twinkling colors that burst high into the air and then fell, disappearing into the lake waters. Again and again, the sky was illuminated with volumes of multicolored, sparkling lights as they stood looking down at the eerie-colored shadows splashing across the agony on Marvin's tearstained face.

CHAPTER 16

The Capture

"MARVIN . . . MARVIN, LISTEN TO me," Cricket pleaded, shaking him with all her strength. "Something awful has happened, and they think you did it . . . something really bad, and you need to come back to the lake and explain that it's all a horrible mistake."

"I know, Cricket . . . I'm really sorry," said Marvin in between sobs. "I did do something bad, but I didn't mean to hurt her. Honest, Cricket, it was a mistake. You believe me, don't you?"

"We know you'd never do anything to hurt anybody," said Cricket, attempting to comfort him. "But you need to tell the sheriff that this whole thing is just a misunderstanding."

"Can you tell us what happened?" Tommy knelt down to catch Marvin's attention.

"I slapped her . . . I slapped her . . . I slapped her really hard," said Marvin.

"You slapped whom?" asked Mike.

"I knew I shouldn't hit a girl, but I couldn't help it. She laughed at me, she made fun of me . . . she made me so mad that it just happened, and now I can't take it back. Oh god, I'm so sorry . . . didn't mean it . . . I didn't mean it. You've got to tell them, Cricket . . . tell them that I'm sorry. She said she would have me put in jail." Marvin had a firm grip on Cricket's shoulders, repeating over and over his admission of guilt and regret.

No matter what they said, Marvin didn't seem to hear them or understand what they were trying to say. He just kept repeating the same disconnected proclamations. It became clear they were going to need help. After a quickly held meeting, it was decided that since Cricket was the slowest runner, Mike, Tommy, and Chris would run back to the lake to seek help while Cricket stayed with Marvin. "Just try to keep him calm, Cricket" were Tommy's instructions. "Just talk to him and keep telling him everything will be all right.

Okay? Can you do that?"

"Sure, I can do that, but I don't think it will do any good." "Just keep talking. He'll listen to you," said Mike.

"Well, all right," she said, "but hurry back, you guys."

Cricket sat on the floor of the fort close to Marvin and tried to console him as he continued his sobbing and rambling conversation. Marvin laid his head in Cricket's lap like a small child seeking approval while clutching her hand with such force her fingers became numb.

"Tell me what happened, Marvin, please," Cricket said in her calmest voice.

"I'm sure everything will be all right just as soon as the sheriff has heard your side. So tell me, I'm your friend, and I'll believe you, honest."

"Oh, Cricket, you don't understand . . . you're too little to know what I'm talking about. No one will understand . . . everyone will think I did it on purpose."

"Marvin, listen to me. Everyone likes you. The sheriff will listen to you. Just tell him the truth, and everything will work out, I'm sure of it, but . . ."

In the distance, she heard voices.

"See, Marvin, I told you someone would come to help.

Everything will be fine now, you'll see." At the sound of the voices getting closer, Marvin's eyes took on the look of a trapped animal; panic spilled over his shaking body as he pushed himself deep into the corner of the fort. Cricket continued her attempts to comfort the terrified Marvin when she recognized her grandfather's voice frantically calling out her name in a tone she had never heard before.

"Annie, Annie! Where are you, Annie?" called her grandfather. "I'm over here, Grandpa, in our fort."

Within seconds, Thad Bane stood breathlessly in the doorway. Before Cricket could even speak, he snatched her up into his arms, kissing and hugging her so tightly she could barely breathe.

"Oh, Annie, my precious Annie, thank God you're all right," said Thad, looking directly into her eyes and brushing her hair from her face. He removed Cricket from the fort, and the sheriff and his deputy rushed inside.

While struggling with the sheriff, Marvin was dragged out of the fort, and as he passed Cricket in her grandfather's arms, he pleaded, "Cricket, tell them I'm sorry. Tell them I didn't mean it. Please, Cricket, tell them!"

When the police car pulled away, sirens screaming, Cricket could see Marvin's terrified face looking at her through the rear window, his lips silently forming her name as he disappeared out of sight. Cricket buried her face deep into the security of her grandfather's strong shoulders, locking her small arms tightly around his neck in an attempt to shut out the vision of the agony etched across Marvin's face as he was taken into custody. Later that night, lying in her bed, Cricket could hear her grandparents in their bedroom, discussing the horrible events of the day in those hushed, muted tones adults think are inaudible to children.

"Lord, Thad, what is this world coming to when our children aren't even safe at a holiday picnic?" Arvilla gave a huge sigh. "You think you know your neighbors, your community, and then something like this happens." "I know, dear, it's just too horrible to fathom. That could have been our little Annie. Jesus, it makes me sick to my stomach to think of it." Thad placed his head in his hands as he sat on the edge of the bed.

"I can't even begin to think how the Toomeys must feel," said Arvilla, shaking her head.

"Did you see Maggie? She was devastated."

"Yes, I saw her. Good thing Doc Miller was nearby. She's really taking this hard, but who wouldn't?"

Thad rose and paced up and down the bedroom floor.

"You know, I was panicked at first for Annie's safety, but after I calmed down and started thinking about the day's events, I couldn't help but feel there was something off-kilter here. I can't put my finger on it, but I just don't see Marvin as a murderer. We've known that boy since he was born, and something just doesn't fit. I know he's had some learning problems since that motorcycle accident, but he's never been in trouble before, not in school or out. Marvin is basically a good kid."

"I agree, dear," said Arvilla. "It doesn't seem like Marvin is capable of doing anything so violent, and to someone who was a friend." Thad looked thoughtful for a long moment. "I think I'll have a talk with Sheriff Davis and see if he feels the same way I do." "Thaddeus Duncan Bane," said Arvilla as she sat up in bed. "What are you up to? That statement sounds an awful lot like a retired judge thinking of taking up the law again, *retired* being the optimum word here, my love. I'm sure the sheriff will sort things out."

"Well, we'll see," said Thad. "But I'm still going downtown to have a talk with him in the morning."

"Oh, Thad, you're impossible, but I love you anyway," said Arvilla as she leaned over and kissed him on the cheek.

Mary Frances had been found under the boat dock just after sunset, raped and apparently strangled. The same boat dock where Cricket and all her friends had celebrated their comrades' victories earlier that day. Under Mary Frances's half-naked body was Marvin's most prized possession: the engraved pocketknife given to him by his father on his fourteenth birthday. And worst of all for Marvin, he was seen running from the boat dock area toward the woods just about sunset by a family walking their dog. Cricket didn't yet know of things sexual or the meaning of *rape*, but she did know that Mary Frances was lost to her forever, just like her father. An overwhelming sting of sorrow rushed through Cricket's young soul, and it felt like her heart had split into a million pieces. Warm tears poured down her cheeks, and uncontrollable sobs escaped her attempt to bury her pain in her pillow.

Cricket's prayers came hard this night. She had to fight her bruised and broken feelings, which made her want to scream, "Why? Why my daddy? Why my friend Mary Frances? How can you be so mean?"

"Hello, God, Cricket here. I'm really confused, and I just don't understand how you can let things like a war and a misunderstanding take the people we love away from us. Don't you know just how much that hurts? Aren't you supposed to love and care for all your children? Please help my grandpa explain all this to me so we can continue to be friends and talk at night, and then I won't be so mad at you. Wouldn't you think, with a name like God, you would have to live by the Ten Commandments too and not let your children kill one another? Thanks for listening. We'll talk again tomorrow. I'm just too sad right now to chat. Love, Cricket."

Just as she finished her prayers, she felt a touch on her shoulder, and then her grandmother's arms closed around her and cradled her close.

"Now, now, my sweet Cricket," she said, rocking her back and forth. "You mustn't feel so sad. Losing a dear friend is a very hard thing to understand at your age, sweetheart, but you know Mary Frances wouldn't want you to cry and feel so bad. I'm sure she is in heaven right this minute with the angels and tucked safe and warm in a big white cloud bed, sound asleep." Cricket's grandfather was standing next to her grandmother. He reached down, lifting her up into his arms. "Would you like to sleep with Grandma and me tonight, sweetheart?"

"Yes, oh, yes, Grandpa," said Cricket as her small frame shook with despair and her tears flowed like a woodland spring.

The three of them headed for the bedroom, and everyone snuggled down into the bed.

"Grandpa, what do you think happens to us when we die? I mean, what really happens?"

"Well, Annie, I truly believe in heaven and that my eternal peace will be with God."

"Is that what you believe, Grandma?" "Yes, sweetheart. I certainly do."

"Do you think we'll all be together again someday in heaven?" asked Cricket.

Grandpa wiped the tears from her damp face and said, "I'd like to believe that someday we will all be together again, living in the house of the Lord. I can't imagine it being any other way, Annie." "I like that idea too, Grandpa," said Cricket. "I really miss my dad, and I'd like to think I'll see him again one day. I've really been mad at God for taking him and Mary Frances. Do you think he'll forgive me?"

"In his graciousness and love, God forgives everyone who truly seeks his forgiveness, so I'm sure he'll forgive and understand how someone so young can feel anger and confusion over the death of a loved one."

Grandma gently rubbed Cricket's back until the sobs subsided and her eyes could no longer stay open. The faint scent of night- blooming jasmine wafted through the bedroom window from the next-door neighbors' yard, and in her half-asleep state, Cricket felt the presence of her mother gently kissing her good-night. For a few lingering seconds, just before the familiar feeling of impending slumber washed over her exhausted body, she felt the sharp stab of homesickness and the need to feel her mother's arms around her. Very soon, the three were sound asleep, each with their own private dreams, sorrows, and sadness of the day's events. But they were together, they were grateful, and they were safe. At least for that night.

CHAPTER 17

The Investigation

THE NEXT DAY, SHERIFF Davis requested that all the neighborhood children and their parents come to his office to give statements. They all assembled in the waiting room: Mike Toomey and his mother, Maggie; Chris and Tommy Wilson and their parents, Myrna and the Fishers, and Kat, who came with Cricket and her grandparents. The waiting room was square-shaped, with tiny black-and-white tile on the floor. Hard, uncomfortable benches lined the walls. Pictures of past sheriffs hung on one wall, while the opposite wall held trophies, awards, and a picture of Franklin Delano Roosevelt. Over the door was a large clock that loudly ticked away every minute of their stay. The air was filled with the stale smell of the sheriff's signature cigar, clenched in his teeth. Abruptly the door swung open, snapping everyone to attention as Mr. and Mrs. Waters entered the room. With eyes directed only to the floor, they quickly disappeared into the sheriff's inner office. From where Cricket and her grandparents sat, they could see through the half-open door to the sheriff's desk and some chairs directly in front of it. They might as well have all been in the same room, since the walls were so thin they could hear every word being spoken.

"Bob, Edith," said the sheriff, gesturing them to sit. "I'm sorry to have to ask you to come down here like this, but I think it's important for your boy that you are here and that we get to the truth of this situation as soon as possible. I'm not going to sugarcoat this. Things don't look good for Marvin . . . finding his knife and all under the girl's body."

Mrs. Waters began to softly cry into her handkerchief. "I know my boy, Jim," said Marvin's father, "and he isn't capable of something as awful as this. I just know it . . . in my gut . . . he didn't do this!" "I hope you're right, Bob. But you've got to trust me and let the evidence tell the story. Now I'm going to tell you what's going to happen here this morning. Pretty soon, my deputy will be bringing Marvin here from the jail, and I'm going to give him the chance to tell his side of the story. Marvin has had all night to gather his thoughts, to calm down, and it's extremely important for him to tell the truth about anything else he knows about the death of Mary Frances."

"Will we be able to take him home after we're done here?" asked Mrs. Waters.

"Well, Edith, I don't think we can clear this up that fast, so he'll have to stay with me for a while until I can get all the facts from everyone involved and determine what needs to be done. But I promise we will release your boy just as soon as possible, all right?" Just then, the outer office door swung open, and Marvin, followed by two burly officers and Deputy Dan, shuffled in, wearing prison clothing, handcuffs, and leg-irons. His head bent, his body slumped, he somehow looked much smaller and very young and afraid. Marvin didn't make eye contact with anyone.

"Sit here, Marvin," said the sheriff, gesturing to the empty chair directly in front of his desk.

"Now, son, you know this is a very serious situation we've got here, and I need to hear in your own words what happened between you and Mary Frances yesterday at the picnic. I want to hear what went on. No bullshit, just the plain truth, you understand?"

"Yes, sir," muttered Marvin. "I'll tell you everything I know." "Speak up, son," said the sheriff. "Yes, sir," repeated Marvin, straightening up in his chair as everyone in the office sat motionless in anticipation.

"Well, after the log-rolling contest and the sack races, Tommy, Chris, Mike, Kat, Cricket, Myrna, and Mary Frances and I all went down to the boat dock. We just hung around, eating ice cream and sitting on the dock and stuff, until the sun started to set. That was when we all headed back toward the picnic grounds so our folks wouldn't worry." Marvin paused, looking around the room, then at his parents, and continued. "About halfway back, I realized I'd lost my knife. I looked all through my pockets, and it was gone, so Mary Frances and I ran back to look for it. We looked all over. That knife is sort of special to me 'cause my dad gave it to me on my fourteenth birthday. I guess the knife must have slipped out of my pocket and fallen through the boards of the dock or something, 'cause we finally found it under the dock. I was so relieved."

Marvin hesitated, and the sheriff said, "Go on, son. What happened next?"

Marvin began to squirm with discomfort as he continued. "Well, uh . . . Mary Frances grabbed my knife, and she wouldn't give it back. She said if I wanted it, I'd have to come get it. We sort of wrestled around under the dock . . . you know, over the knife . . . just in fun and all, then . . ." Marvin's uneasiness began to elevate. "What happened then, Marvin? I know this is difficult, but it's important that you tell me everything, no matter how awkward or uncomfortable it is to talk about. Do you understand?"

"Yes, Sheriff, I understand," said Marvin, "but do I have to tell the rest of the story in front of my mother?"

Sheriff Davis spoke in a gentle voice as he addressed Marvin's mother.

"Edith, could you please excuse us and wait in the other room for a moment?"

Edith Waters reluctantly exited the room and took a seat on one of the wooden benches in the outer office, where she could still hear what Marvin had to say, saving her son obvious embarrassment. "Well, as I said, we were just fooling around, and somehow, the fooling around turned into kissing and stuff, then Mary Frances pulled off her bathing suit top and asked me to touch her. She scared me near to death . . . ain't never had a girl do that before . . . I didn't know what to do or say."Marvin found it difficult to sit still. He continued, his cheeks and ears bright red.

"She slid her hand down the front of my swimsuit, and that really startled me, and I guess it was just a reaction, but I grabbed her hand and pulled it away. That really made her mad, and she slapped my face very hard. I asked her what was wrong, and then instead of being mad, she started to laugh." Now Marvin's discomfort level was off the charts. His face was completely flushed, and he was sweating profusely.

"She said, 'You've never done it before, have you, Marvin?' and she was all sarcastic. 'You're a virgin, aren't you?' And she kept making fun of me. I told her to stop laughing at me . . . that it wasn't funny . . . but she wouldn't stop. So I slapped her hard, but she just kept laughing. I ain't never hit a girl before, Sheriff. I know it wasn't right, and I felt just awful, but she made me so mad."

"Is that when you lost control, Marvin?" asked the sheriff, moving his chair closer. "Is that when you couldn't stop yourself from what happened next?"

"I guess so, Sheriff. I was so embarrassed I could have died. She just kept laughing and laughing . . . she wouldn't stop! Finally, I just told her I was done with the stupid games she was playing, I was leaving. That stopped her laughing, all right. Now she was hopping mad—I mean mad as hell again. Then she hauled off and smacked me right in the face again, calling me every name in the book. I tell you, Sheriff, that girl had a mouth like a dockworker."

"What kind of things was she saying, accusing you of?" asked the sheriff.

"What do you mean?" Marvin fidgeted in his chair.

"Was she accusing you of doing something? What in general made her so angry?" "I don't know, Sheriff . . . just crazy stuff that didn't make any sense to me. She said I was just like all the others . . . dumping her and using her . . . not man enough for her. After a while, she seemed to be talking about someone else. She even rambled on about something to do with Adder Toomey and a sick, twisted friend of her father's . . . just stuff that made no sense to me." Marvin looked genuinely puzzled.

"Was that it? Did she talk about anyone else?"

"Not that I remember, but I swear, Sheriff, when I left, she was alive and yelling after me that she was going to tell everyone that I raped her and I'd go to jail for life. I was so scared I just ran . . . I ran and hid in our fort. I didn't want to go to jail, and I swear I didn't mean to slap her so hard. Honest, I didn't mean to." Marvin lowered his head and began to sob.

"Then how do you explain that right after you ran away, Mary Frances was found dead, raped, and half-nude just where you say you left her?" asked the sheriff.

"I can't, Sheriff," said Marvin between sobs. "All I know is that she was alive and screaming mad at me as I was running away."

"Do you have any idea what time it was when this all happened?" asked the sheriff.

"No, not exactly. The nearest I can guess is that it was sometime around sunset."

"Did you see anyone at the dock who can verify that they saw you leave Mary Frances alive?" asked the sheriff.

"No, but I felt like there was someone watching us. Even Mary Frances said she felt like someone was watching, but we never saw anyone," answered Marvin.

"I sure wish I had seen someone, then they could tell you what I am saying is the truth." Marvin bent his head and softly began to cry at the sight of his mother re-entering the room. His body was shaking in a state of pure hopelessness.

Mrs. Waters slowly walked to her despondent son, putting her arms tenderly around his trembling shoulders, and quietly said, "It will be all right, Marvin. It will be all right, dear . . . don't cry." Marvin's sobs grew muffled, but nothing could stop the shaking, the trembling of his entire body as he fought to keep his despair inside. The sheriff left the room and joined the summoned collection of witnesses in the seating area to give Marvin and his parents a few minutes alone. After the Waters left and Marvin had been removed from the sheriff's office, it was time for those assembled in the waiting room to take their turns in the chair in front of the sheriff's desk. Tommy, Chris, Mike, Myrna, and Kat confirmed Marvin's account of the day's activities up until the time Marvin and Mary Frances left to return to the boat dock to look for Marvin's knife. The sheriff took their statements, and they were excused and left the building.

Last to be questioned was Cricket, accompanied by her grandparents. "Now, Cricket, you've heard what the others had to say about what they remember of the events. Do you have anything to add?" asked the sheriff as he settled back into his overstuffed desk chair and lit another cigar, as if interviewing her were just a footnote to the day's investigation.

"No, sir, that's pretty much what happened, all right. When we left the boat dock and headed back to the picnic grounds just a little before sunset, Marvin and Mary Frances were right behind us until they went to look for Marvin's knife . . . and everything seemed just fine. That's pretty much all I know," said Cricket as she sat tucked tightly in her grandfather's lap.

"So you didn't see anyone else in the area, and you didn't return to the boat dock again? Is that right, Cricket?" said the sheriff.

Everyone seemed surprised when Cricket hesitated to answer the last question.

"Well . . . I mean . . . well, sort of." Cricket leaned even farther into her grandfather's lap. The sheriff went from relaxed to straightening up in his chair, and he bent toward Cricket and her grandfather. "What do you mean *sort of*, Cricket?" She looked at her grandparents, unsure.

"Go ahead, Annie," said her grandfather. "Tell the sheriff if you have anything to add."

She was in a quandary about how much she should divulge after promising Mary Frances not to tell anyone about Mr. Toomey's on-and-off rages.

"Grandpa, I made a promise not to tell something, and I don't know the rules about when or if you can break that promise."

"Well, let's see now. You're right, a promise is a very special oath, and breaking it is not to be taken lightly. Who asked you to keep this secret?" asked her grandfather.

"Mary Frances," she answered.

"Is the content of this promise something that might, in any way, help the sheriff find the person that hurt your friend Mary Frances?" asked Grandfather.

"Maybe, Grandpa. I don't know for sure," said Cricket.

"Well, let me ask you this, If telling this secret might help the sheriff and keep something bad from happening to someone else, don't you think Mary Frances would tell you it was all right to tell under the circumstances?" said Grandfather.

"Yes, Grandpa, I think after what has happened, she would tell me it is okay to tell the sheriff. Thanks, Grandpa. I feel better now." "All right, Cricket," said the sheriff. "What is it you have to say?" "Well, just about sunset, Grandma asked me to go get my sweater and bring her a blanket from our picnic table. Just a little way away from our picnic table was a large pile of kindling wood, and when I went to get a few pieces for our campfire, Mr. Toomey jumped in front of me."

"Did he say anything to you?" asked the sheriff.

"Yes, sir, he sure did. He was looking for Mary Frances, and he was awful mad at her," she answered. "Why didn't you say anything about this before?" said the sheriff as he quickly stood up from his chair, startling Cricket, who drew even closer into her grandfather's arms.

"Well," Cricket said with a gulp, "Mary Frances asked us all not to tell anyone about Mr. Toomey's temper, like the night of Mary Frances's birthday party, when we saw Mr. Toomey hit Mrs. Toomey. She said something awful would happen if we told anybody, and we all promised her we wouldn't say a word. My mom says you must always keep a promise."

"Your mom is right, Cricket. A promise is a very special thing, but there are times, when someone's life depends on that information, that we're allowed to break that promise. Now help me get this straight. You saw Mr. Toomey hit Mrs. Toomey, is that right?"

"Yes, sir, all of us girls saw it happen," she said. "It was a terrible argument in their kitchen that woke us up from a sound sleep in our tent in the backyard. We ran to the porch and saw it all happen. They called each other names . . . they yelled at each other, and finally, Mr. Toomey hit her so hard her lip bled. But the next morning, everything seemed fine. When you dropped by at breakfast, you didn't notice anything wrong, did you?"

"That's true, Cricket. Now tell me what Mr. Toomey said that made you believe he was mad at Mary Frances."

"Well, his face looked mean, and his voice sounded very angry, and when he grabbed me by the arm, it hurt," said Cricket.

"He grabbed you by the arm?" repeated the sheriff as he moved closer to Cricket and her grandfather.

"Yes, sir, and he wouldn't let me go," she said as she pulled up her sleeve to reveal a set of black-and-blue bruises that took the shape of fingers encircling her small arm.

"Thad, Arvilla, did you know about this?" asked the sheriff. "No, absolutely not. Cricket, why didn't you say something to us?" said Grandfather as he examined the bruises. "Now, Cricket," said Sheriff Davis, "listen very carefully to me. It's very important that you tell me exactly every word that Mr. Toomey said to you, okay?"

"I'll try . . . but I don't know if I can remember everything he said. I was pretty scared. Okay, here goes . . . he said something about Mary Frances being a hobo." Upon reflecting on the conversation, she added, "No, tramp . . . that's it. *Tramp* was the word he used. He said she was probably in the woods, screwing studs, but I told him no, because Mary Frances didn't know anything about tools. Marvin had to redo practically everything she tried to do on the fort we built, so I know she wasn't doing anything with tools in the woods. I told Mr. Toomey Mary Frances and Marvin had gone back to the boat dock to look for Marvin's knife."

The sheriff struggled to hold back a slight smile as he approached Cricket, asking her if there was anything else she could think of. She hesitated, trying to ensure she wasn't leaving anything out.

After a brief pause, she added, "He did call her some kind of a tease, but I can't remember the exact word he used . . . maybe it was a thick-teaser . . . yes, I think that is right."

"That's okay, Cricket, I get the general idea, and you've been a great help. Thank you. You can leave now, but if you think of anything else, have your grandfather call me, all right?"

"Yes, Sheriff, I will," said Cricket. They were thanked again for coming and excused, and the sheriff's office became abuzz with activity. The sheriff sent his deputy to Murphy's Pub to search out Adder Toomey, and the sheriff himself was going to the Toomey home to talk to Maggie. The story seemed to have no end, and there was definitely much more than what was first expected. The fact that Adder Toomey was now in the mix seemed to add another layer to the events of the Shingle Weavers Picnic. And as Cricket's grandmother expected, Thaddeus Duncan Bane could be found right in the middle of the developing riddle that, before its resolution, would put several lives in danger.

Getting Ready For Trial

THE ENTIRE TOWN WAS on alert. Nothing like this had ever happened before. An honest-to-God, impending murder trial with all the aspects of a supercharged Hollywood movie. It sent electricity into every sector of the community. Thaddeus Bane's name was again on the top of the gossip list almost to the degree it was when he took on the whole town over the local Japanese farmers being shipped out to internment camps. It was quite an experience for Cricket to be able to watch the process of just how a defense was put together. She was seeing Thaddeus Bane not only as a grandfather but also as Thaddeus Bane the man, the lawyer, the judge, and the advocate of justice and champion of the downtrodden. She saw her living hero in action, and he was everything she thought him to be and more. Thad converted his wife's little sewing room into a temporary office since he was expecting to put in some long hours during the trial. He also arranged for another retired judge to take over his duties as a traveling judge to small outer communities that had no permanent judge to adjudicate their matters of law. Thad's list of people he intended to interview was extensive. The obvious first person on his list was Miss Perkins, for Lord only knows, if there was any one person in town who had a bevy of information (albeit fact or fiction), that one person was definitely Miss Perkins. Miss Perkins gave Thad a blow-by-blow description of the event in the park between Marvin and Frankie Baker. She said she was working in her garden at the time and even overheard much of the conversations that took place.

"You should have seen the brutality that Waters boy used. Why, as much as I can't stand that little sneak thief Frankie Barker, I was afraid for that boy's life. I'm not at all surprised that roughneck was responsible for that poor little girl's death. He's a menace to society and should rot in jail. And you, Thaddeus Bane, should be ashamed of yourself for even thinking about defending that murderer," stated Miss Perkins with an arrogant turn of her head.

(Well, so much for Miss Perkins's unbiased opinion.) Without so much as drawing another breath, Miss Perkins continued her diatribe by suggesting that if he really wanted to do the community a service, he would be putting Adder Toomey in jail too for his mistreatment of his wife, and did he also know that she had seen Adder and Mary Frances parked over by the park swings, laughing and drinking alcohol?

"Can you imagine a full-grown, married man feeding a young girl alcohol right in the middle of a public park? Heavens to Betsy, what is becoming of society these days? And furthermore—" "Thank you, Miss Perkins, I appreciate your help," interrupted Thad.

"I may need to talk to you again. Would you be willing to testify at trial as to what you might have seen or heard?"

"Why, yes, I certainly will. I see everything that goes on in the park, and I hear what goes on there too. And I certainly have a few other things I can say about what I've witnessed in this town, I can tell you . . ."

"Thank you, Miss Perkins. I'm sure you'll be most helpful. I'll get in touch with you if I feel your testimony is essential."

Next on Thad's list of interviews was to get the other side of the story in a statement from Frankie Baker. Cricket had already told her grandfather the story of what happened in the park that day between Marvin and Frankie, but Thad was curious about what kind of a slant Frankie might put on the incident if he was called to testify in court as a character witness against Marvin. Frankie's statement declared that he and his friends were just minding their own business, playing a game of chase, when they accidentally ran into Cricket on her bike and she fell. As they were helping her up, Marvin appeared out of nowhere, accused them of terrorizing her, and began his uncalled-for, unrelenting physical abuse of Frankie. Marvin was a bully, and they had done nothing to deserve such treatment. Frankie's friends Sam, Walt, and Barney were more than willing to put in their two cents' worth, even adding that they tried to help Frankie but were threatened by Marvin and could only stand by, being innocent observers, making Marvin sound like some crazed, wild man beating up on their poor friend. The next thing on Thad's agenda was to query the town's residents to see if he could find anyone in that area of the boat docks who might have seen Marvin leave while Mary Frances was still alive or anyone who might have seen what transpired between Mary Frances and Marvin. The whereabouts of Adder Toomey was a growing concern for all involved in this case. Maggie hadn't heard from him; no one in the office had seen him. He hadn't been seen by anyone since the picnic, and even though he had been known to be absent during an occasional bender, more than overnight was unusual for him. It gave those involved pause to wonder, *Did his disappearance have anything to do with Mary Frances's death?* The sheriff was also out and about, investigating the crime scene, the fort, and anywhere Marvin had been seen the day of the picnic. He questioned the Waters about Marvin's movements and spoke with several families who had been near the boat dock that day. Nothing! Doc Miller read over the coroner's report and said it didn't seem to indicate that Mary Frances was raped. Oh, yes, there had been sex, all right, but the report seemed to indicate that the sex was consensual, not forced. That presented quite a puzzle, for the scene certainly appeared to represent a rape. Clothing removed, bruises on her neck, sand indicating there had been a struggle. It was going to take some work to make sense of all these mixed signals. The Waters became withdrawn after Marvin's arrest. Facing the town and the criticism of their son was difficult for them. They were positive that Marvin was telling the truth and that he was incapable of any kind of brutality, let alone murder. Kat in particular was suffering. She was supersensitive, bearing the pain and heartbreak of her parents and, most assuredly, that of her brother, Marvin. Kat put on a brave face, but to those who knew her, her anguish was apparent. Thad worked long into the nights before the trial. The more questions he asked, the surer he became that this was a puzzle that just did not fit. Thad agreed with Marvin's parents in his belief that Marvin was incapable of brutality and certainly incapable of murder. Had Marvin been right about his feeling that someone watched him and Mary Frances at the boat dock? If so, who could that person be? And why hadn't that person come forward? What was Adder Toomey's part in all this? Did his disappearance have anything to do with Mary Frances's death? Was Miss Perkins right for a change, and had she really seen Adder and Mary Frances together in the park, seemingly drinking? Or was that just an innocent situation that Miss Perkins interpreted as something evil, as she often did? So many missing pieces that just didn't make sense, and Thad was determined to find those pieces and see just exactly what they looked like. The answers seemed like familiar shadows in darkness, waiting for the daylight to expose the truth. He could almost reach out and touch the explanation.

CHAPTER 19

Marvin's Trial

THE FIRST DAY OF Marvin's trial found the citizens of Everett suffering from some rare malady, a community pandemic that seemed to have infected every employee and employer alike for miles. All the local hangouts, some of which were open even on holidays, mysteriously closed. The lawn in front of the courthouse looked like the crowd for the Fourth of July parade, as interested citizens milled about since the small courtroom had limited seating. Roscoe Malbee, who wrote the obituaries and was all-around substitute reporter for the local paper, the *Everett Tribune*, stationed himself in the last seat next to the door and took it upon himself to deliver a blow-by-blow description, in bits and pieces, to the public waiting outside. Everett had dealt with normal, run-of-the-mill infringements of the law, such as the occasional burglary, odd assorted incidents of disturbing the peace, driving under the influence, property disputes, minor vandalism, and the occasional Peeping Tom, but never had there been a murder. The town was both appalled and fascinated. The courthouse was located at the south end of town directly across the park from the sheriff's office. It was a classic, turn-of-the-century brick building with marble steps, impressive entrance pillars, and the prototype statue of Lady Justice blindfolded and holding her scales. To the right was the registrar and county clerk's office, small but adequate for the volume of business they needed to handle. To the left of the entrance was the office of the jury commissioner, the county prosecutor, the judges' chamber, and the jury deliberating room. Directly ahead was the entrance to the courtroom and the center of a whole community's attention. The courtroom's walls were paneled in a rich, dark oak, with tall narrow windows lining the one outside wall. The public seating was divided from the trial and jury area by a hand-carved railing that consisted of hard, uncomfortable oak benches. The judge's chair and mammoth desk were slightly elevated and looked down upon the prosecutor and defendant's tables. The Italian marble floors echoed every footstep and carried the voices of the participants throughout the room so even a whisper could be heard in the last row of public seating. Three equally spaced fans hung like large hovering birds from the vaulted ceiling, distributing the smoke and warm air into equal portions throughout the room for all to share. As the day progressed, the sun glowed through the tall stately windows, and the courtroom took on an interesting scent of oiled wood, musty old books, and uncomfortable, warm wool suits. A small balcony area of about six benches deep overlooked the entire courtroom, where every move and gesture could be observed. Cricket and her grandmother were seated in the first row of the balcony, where they could watch Cricket's grandfather direct his defense of Marvin like a well-scripted play. Grandfather's opponent, an ambitious young prosecutor by the name of Avery Morris, was full of hellfire and righteous indignation, which was equally as interesting to watch. The fire of youth and the calm of experience were a dueling combination hard to beat. The first day of the trial was pretty much true to form, selecting and seating the jury and the opening statement of both the prosecutor and the defense, which took most of the morning and into the early afternoon. Avery Morris presented an Ichabod Crane–like stature: tall, lean, with sharply defined facial features. He paced back and forth in front of the jury, stopping only to punctuate a point of law or emphasize a statement of guilt by turning abruptly and pointing a long bony finger at the defendant. He had the habit of hooking his right thumb into his vest pocket and tapping his left index finger on the handrail in front of the jury box. His voice ebbed and flowed with just the right amount of emphatic volume to snap the jury back to attention. He ended each sentence with a turn of his head, casting his eyes upward, as if expecting a replay from the Almighty. The prosecutor's case took the position that this was a blatant, open-and- shut case of a brutal murder carried out by a young man rejected by the victim. He hammered away at the facts of Mary Frances's youth and innocence and the location where Marvin's knife was found. He promised to produce witnesses who had personally experienced Marvin's brutality. Witnesses who heard Marvin beg for forgiveness when he was captured. Then there was Marvin's attempt to hide to elude the police, an act not of an innocent man. He promised, by the end of the trial, the jury could absolutely find, beyond any reasonable doubt, that Marvin was guilty as charged. Thad's opening statement was brief in comparison to the prosecutor's long diatribe of condemnation. He stated, very simply, that things are not always as they seem and reminded the jury to hear all the facts before coming to any conclusions. Thad stated his faith and trust in the justice system and the jury's ability to seek out and recognize that truth, for facts would be presented to prove Marvin completely innocent of all charges.

The opening statements having been given, the judge turned to the prosecutor and stated, "Mr. Morris, you may call your first witness."

"Thank you, Your Honor. The prosecution calls Frankie Baker," said Mr. Morris.

Cricket was astonished; she could barely recognize Frankie. Instead of the slovenly, dirty-faced creep that used to terrorize the park, up stepped a well-scrubbed young lad, dressed in neatly pressed navy-blue pants and a crisp white shirt. He really was a pretty good-looking person once he had a bath. Cricket thought to herself that it was the first time she had ever seen him with his hair combed. But even a complete hygienic makeover couldn't remove the swagger and contempt for authority he always wore like a badge of honor. He stood in the witness box with a supercilious smirk on his face, looking over the courtroom.

"Place your right hand on the Bible," said the bailiff. "Do you swear to tell the truth and nothing but the truth, so help you God?"

"You bet. I sure do," said Frankie.

"Do you realize the seriousness of a sworn oath, young man?" interrupted the judge.

"Yes, sir," answered Frankie with a sheepish grin. "Please state your name for the court," said the bailiff.

"Frankie Baker, sir," said Frankie, attempting to maintain his courtroom persona.

"Please be seated," said the bailiff.

"Now, Frankie," said Mr. Morris, "do you know the defendant, Marvin Waters?"

"Yes. We are in the same class at school," answered Frankie. "Did you have a chance encounter with Marvin in the park sometime during the last week of June of this year?"

"Yes, I sure did," said Frankie, sitting as straight as an arrow, with a constant smug expression on his face.

"Will you please, in your own words, tell the court what took place the day of this encounter?"

"Well," began Frankie, "my friends and I were just minding our own business when, all of a sudden, I went around the statue and there, out of the blue, was Cricket riding her bike right in front of me. We crashed into each other, and while I was trying to help her get up, out of nowhere Marvin showed up and accused me of being responsible for Cricket's fall. He grabbed me around the neck so tight I could hardly breathe, and then he started beating me up. He rubbed my face into the dirt, made me take off my clothes, like he was some kind of pervert."

"What did he make you do with your clothes?" Mr. Morris said. "He made me get them wet in the fountain and wash Cricket's bike with them," said Frankie.

"During this encounter, what, if anything, did Marvin say to you?" said Mr. Morris as he tapped his fingers along the railing in front of the jury box.

"Marvin started calling me all kinds of names and threatened to beat the crap out of me if he ever saw me in the park again. I got as much right as Marvin does to be in that park," said Frankie with exaggerated indignation.

"And how did this encounter end?" inquired Mr. Morris.

"I finally pulled myself loose, and I told Marvin a thing or two, like he was lucky he caught me off guard like he did, trying to help poor little Cricket and all. Otherwise, I would have cleaned his clock," said Frankie.

"Do you recall any reason or incident that might have caused this aggression?" asked Mr. Morris.

"No, sir," said Frankie, raising his voice level. "He's just plain mean . . . downright dirty. I ain't ever done nothing to Marvin."

"Objection, Your Honor," stated Thad.

"Objection sustained," answered the judge. "Just answer the questions, young man. Don't offer your opinions."

"Yes, sir," said Frankie. "No further questions at this time, Your Honor," said Mr. Morris.

Frankie got up from his seat with a big smile on his face and was looking around the courtroom as he began to strut down the aisle on his way out when the judge said, "Just a minute, young man. Not so fast. You've not been excused. Now, it's the defense's turn to ask you questions."

Frankie, looking very embarrassed and awkward, returned to his seat in the witness box.

"Remember, young man," said the judge, "you are still under oath."

"Yeah, yeah, I get it, Judge," muttered Frankie. Cricket was aghast that Frankie had just told huge, out-and- out lies and got away with it. She was about to share her shock with her grandmother when she patted Cricket on her hand and whispered, "Don't get upset, sweetheart. Just wait and see what your grandfather does."

"Mr. Bane, your witness," said the judge.

"Thank you, Your Honor." Thad stood up and walked toward the witness box.

"Good afternoon, Frankie. My name is Mr. Bane, and I have just a few questions to ask you. Now, let's review your testimony. You say that you were minding your own business, playing in the park with friends, and trying to help little Annie, who had fallen off her bike, when out of the blue, Marvin Waters appeared and began to beat you up, for no good reason whatsoever. Is that right?"

"Yes, sir," said Frankie, "that's exactly right."

"For the record, Your Honor, I would like the witness to identify the little girl in question," said Thad.

"Any objections, Mr. Morris?"

"No, Your Honor," said Mr. Morris.

"Annie Elizabeth Jordan, will you please stand," said the judge. Cricket stood up, hoping her glare would burn a hole in Frankie's soul for telling such a pack of lies.

"Frankie, is this the little girl that fell from her bike on the day in question?" said Thad.

"Yes, sir," said Frankie. "Cute little thing, ain't she?"

"Please, young man," said the judge, "just answer the questions and nothing more. I don't want to warn you again. Continue, Mr. Bane."

"Thank you, Your Honor. Now, Frankie, would you please describe her?" said Thad.

"What do you mean?" asked Frankie.

"Just describe what she looks like . . . for the record," continued Thad. "Well, okay," said Frankie. "She's blond, with blue eyes." He was still puzzled by the question.

"Let's get a little more detailed than that, Frankie," urged Thad. "Let's say she is blond, right? Blue eyes, right? About four feet tall, maybe fifty pounds, seven years old, with a newly healed scar on her right knee and right elbow. Is that a pretty fair description, Frankie?"

"Yeah, I guess so."

"And would you agree you are, shall we say, maybe four times her weight and considerably taller?"

"Yeah, I guess so," said Frankie.

"Now, considering your gallant behavior that day, do you believe that if I called Annie Jordan to the witness stand, she would agree with your version of the events in the park that day?"

Frankie began to squirm in his seat and perspire profusely. "I don't know . . . she's just a little kid and probably would say anything Marvin asked her to. You can't believe anything she might say."

"All right, Frankie, perhaps you're right. She is very young and could be confused about the facts," said Thad. "Let us look to a more mature witness since they are probably more reliable. Are these the three friends you were playing with in the park on the day in question here in the front row?"

"Yes, sir," said Frankie as his comfort level continued to shrink. "Let the record show, Your Honor, that the witness has identified

Sam Lock, Barney Swanson, and Walter Mode," said Thad. "Now, Frankie, if I should call any of these three young men to the witness stand, do you believe they would agree with your testimony?" said Thad.

"Objection, Your Honor," stated Mr. Morris. "What the witness believes or does not believe is not pertinent."

"On the contrary, Your Honor, what this young man believes to be true is very pertinent to this case," stated Thad.

"Very well, Mr. Bane, I'll overrule the objection, but please get to your point," said the judge. "Well, Frankie, would they agree?" said Thad.

By this time, Frankie's ears were bright red, and he was sweating large damp circles under the arms of his once-crisp, clean shirt. Sweat was also rolling down his forehead in sheets, into his eyes, causing him to squint and rub his stinging eyes.

"Answer Mr. Bane's question, young man," ordered the judge. "I can't guess what they would say . . . they ran off like a bunch of chickenshits," whined Frankie.

"Watch your language, young man," cautioned the judge. "Sorry, Judge," muttered Frankie under his breath.

"Well, Frankie," said Thad. "Let me get this straight. It looks like you feel Annie Jordan is too young to be a credible witness to back up what you say happened that day in the park. Your three buddies here, Sam, Barney, and Walter, ran off and deserted you in your time of need. So what about Miss Perkins, seated across the aisle from your friends? She lives just across the street from where the incident took place, and she might have heard and seen everything. If I should call her to testify, do you believe she might confirm your description of what happened or perhaps have even more to add to your testimony?"

"Objection, Your Honor," said Mr. Morris.

"I repeat, the witness can't possibly know what other witnesses might know or add to this testimony."

"Mr. Bane, where are you going with this? And is there an end in sight?" asked the judge.

"Yes, Your Honor. I just want to know if the witness feels anyone of all these many people who also witnessed his brutal attack might want to add some significant information or corroborate Frankie's version of the event . . . anyone! And I just want to give the lad the opportunity to add, change, or correct his testimony before he leaves the stand."

"Very well, objection overruled," said the judge with a glare toward the witness. "Do you have anything you want to change or add to your testimony, young man?"

"Well," stammered Frankie. "Maybe I . . . I mean . . . I could have exaggerated a bit . . ."

"Let me help you, Frankie," said Thad. "Isn't it true that you didn't observe Annie fall from her bike but, in fact, you jammed a stick into the spokes of her bike, causing her to be thrown from it, badly scraping her knee and elbow, all just to show off in front of your friends?"

"It was really an accident, see . . . and I . . .," stammered Frankie.
"Isn't it also true, Frankie, that Marvin just happened to come through the park and saw what you had done to Annie and he decided to teach you a lesson, once and for all, for being such a bully and hurting a little girl for no reason whatsoever, contrary to what you've sworn to?"

"Maybe I could have forgotten some stuff . . . or maybe added a few things," said Frankie, still rattled by being caught in his lies. "I didn't hurt her that bad, and Marvin didn't have to beat me up like that."

"A large fourteen-year-old boy hurts and terrorizes a little seven-year-old girl, and Marvin steps in and gives a bully a taste of his own medicine. Sounds like a hero to me," said Thad.

"Objection, Your Honor!" shouted Mr. Morris.

"Objection sustained. The jury will disregard the statement," ordered the judge.

"I withdraw the statement, Your Honor. No further questions," said Thad.

"The witness is excused," said the judge. "Due to the lateness of the hour, we will adjourn until Monday, 10:00 a.m. Frankie, I want to see you and your parents in my chambers. *Now*! Court dismissed."

And the irritability of the judge's disposition came across loud and clear, as the smack of the gavel could be heard all the way out to the front lawn. Frankie and his parents headed off to the judge's chambers; Marvin was escorted from the courtroom and returned to jail. The courtroom observers began to exit the room among a buzz of opinions and suppositions. Grandma and Cricket waded through the exiting onlookers toward the courtroom to meet up with Grandfather.

"Grandpa! Boy, you sure showed that fink Frankie a thing or two. How did he and the defense attorney think they could get away with all those lies?"

"Mr. Morris is a decent man. He doesn't know Frankie as we do, and I'm sure he lied to him just as he lied to the court. I pretty much knew Frankie would show his true colors if I could keep him on the stand long enough. Frankie is lacking the most important attributes of a truly talented liar, a quick mind and a good memory. It's easy to remember the truth, but remembering your lies takes a true talent." Grandpa said this last part with a wink.

"What will the judge do to Frankie?" asked Cricket.

"My guess is it will be a good, old-fashioned come-to-Jesus meeting that Frankie will not likely forget very soon, and maybe even some juvenile hall time. We'll see," said Grandfather.

Cricket's first experience with the justice system definitely left a lasting impression on her and only added to the deep regard and admiration she had for her grandfather. One thing that did bother her and she found very hard to understand was, how could a jury *disregard* something that has already been said? Perhaps it was just another one of those grown-up things that she wouldn't be able to understand until she was older. For now, it just didn't make any sense whatsoever.

That night, Cricket retrieved her dad's wings from under her pillow and began her prayers. "Dear God, Cricket here. It's been a little while since we really had a good, long talk, not just the usual 'Please bless Mom and my loved ones.' You might have been too busy to take notice, but Marvin's trial has started, and today was the first day in court. Grandpa was wonderful. He really outfoxed Frankie and got him in bad trouble with the judge for telling all those awful lies, especially because he promised, with his hand on your book, to tell the truth and nothing but the truth, so help him you. "I think when you have some spare time you should have a talk with Frankie. Grandpa says he is going to have a come-to-Jesus meeting with your son and the judge, so maybe you could drop by and make it a come-to-God meeting too. "Anyway, I've got great news. I think I know what I want to be when I grow up. I want to be a lawyer first and then a judge, just like my grandfather and you. I'll study extrahard while I'm in school so I can be the very best lawyer and judge that ever was. What do you think, God? Sound like a good plan? "Well, God, that does it for now. Please bless my dad, my mom, and our baby. Take care of Grandpa George until I get home, bless Grandma and Grandpa Bane, and one more blessing, God, an extra big one for Marvin, who is still in jail and needs all the help you can give him. Good night, God. Love, Cricket."

Cricket drifted off, indulging herself in her newly acquired career path. She saw herself wearing a dark business suit and a bright-red cape with a huge initialed *S* in the center. Super Lady Lawyer was her title. Her cape enabled her to fly wherever evil threatened the innocent and downtrodden. Could she be taken more seriously, look more wise and studious if she wore horned- rimmed glasses? She hoped so.

CHAPTER 20

Puzzle Pieces

AS CRICKET AND HER grandfather walked through the post office doors, the usually bustling general public became pin-drop quiet, and people stood in small groups and began to whisper and stare.

"Thad . . . Thad, hold up," said Sheriff Davis. Pulling them into a corner, the sheriff continued.

"Thad, do you really know what in the blazes you're doing? Why are you getting yourself involved in this mess? This kid could be as guilty as sin. Ever think about that?"

"Sorry, Jim," said Thad, "but I think you're wrong. I've known this boy since he was born, and as moody as he may seem at times, I just don't see a killer here. I really don't."

Looking around at those staring at them, the sheriff continued to whisper. "The town is really riled up . . . an innocent young girl and all. There's been some pretty ugly talk about Marvin never making it to a verdict. The word *vigilante* has come up often, along with good, old-fashioned hometown justice, if you know what I mean. You better take care. I mean, tempers are really flaring. This is the biggest thing that has happened in this town for years, and people's feelings are pretty strong on this, on both sides." "Look, Jim," said Thad, "I appreciate your concern, I do, but there will always be a few malcontents whenever anything of this magnitude happens. We'll be just fine, and thanks for the heads-up." "Don't be such a dad-gum, hardheaded, bleeding heart again." Sheriff Davis smacked the wall, and everyone in the post office froze. "Have you forgotten the dust you kicked up by taking on half the town over the Japanese farmers being shipped out to internment camps? That didn't exactly earn you any goodwill among other farmers around here. Adder Toomey is still pissed off at you to this day, and so are a few others who planned to make a killing on those farms. Toomey all but had the entire Eto farm set up for a housing development, and you snatched it right out from under him. Plenty of folks felt you stood on the wrong side of that issue. Defending

Marvin will just fuel up all those old feelings."

"The Eto situation is old news, Jim," said Thad. "The government had no business taking the land and possessions of people just because they are of a different culture, and the war is no excuse to enforce actions that discriminate and ruin lives and families. I did what I had to do to look myself in the mirror in the morning, and the same thing goes in Marvin's case. That boy deserves a defense no matter what the anger factor of the town's troublemakers. Let the evidence prove him innocent or guilty, not the consensus down at Murphy's Pub. Speaking of which, what's the latest on Adder? Any news?"

"He was spotted over in Bellingham. We're hoping to get the chance to question him soon," said the sheriff.

"Keep me up-to-date. I'm very curious to hear what he has to say."

"Sure, but keep in mind what I've said. And keep your eyes open, okay?" The two men shook hands, and Cricket and her grandfather went on their way. Cricket had listened intently to her grandfather's conversation and had all sorts of questions to ask as they walked home.

"Grandpa, what's a *malcontent*?" "Well . . .," said Grandfather, "it refers to a person who is a grumbler, a complainer. Someone who is always dissatisfied, someone impossible to please."

"Oh, I get it. Someone like Grandma's sister Gertrude. She is never happy, and every time she visits, all she does is grumble that the tea is too hot or not hot enough, the house isn't clean enough, I'm not quite enough, children should be seen but not heard . . . what's that supposed to mean? Grandma calls her a nitpicker."

Grandfather chuckled and answered, "Yes, Annie, that's it exactly, just like Aunt Gertrude, but don't tell your grandmother I said so."

"And, Grandpa, what's *internment*?"

"That's a little harder to explain," he said. They stopped at a bench in the park and sat down.

"After the bombing of Pearl Harbor, people were very frightened that the Japanese soldiers would just keep coming and drop bombs here on the West Coast. They didn't, of course, but the fear that it stirred up was intense. The government had fears that those of Japanese descent living along the coastal areas might be spies for their native country and helping the Japanese invade America's West Coast. So all those of Japanese descent were forced to give up all their possessions and move farther inland, away from the coast, and into restricted areas that were called internment camps for the duration of the war." The look on Thad's face was plaintive and troubled as he continued. "It was a very terrible injustice to these people who were just as American and loyal as you and me. They had to leave behind almost everything, their homes, their land, their friends. There were Americans, their neighbors and so-called friends, who took advantage of this injustice to benefit their greed. It was a sad and disgraceful period in our history, Annie. One I pray I never see repeated."

"Is that what happened to Mr. Eto and his family?" "Yes, Annie, I'm sorry to say that is what happened." "That's so sad, Grandpa. I'm glad you tried to help them." She squeezed his hand and felt a sense of pride in this man, her true hero.

"It wasn't all my doing. There were many decent people in this town that joined me in the effort to save the Eto farm until after the war."

Cricket and her grandfather proceeded on their way home. She questioned him about the trial and his ability to prove Marvin innocent. Grandfather assured her that he would do his best. She felt that on the first day of the trial, her grandfather sure showed that liar Frankie Barker a thing or two about telling the truth. Grandfather said he had the inside track on this issue, being personally related to the object of Frankie's bullying, by having facts about Frankie that the prosecutor didn't. They tried to paint Marvin as some sort of a violent, unreasonable, uncaring monster.

"We won the point that day, but there is a lot more to come, and not all of it will be as easy to prove in Marvin's favor."

Cricket wanted to know if Grandfather thought Mr. Toomey had anything to do with all this.

Grandfather said, "It's very difficult to second-guess what someone else may think or do, and only time will bring out all the facts."

That evening, Cricket crawled up on the sofa next to her grandfather, as she did most nights, and she read aloud a chapter of her book *The Wizard of Oz*, then Grandfather read aloud an article or two from the newspaper.

"You've got to keep up on current events," he said.

Just as Cricket finished her chapter and Grandfather was about to read his two chosen articles, a huge crash rang out. Splintered glass shot across the room. The glass had been shattered by a brick with a note attached. Cricket lay slumped over in the corner of the sofa, and a large lump began to swell and grow on her forehead. Blood streamed down her face onto her white bunny Tshirt. Arvilla screamed and threw her body over Cricket, whose injury continued to bleed profusely. Thad jumped up, scrambled his way to the closet door, retrieved his shotgun, and rushed into the front yard. All he could see were the taillights of some undetermined vehicle disappearing in the distance. He returned to the house to find Arvilla on the phone to the sheriff, who arrived almost before she could hang up. Cricket sat curled in her grandmother's lap, dripping wet, as Arvilla had kept Cricket's eyes closed long enough to dunk her completely in the tub to remove all the glass splinters from her face, eyes, and body. The ambulance arrived and attended to Cricket. Her grandparents were assured that her eyes were unharmed and the other scrapes and cuts were minor. The lump, however, was of some concern because of a possible concussion, and they recommended a night in the hospital just to make sure.

"I'll go with Cricket, and you come get me, Thad, when you're through here," said Arvilla.

"I'll be right along, dear," Thad assured her with his usual calm demeanor.

The ambulance departed, and Thad turned to the sheriff. "What in hell is going on here? That brick could have killed Annie or any of us."

"Thad, I warned you that this is a real heated issue you've got yourself mixed up in. No kidding! You can't take this lightly. I'll bring a couple of my reserve deputies out to keep an eye on the house and escort you to trial until this is resolved."

The sheriff dug through the broken glass and retrieved the brick and unwrapped the note: *Murderer-protecting, Jap-loving attorneys belong on the bottom of the sea, and there's more to come.*

The sheriff helped Thad clean up the glass and board up the broken window, then Thad headed for the hospital to check on Annie. When he arrived, he stood at the door to her room and stared at her lying in her bed, so small, so precious, glass wounds on her face and arms and a fresh white bandage over the lump on her left temple. Arvilla sat asleep in a large overstuffed chair next to the bed, holding Annie's little hand. Thad couldn't hold back his tears at the very idea of his beautiful little Annie receiving any harm on his watch. The questions began to fill his thoughts. Had he gotten himself into something he couldn't handle? Could he really follow his conscience and still protect his family at the same time? He gently picked up his granddaughter and settled into the other large chair across from Arvilla, holding her tenderly in his lap.

Annie slowly opened her eyes and whispered from her drug- induced dreams, "I love you, Grandpa."

Thad's eyes filled with tears again as he answered in a private whisper, "It's all right, little Annie, Grandpa's here. No more harm will come to you, I promise. Go back to sleep, dear."

Thad wrapped the blanket snugly around Annie, held her close, and rocked her slightly back and forth until her breathing indicated her sleep was deep and peaceful. He dozed off, embracing his beloved grandchild, praying for the ability to keep the promise he had just made. The moon began to travel from behind the parting clouds. The sky and the earth below were bathed in the moonlight of this night. Cricket's hospital room window framed the moon's ascent like a large painting on the wall, and its light, like the closing of a three-act play, illuminated this tender tableau of a family in peaceful slumber, a peace and sense of safety that would one day soon change forever.

CHAPTER 21

Adder Toomey's Back in Town

THE ENTIRE TOWN WAS engrossed in Marvin's trial. After the brick incident that hospitalized little Cricket, the town's interest rose to a whole new level. It was the main topic of conversation at the post office, Sue Sue's Café, Barney's Barbershop, Elks Lodge, Wilson's Market, Madge's Beauty Parlor, Yadkin's Butcher Shop, and Pine Hill Quilting Society, to name just a few. The Barstow sisters had their hands full just keeping all the gossip and speculation in order. Their switchboard lit up like a multicandled birthday cake for Methuselah. Miss Perkins was whirling around town like a top, and Doc Miller kidded by saying that if this trial went on much longer, Miss Perkins was going to explode like an old fuse box carrying a very heavy load of information. She was indeed in her glory, and her enthusiasm was unmatchable. The speculation about Marvin's guilt or innocence pretty much divided the town into several camps. Those who still held a grudge toward Thad Bane thought he was meddling in things that shouldn't concern him. Another camp, a large number of the town's citizens, was willing to wait out the evidence before offering an opinion. Then there was the camp whose adherents, like Thad Bane, firmly believed Marvin to be completely innocent. Because feelings, pro and con, were running so high in the community, Judge Taylor had the prosecutor and Thad Bane select a jury from Marysville, about fifty miles north of Everett. The judge made arrangements with the local school board to provide a school bus for the jury's daily transportation to and from the courthouse. This cautious act of jury selection caused even more of a stir, but the judge was determined the fairness of any verdict would be beyond question. To guarantee Marvin's safety and take the burden of protection off the shoulders of Sheriff Davis, the judge also made arrangements for Marvin to be housed out of town in a jail in the small community of Pinehurst, twenty-five miles south of Everett. The judge was determined to take no chances that the situation could go terribly wrong in a New York minute. The Bane phone rang incessantly with calls from supporters, detractors, and occasional threats of a reckless nature. The sheriff placed two of his best reserve deputies at the Bane home from dusk to dawn. Nevertheless, Thad was undeterred in his relentless belief in Marvin's innocence, and his research and preparation for each day in court went long into the nights.

"Thad," said Arvilla, "you're looking very tired, dear. Why not call it a night and get some rest?"

"I only have a few more things to attend to. You go along, sweetheart. I'll be to bed soon."

"How's the case looking, dear?" said Arvilla.

"Well, I've got some great points to work with, but I sure could use a witness on Marvin's behalf. Someone who saw him leave the dock area while Mary Frances was still alive."

"Do you think it's possible that someone may come forward?" "It's looking pretty bleak along that line, but I'm not giving up hope." Thad removed his glasses and rubbed his tired eyes. "Has anyone seen or heard from Adder yet?" asked Arvilla.

"No, not yet, but the sheriff is working on that. I'm sure interested in what he may have to say. I'm sure Adder knows more about all this than we think. Now, you run off to bed and let me get back to work, and I'll be along in a little while." Thad kissed Arvilla tenderly on the cheek. "Very well. Try not to be too long." Arvilla walked down the hall and disappeared into the bedroom.

Something woke Cricket, and she lay, listening to see what sounds she could hear in the house. She was just about to turn over and return to her sleep when she heard the sound of papers being shuffled in her grandfather's office.

"Say, what are you doing up so late, little miss?" said Grandfather, leaning back in his big office chair, stretching his back and removing his glasses.

"I saw your light on and wondered if you are lonely." Cricket crawled up onto her grandfather's waiting lap.

"You know," said Grandfather, setting down his papers, "I was just thinking how nice it would be to have a little company. How about we have a nice, hot cup of cocoa and a couple of your grandmother's yummy peanut butter cookies?"

"Hmmm," purred Cricket. "It sounds good to me."

Sitting around the kitchen table, sipping her warm, sweet cocoa, she said, "Grandpa, I'm really worried about Marvin. I just know he couldn't have done anything to hurt Mary Frances. He's just not that kind of a person. If he was ever going to hurt someone, it would have been Frankie that day in the park, but he just roughed him up and let him go. Doesn't that prove Marvin isn't capable of murder?" "Well, sweetheart, when it comes to the law, it doesn't matter what you feel or know. It's only a matter of what you can prove, and that's exactly what I'm trying to do, prove Marvin didn't do this awful crime."

"How's it going?" she asked.

"Things are coming along. We'll just have to wait and see what comes up."

Halfway through their conversation and cocoa, the doorbell rang, startling both Grandfather and Cricket, considering the late hour.

Sheriff Davis was at the door.

"Jim, what's up? Is something wrong?" asked Thad. "Sorry to bother you so late, but we've located Adder Toomey," said the sheriff, taking a chair in the kitchen.

"He got into a barroom brawl outside of Ferndale. Hit a cop with a whiskey bottle and made a run for the border. They finally caught him. Ran his truck off the road and took him into custody. We're bringing him in for questioning in the morning. I thought you might want to be there to hear what he might have to say."

"You bet," said Thad enthusiastically. "Thanks, Jim."

"That old football injury to Adder's knee might have kept him out of the army, but it sure didn't keep him from beating the blazes out of two cops who tried to cuff him."

"Anyone seriously hurt?" asked Thad.

"Several stitches, a broken nose, one cracked front tooth, a black eye or two, but nothing needing an overnight hospital stay," replied the sheriff.

"Adder can be a real wild man when he's been drinking." Cricket looked deep into the chocolate swirling in her cup and thought of her last meeting with Mr. Toomey. A *wild man* was the perfect description.

"Did he say anything when they brought him in?" asked Thad. "No," said Sheriff Davis. "He was pretty riled up, and nothing he had to say made any sense. He should be calmed down by morning." He went quiet for a moment. "Well, it's late, I better get going and let you two get back to your cocoa. See you in the morning. Around eight okay for you?"

"Fine, Jim, eight is just fine. I'll walk you to your car."

Cricket turned to see her grandmother sleepily enter the kitchen. "Who was that, dear?"

"It was Sheriff Davis. They found Mr. Toomey and are bringing him back to town tomorrow morning for questioning." Thad entered the kitchen and joined Cricket and Grandmother at the table.

"Thad," said Arvilla, "what does that mean for Marvin?" "We'll have to wait and see what Adder has to say. There isn't anything physical to connect Adder to Mary Frances's death, and going on a month long bender doesn't automatically make him a suspect or guilty of anything, now, does it?"

Thad now seemed to drift into deep thought.

"Do you have any idea what he might say?" asked Cricket. "Not a clue, not one idea of what he might know or have to add, not until I talk to him in the morning. Now, you ladies get back to bed. I've got a lot to think about and notes to make before morning. Scoot." Thad gently kissed them both on the forehead, and they obediently, hand in hand, headed down the hall to return to their beds.

As Cricket snuggled back down in her bed, she suddenly shot upright, remembering something she wanted to add to her prayers. "PS: God, Cricket here. I have something important to add to my prayers. This is a big break for Grandpa and his case for Marvin. Please give him a new clue as to what happened to Mary Frances. Mr. Toomey may not be a suspect yet, but from my experience with him, he sure has a temper worth investigating. Oh, I meant to thank you for letting Grandma and Grandpa know that Uncle Ken wasn't killed in the war and that he is in some prison camp with the Japanese. I hope they are as nice as the Eto family, who used to live just outside town before the war started. If you have time, could you please add him to my prayers and look in on him once in a while? Thanks, God. Sleep tight. See you in the morning. Love, Cricket."

CHAPTER 22

The Visitor

IT WAS A BEAUTIFUL morning. The sky was clear, with the exception of a few ice cream clouds, and summer was doing her best to spread her joy in every flower while the birds filled the air with song and preened their feathers preparing for their day. It was even unusually warm and sweaterfree for this time of year in the Northwest. Cricket went about her normal chores, sweeping the back and front porches, a continuous job with the lumber mills spewing cinders into the sky daily. She was in charge of emptying the garbage, filling the bird feeder, and picking a small bouquet of sweet peas for her grandmother, who loved to keep her favorite flowers on the kitchen table while their blooming season lasted. Grandma was listening to her favorite radio program, *Stella Dallas*, as she finished up baking several pies and a batch of her famous zucchini bread. In this episode, Stella was accused of stealing a mummy, as the pipe organ emphasized the growing tension of the situation. Cricket just loved to listen to the radio as she did her chores, and *Stella Dallas* in particular, because Stella was endlessly in some sort of trouble but she unfailingly managed to escape her plight.

"Cricket, are you finished with your chores yet?" Grandma called from the kitchen. "Almost, Grandma. I just have the garbage to empty and then I'm done."

"That's good, dear. When the pies and bread cool, I'd like you to take a basket down to the Toomeys. I'm sure Maggie isn't up to much cooking these days, and I hear her mother was coming for a visit to help her out." Grandma began setting the kitchen table for Thad's arrival for lunch at noon sharp. No sooner had Arvilla finished talking to Cricket than Thad walked through the backyard gate.

"Thad," said Arvilla, somewhat surprised. "You're home early. Is everything all right? Did you get the chance to question Adder?" "I'm fine," said Thad, kissing Arvilla on the cheek, "just a little tired. Not much sleep last night. The sheriff didn't get much out of Adder. He was pretty incoherent. He needs more time to sober up. I guess he's been on a marathon bender since he left Everett." "Oh, I'm sorry, dear. I know you were hoping he has some pertinent information that will help shed some light on your case." "He still may, but not for a few days. He offered a bunch of ravings about being made a fool of, about Mary Frances being a lying little witch, except he spelled it with a *B*. Of course, the same complaints he's had for years about his failed development scheme being my fault, and a lot of other nonsense. This man hangs on to a grudge like a dog with a bone. Lord, will he ever get over his angst?" "I'm sorry, Grandpa," said Cricket, taking her grandfather's hand. "I know you hoped for more."

"It's all right, ladies. Not to worry. I think I'll take a short nap before getting back to work. With the trial in session tomorrow, I'll have a lot of work to do this afternoon. Wake me up around one, will you, dear? I'll eat lunch then." He patted Grandma on the shoulder as he passed.

"Certainly, dear." Grandma smiled. "Get some rest." "Do you want me to read you a story, Grandpa?"

"No, thank you, sweetheart. Maybe later tonight, okay?" "Sure, Grandpa, tonight will be just fine. I love you." Cricket gave him a hug as he passed her in the hall.

"Cricket," said Grandma, "here's the basket, dear. Take it directly to the Toomeys and then come right back. Maggie has enough on her hands, and she doesn't need any extra children around the house for now."

"Sure, Grandma, I'll be right back." Cricket walked down the porch steps toward the sidewalk.

"Hey, Cricket," called Myrna, "where you going?" "I'm taking some things my Grandma baked over to the Toomeys," said Cricket.

"Have you heard the latest news?" asked Myrna. "No. What news?"

"Well," said Myrna, "the rumor is that Marvin and Mary Frances got into a fight because she was pregnant and it's Marvin's fault. Do you know what *pregnant* means?"

"Of course I do," said Cricket, somewhat offended. "It's having a baby growing in your tummy. But that couldn't have been the case with Mary Frances. She was too young."

"Not necessarily. Once you start your periods, you can get pregnant."

"You're kidding. I thought you had to get married first." "Well, that's for your mom to talk to you about. But I heard Miss Perkins telling my mom at the bank the whole story," said Myrna.

"Well, is it any wonder? No one believes anything Miss Perkins has to say," said Cricket in defense of Mary Frances's good name. "She's always starting some kind of a rumor or another. She's always causing trouble."

"I don't know . . . she seemed pretty sure. She said she heard it from Doc Miller's nurse."

"Okay, there you have it. You know Nurse Wallace is known around town as the Vault. She is so good at keeping quiet about what goes on in Doc Miller's office. She won't even tell anyone Doc Miller's middle name, and the guys down at Murphy's Pub have been trying to get that out of her for years."

"Maybe so, but she sure sounded like she knew what she was talking about," said Myrna.

"I've got to get going. I'm supposed to get these things over to Mrs. Toomey. Do you want to come with me? I won't be long. Grandma said they don't need extra company, so this will just take a few minutes."

"No, thanks," said Myrna. "My mom would skin me alive if I went over there with that crazy Adder Toomey back in town."

Myrna waved goodbye as she ran up the steps and through her front door. Standing on the Toomeys' front porch, Cricket could hear kids inside and two adults talking.

She rang the bell several times, and finally a voice on the other side of the door said, "Yes, who's there?"

"It's me, Cricket, Mrs. Toomey. Grandma has sent you some pies and bread." The door slowly opened, and to Cricket's utter amazement, there stood Mrs. Parker, the lady she had met on the train.

"Mrs. Parker," said Cricket, totally bewildered. "What are you doing here?"

"Why, Cricket, what a nice surprise!" said Mrs. Parker. "I'm here visiting my daughter, Margaret. Remember, I told you I had a daughter living in Everett? Come in, child, and let me help you with that heavy basket."

"I had no idea that Mrs. Toomey was your daughter. My grandparents live just down the street," said Cricket, still stunned by the coincidence.

Mrs. Toomey entered the room. Her face was drawn and pale. She made an honest attempt to portray a woman smiling, but it was easy to see, even to Cricket, she was very much on the verge of tears. "Hello, Cricket. Please thank your grandmother for us. This is most kind of her to take the time to bake for us. Tell her how much I appreciate her kindness." Mrs. Toomey eased herself into a chair, as if one more second of standing would have sent her into a rumple on the floor.

"Let me fix us all a nice cup of tea," said Mrs. Parker. "I know how much Cricket enjoyed our tea on the train, and I think a cup will be good for all of us. Right, Maggie?"

"Thanks, Mom. That would be great," said Mrs. Toomey.

"I can't stay very long, Mrs. Parker," said Cricket. "Grandma said you had enough going on and I shouldn't add to the number of children you have to look after for now."

"That's very thoughtful of your grandmother," said Mrs. Parker, "but a small cup of tea couldn't hurt, don't you agree?"

"Okay, then. That would be very nice," said Cricket.

Just as Mrs. Parker was about to reply, a loud sound and smashing of glass came from the kitchen.

"What on earth?" Mrs. Parker said, turning toward the kitchen door.

There was more crashing, banging, and smashing of breakables. Then the kitchen door burst open with such force it smashed a hole in the plaster wall, and in staggered Adder Toomey. He was a mess, extremely dirty, with his shirt in tatters. He sported an unkempt growth of beard, with dried bloodstains on his forehead and his right eye badly swollen. Attached to his left wrist was a pair of handcuffs, open and dangling. He had a wide-eyed, wild look about him as he stood slightly swaying and surveying the room and the people in it with a penetrating sweep of his bloodshot eyes.

"Well, well, what do we have here? My three favorite females, the witch, the bitch, and the lying little snitch that told the cops I was out to get Mary Frances the day of the Shingle Weavers Picnic." Adder had a twisted smirk on his distorted face. Cricket was struck speechless. A sense of fear and foreboding shot through her body. She found herself moving ever so close to Mrs. Parker, who seemed totally unflustered by her son-in-law's arrival and threatening attitude. "Please, Adder," said Mrs. Toomey, stepping in the path of her menacing husband. "The children are upstairs, and I don't want them to see you like this." She reached for his arm. With one swift movement, Adder slammed her against the wall. Like slow motion in a movie, she slid down into a heap on the floor, bleeding profusely. Adder continued his raging advance as Mrs. Parker pulled Cricket behind her. Cricket's heart was pounding, her mouth parched and dry. When she opened it to speak, nothing came out.

Mrs. Parker straightened her small stature into its tallest posture, looked Adder directly in the eye, and in her calm but intense best Southern accent, said, "Listen to me, you no-good son of a rattlesnake. I know what it's like being married to a lowdown, contemptible skunk like you. No wonder Maggie's father didn't trust you. You're just like him, and he knew it. You've laid hands on my daughter for the last time, and if it's the last thing I do on the face of this earth, I'll see to it your spineless, cowardly, woman- beating hide spends enough time in jail to rue the day you ever hit my child. Do you understand me, Adder Toomey?"

Her barrage of insults temporarily halted Adder's forward advance, and for a few seconds, he seemed somewhat intimidated. Then a strange, twisted smile came over his face, and he glared at Cricket and Mrs. Parker.

The quiet tension in the room was explosive. Without hurry, Adder adjusted his ripped and tattered shirt, tucking it neatly into his pants. He slicked back his unkempt hair. Then looking directly at Mrs. Parker, he said in a low and slowly intensifying voice, "You meddling old fool! Do you think I give a shit what you or this whole town think about me? I'm not going to take any more crap, not from your pathetic ice queen of a daughter, not from a thirteen-year-old bitch, and certainly not from the high and mighty Thaddeus Bane and his snooty granddaughter."

Adder began to pace the floor in front of them, and his voice became louder and louder as he continued his maniacal ranting. "I already showed that little prick-teaser Mary Frances the cost of messing with me. Yes, I showed her, all right!" he shouted as he began to laugh and clap his hands in a manic, frenzied applause. "She'll never smart-talk me again, that little whore."

Adder was startled when Maggie rushed up behind him, sobbing. She grabbed his arm. "What have you done, Adder? What in God's name have you done? Did you murder Mary Frances, an innocent young girl, your brother's only child? Answer me, Adder! Did you do this awful thing?"

Without hesitation, Adder lifted Maggie off her feet and flung her across the room so forcefully that when she hit the kitchen door, it came off its hinges. "No more, no more!" he screamed. "I'm not taking any more crap from anyone." He paused for a moment, and then he slowly turned. His eyes narrowed, his glare intensified, and his attention turned to Cricket, who stood shaking behind Mrs. Parker.

For Cricket, this whole scenario began to slow to a snail's pace. Mrs. Parker shoved her toward the front door as her usual cool demeanor took on a more sinister tone. "Cricket, run home now, dear. *Now*!"

Adder violently shoved Mrs. Parker aside as Cricket turned to make a run for the front door. Unexpectedly, a huge hand grabbed Cricket by the back of her shirt, roughly snatching her off her feet and up into the air. She found herself face-to-face with Adder, who was screaming obscenities about her and her grandfather. Adder's grip was strong and intense, and Cricket's heart pounded faster and faster against her chest until her breath felt short and forced. She swung her arms and kicked her feet, hitting him in his swollen eye and accidentally kicking him in the groin. Bent in pain, Adder dropped her to the floor like a hot stone, which knocked the air out of her. She was stunned and unable to move. He stood unmoving and silent for a few seconds, then with full anger erupting, he regrouped, bent down, and raised his clenched fist. Cricket shut her eyes and held her arms over her head to forestall the blow she knew was coming. Suddenly, she heard a startling, unfamiliar explosion. She opened her eyes to see Adder standing over her with a look of total shock on his face, and then he slowly fell backward onto the floor. Cricket looked up from the heap that was Adder Toomey's motionless body.

Mrs. Parker stood there with her pearl-handled pistol in her hands. Maggie Toomey had come out of her daze and was leaning against the wall in disbelief.

"Dear," said Mrs. Parker, who had regained her composure, "now pull yourself together and call the sheriff and Cricket's grandparents. Margaret, do you hear me, dear?"

Her mother's command brought Maggie back from her stunned state. "Yes, Mother, I'll call right away." Hands shaking, Maggie reached for the phone. "Miss Millie, this is Margaret Toomey, would you please connect me with the sheriff's office, please?"

It seemed like the sheriff arrived in just seconds, and quickly the neighborhood became a river of excitement and bewilderment. The neighbors came out of their homes one by one until the sidewalks were filled with neighbors whispering and chatting in amazement and supposition. Cricket's grandparents arrived within seconds too, with Cricket's grandmother in near hysterics and her grandfather looking pale and ill, although his exterior appeared calm and authoritative. At the mere sight of her grandfather's face, Cricket's facade of bravery fell to pieces and tears of relief spilled down her face. Grandfather grabbed her up into his arms and rocked her back and forth. It was then that she realized that the warm tears she felt on her checks were those of her grandfather's, not hers.

"Annie, my precious Annie, if anything had happened to you, I'd . . ." Her grandfather's voice choked as he hugged Cricket even closer.

"Grandpa, Grandpa, I'm all right. Please don't cry," Cricket said, trying to console him, hugging him back with all her strength. Thad carried his granddaughter outside, and they sat on the front steps as he continued to hold her tight in his arms. "Annie, are you okay?" he said, releasing his grip to look into her face. "Yes, Grandpa, I'm fine." Then she let the tension of the event drain from her body.

The sheriff approached. "Thad, is Cricket okay?" "Yes, thank God. She's all right," said Grandfather.

"What in the hell happened, Jim? I thought you had Adder locked up in jail."

"We were taking him from the office back to the jail when he overpowered Dan, split his head open on the car bumper, and ran off toward the highway. Someone reported seeing him north of town, and we thought he was headed for the border again. Never thought in a million years that he'd be dumb enough to come back home."

"How's Dan doing?"

"He had six stitches, but you know what a hardheaded Swede he is. According to Doc Miller, he'll be just fine," said the sheriff with a smile.

"That's a blessing," said Thad, shaking his head.

"I guess we can all thank God that no one else was hurt or killed."

"Lucky for Cricket that Maggie Toomey had a gun-toting mother with the guts of an army mule, or this might have had a very different ending for a lot of people," said the sheriff, patting Thad on the shoulder.

The neighborhood crowd was abuzz with speculation on what might have happened. Who shot whom? What was going on? The ambulance arrived and attended to Adder's wounds and placed him on a gurney. The onsite prognosis was he was in critical condition but had a chance of surviving. As they placed Adder in the ambulance, the neighborhood that had been awhirl with conversation fell eerily silent, watching the ambulance race away toward the hospital. Slowly the crowd began to disperse. Some neighbors stopped by Thad and Cricket, commenting on the abhorrent event and how they knew Thad was right in his belief of Marvin's innocence. The sheriff passed on taking a statement from Maggie Toomey, who was in such a state she could barely speak. He took a brief statement from Mrs. Parker instead. In her usual cool, calm, and collected manner, Mrs. Parker related every detail to the sheriff. Without a hair out of place, she turned her attention to her distraught daughter. The sheriff requested that all interested parties show up at his office the next morning to offer a more detailed and precise account of the events, to finish up the report of the shooting of Adder Toomey.

The mystery of the death of Mary Frances Toomey, which had held the town captive since it began, seemed to have been solved. There was little doubt within the community about who had killed Mary Frances, and it was just a matter of formality before Marvin would soon be released from jail.

"You think you'll be able to talk about what went on here tomorrow down at my office, Cricket?" said the Sheriff.

"Yes, sir, I'm fine," she said.

"How about 9:00 a.m., Thad?" asked the sheriff. "That will be fine, Jim. See you tomorrow."

Arvilla, who had been attending to the Toomey children upstairs, out of sight of their father's bleeding body, arrived on the porch and whispered into Thad's ear, "Let's go home now, please, dear."

That night, just like the night of the Shingle Weavers Picnic and Mary Frances's murder, Cricket slipped into her grandparents' bed, and she remembered the safe, warm comfort of falling asleep tucked in the loving arms of her grandparents. But tonight, she missed her mother and yearned for her loving touch and that smell of jasmine and lavender. Listening to the two steady heartbeats on either side of her, Cricket began her prayers. "Dear God, this is Cricket here. I hope by now you feel you can call me Cricket. Someday you'll have to tell me your nickname. I bet it's something really wonderful, like himself, the Almighty or his godship, not something silly like a relative to a grasshopper. I really want to thank you for looking out for all of us today. I don't know what any of us would have done if you hadn't been there. I was so scared, God. If there is anything I can do in return, please let me know. I owe you a big one. I'm really awful tired tonight, God. We'll talk more again tomorrow night. I have a lot of questions about evil, death, and other hard-to- understand stuff. Thanks again, God. Sleep tight."

The next morning, everyone arrived at the sheriff's office, and detailed statements were taken from everyone except Mrs. Toomey, who was excused from the procedure and under the care of Doc Miller, at home in bed. The statements were taken to the courthouse. Though Adder Toomey practically admitted to killing Mary Frances, it might be a while before he could be questioned, if at all, so Thad made a motion to release Marvin from jail into the custody of his parents until all the details could be made available. The prosecutor agreed to this request, and the judge granted Thad's motion. The strange and unforeseen probable conclusion of Marvin's trial caused as much of a stir as the original trial had. There were those who said, "I told you so," those simply aghast with amazement at this strange twist, and those who thought Marvin's release was way too premature. After all, Adder hadn't made any kind of a formal confession or statement yet. Miss Perkins was again in full gossip mode almost to the state of exhaustion. She made her rounds gathering and spreading the latest suppositions, giving no more thought to what was true or false than she ever did. Her only regret was that the newspaper's presses didn't break down and allow her to be front and foremost in the information business. One big question now was, what would happen to

Mrs. Parker? Would she be charged with anything? Considering the fact that Adder was abusing her daughter, might she have taken advantage of the situation? Was it a clear case of self-defense, or were there darker forces at work? The rumors, with or without Miss Perkins, ran rampant. No other subject could hold a candle to the constantly changing and infamous murder at the Shingle Weavers Picnic. More than the usual number of the community could be seen out and about. Sue Sue's Café was filled every day. At night, Murphy's Pub overflowed with speculation and, in some cases, betting on the end results of one outcome versus the other. No one dared miss the after-church coffee and cake socials, for fear some new, exciting piece of news might be available for discussion. Few places in town escaped the gathering of the townsfolk. If nothing else, this awful situation had been good for business, though merchants were slow to admit that they hated to see the curiosity of this subject end. No one could have known the situation was far from resolved and that there were more twists to come, more changes, more finger- pointing, more surprises than they could possibly imagine.

CHAPTER 23

The Finale

THE SUMMER WAS DRAWING to a close, the trees had begun to dress for fall, and the start of school was just around the corner. It had been, without doubt, a summer to remember without measure, and one that had changed so many lives. As much as Cricket loved visiting her grandparents, this year she was looking forward to going home and promised herself that never again would she ever complain if life seemed a little boring for lack of adventure. She had her fill of excitement to last a lifetime, and the nice, safe routine of school, homework, dinner, and bedtime sounded like a routine of pure delight. Another reason she looked forward to returning home: she missed her mom. It seemed like years since she had left home, and the events of this particular summer left her with an unusual longing for home and Mom. This had been the longest summer she could remember, and now that the new baby had arrived, Cricket could hardly wait to be there to share the new life they would all have together. The baby was a boy, the little brother she had so wished for, and his name was Max, after their dad. Arvilla and Thad were elated and relieved to hear from the Red Cross that their son Kenneth had survived the Bataan Death March and the Red Cross believed that he had been shipped from San Fernando in the Philippines to a prison camp located somewhere north of Akita in Japan. There was a grand jury hearing concerning the culpability of Mrs. Parker in the shooting of Adder Toomey.

After they had spent several days going over the facts and listening to the testimony of witnesses, Mrs. Parker was cleared of all criminal responsibility, and the jury deemed it an unfortunate case of self-defense. Formal charges of murder were filed against Adder Toomey based on his statements at the time of the shooting and the comments he made to doctors, nurses, and other professionals. The court agreed that, at present, he was not capable of aiding in his defense; therefore, he would be sent to Walla Walla Hospital for mental and physical evaluation as soon as he was physically capable. A hearing to determine his competency was put on hold for three months. Marvin was exonerated and released from all court conditions and restrictions. Cricket was scheduled to leave in two weeks, which would put her at home just in time to start school. That still left plenty of time to enjoy the county fair, a big event in these parts, with eager participation by many in the community. Cricket's grandmother had entered the quilting competition. Her design had been handed down from mother to daughter for over four generations, and she took great pride in her ability to continue the tradition, winning five first places and three second places over the years. Her latest design was a depiction of her family's immigration from France to Canada and on to the United States. Arvilla's family name was Langois, a well-known name of cheese makers in the countryside just outside of Toulouse, France. The younger generation saw great opportunities in the New World and took their knowledge to this new land. Other patterns entered portrayed historical events, family history, patriotic statements, and sentimental subjects often depicted in the quilts for new brides. Darling smaller quilts for newborns or small children or someone of sweet sixteen were also entered. Mrs. Landry, Arvilla's friend, was a shining star when it came to gardening. Whoever invented the term *green thumb* had to have had her in mind. There wasn't a thing she couldn't grow bigger and better than anyone else. Her vegetable garden filled the competition with an outstanding assortment of oversize, prize-winning entries. One year, she even grew a prizewinning pumpkin for the Halloween festival that weighed in at well over two hundred pounds. But her favorite and most exquisite talent was her ability to grow the most extraordinary exotic orchids. Cricket had never seen such beautiful and unusual flowers. Walking through Mrs. Landry's little hothouse near her fountain in the backyard was like taking a stroll into some faraway planet where plants and vines looked nothing like any plant anywhere in the galaxy. The atmosphere was warm and humid, like in a tropical island filled with strange and unique flowers that time had forgotten. There were dainty petite flowers in white, yellow, and purple lady's slippers, also calopogon, violet-pink arethusa, calypso, and the very fragrant pale-pink moccasin flower. Flowers in the shape of butterflies, doves. Cricket's favorite was the showy orchid, a small ivory-colored bloom with a lavender face; this was the kind of orchid that could only be pollinated by female bees. Mrs. Landry's selection was so varied and unique that she was constantly being asked by artists, some of whom had acquired fame, if they could paint her collection. Her friendly, welcoming nature allowed all who asked. Seeing her exquisite display at the fair was one of the favorites for the flower show, and few of those entering this arena could even begin to compete. Then there were the jam, pie, and cake entries. Oh, so many varieties—probably the most hotly contested entries of the entire fair. Even to be named a judge of these prestigious events took on the appearance of a national presidential campaign. A judge must have an expertise in all three categories, and the name of the actual judge of a specific event was not announced until the day of the event to avoid any suspicion of bribes or tampering with decisions. The crowd gathered in the fair's amphitheater as the judges arrived onstage at the display tables. A hush came over the crowd as each judge moved from one entry to another, slowly letting his or her taste buds relish the flavors, texture, and scent of the category being judged. Then there was a cleansing of the palate and a second tasting, just to make sure.

Finally, the ribbons were collected and the judges made known their decisions. The audience was on their feet, cheering the announced winners, who proudly bowed, holding up their ribbons of distinction and mingling with the crowd, showing off their prize. This was all very well and good for the adults, but Cricket and her friends loved the midway and all the fun and scary rides. This year, things seemed slightly different. Where in past years they were allowed to wander unsupervised, this year, parents held close to their children and they were not allowed to be left to their own devices. Wherever they went, they were under the watchful eye of some adult. There was a certain anxiousness that hung over the festivities, a lack of casualness, an absence of assurance that kept parents' eyes and attention directly on their children at all times. But nonetheless, stricter adult observation didn't diminish their enthusiasm or negate their pleasure in enjoying the fair. All of Cricket's friends from the neighborhood were attending the fair except Myrna, whose family was visiting relatives in Oregon. It was wonderful to have Marvin back in their company again. Although he seemed happy, there was something about him that was missing, changed, somehow different. Marvin's buoyant, easygoing, airy attitude was diminished, as if he only had a limited amount of it to give and needed to ration it out while hoarding an abundance in reserve for some secret need. The conspicuous absence of Mary Frances left a large hole in their inner circle. Even Kat seemed reserved and quieter than usual, but even with all the pain and grief of this summer's events, they still managed to make this (unbeknownst to them) last of their summers together a gathering of friends they would not soon forget. The Ferris wheel was everyone's favorite ride, a huge wheel standing about forty-five feet high, with sixteen seats carrying two people each. Although the ride seemed fairly brief, the height and swinging of the seats gave goose pimples to even the most stalwart of their group. Around and around they went, dipping and rising to the sky, with chills of excitement charging through their bodies. No matter how thrilling or scary, they always managed to fit in at least one more ride before the day's end. Another favorite, particularly among the girls, was the merry-go-round. Trying to catch the brass ring and toss it into the clown's mouth was always a challenge. On a few occasions, Marvin would join the girls, and his ability to hit the clown's mouth was amazing. Being so big and strong, he never missed getting the ring, and his powerful throw was always on the mark. Tommy and Chris were pretty good at tossing the ring too. Cricket didn't know why they avoided the merry-go-round. Maybe they felt it was just for girls or some thinking along that line, she deduced. They were all standing in line at the cotton candy machine when Frankie Barker swaggered up to Marvin.

"Hey, jailbird, what they got you doing now, babysitting?" said Frankie, looking directly at Cricket.

"Get lost, bugger face," said Marvin, turning his back to him.

Frankie made the mistake of grabbing Marvin by the arm.

"Not such a big man with adults standing around, are you, Marvin?"

Marvin grabbed Frankie's wrist and twisted it. "Listen, you baboon ass, I'm going to say this once. I'm not looking for trouble, but if it's trouble you want, let's go down behind the cow barns and I'll give you just what you're looking for."

With that, Marvin released Frankie's wrist. Frankie pulled away and backed off out of swinging range. "You ain't so tough, Marvin. 'Stop laughing at me, stop laughing at me, Mary Frances!' You even ran scared from a girl," said Frankie mockingly.

That did it. Marvin lunged at Frankie and knocked him head over heels into the dirt. Marvin was punching him left and right when, out of the blue, Thad Bane appeared and broke up the fight. "Hey now, boys, break it up," said Thad as he helped Frankie up and strong-armed Marvin to keep the two apart. "What's going on here?" he asked. "Marvin started it, Mr. Bane," said Frankie.

"I was just minding my own business and he jumped me."

Before Marvin could answer, Cricket chimed in, saying, "That's not true, Grandpa. We were all just standing around, having fun, and Frankie walked up and started the trouble."

"Yeah, that's right, Mr. Bane," everyone agreed.

"You two cool off now. Frankie, you go about your business and let's have no more of this tough-guy stuff. From either of you, hear me?" said Thad.

"Yes, sir," both boys said, and Frankie walked away to join his friends, who were standing on the sidelines of the encounter. They circled around each other, and you could hear them laughing as they turned to look at Marvin before they strutted away and disappeared in the crowd.

"What was that all about, Marvin?" said Thad.

"He's a jerk, sir. He really knows how to fire someone up," said Marvin.

"Every town has one, Marvin." Thad patted Marvin on the shoulder. "You'll just have to learn how to handle this guy without having to punch him in the face every time you meet."

"Yes, sir. I'll try," said Marvin.

"Hey!" Mike pointed to another ride. "Let's go on the octopus before we go to the show."

"Ugh, that ride makes me sick to my stomach," said Kat. "Me too. Let's go and just watch," said Cricket.

"Okay, make it fast," said Thad. "We want to get good seats for the show."

"Okay, Mr. Bane, we'll hurry." And off they ran.

That evening, the last day of the fair, the show took place just after dark. They all took their seats as the entertainment began. Comedians, dancers, singers, acrobats, and the final act was always someone with a big name. This year, the main attraction was Jo Stafford, who was in Seattle with the USO, on her way to entertain the troops overseas, and took the time to perform at the Everett fair. She sang a wonderful medley of her best-selling songs, like "The Trolley Song," "Long Ago and

Far Away," "I Love You," and although Bing Crosby's recording from the movie *I' ll Be Seeing You* was a big hit, Jo Stafford's rendition would always stay in Cricket's mind and heart. This rendition brought tears to the eyes of everyone in the audience, particularly those who had lost someone in the war or had a loved one serving overseas. Miss Stafford finished her performance with a thrilling version of "God Bless America," which brought everyone to their feet for a ten-minute standing ovation. It was a glorious ending to the day at the fair. That night, as Cricket collected her thoughts to say her prayers, she felt a rather-confusing sadness, a feeling that, although she was anxious to be home, she was also torn about leaving her grandparents.

"Dear God, Cricket here. Thank you for this wonderful day, and thank you for giving Grandma first place in the quilting competition. She was very proud of this particular quilt, and it meant a lot to her. I'm sure Mrs. Landry loved her blue ribbons too. You and she certainly do a fantastic job growing all those beautiful flowers. Was this something your mother taught you when you were a little boy? "Thanks for a baby brother. He's just what Mom and I prayed for, and I'm looking forward to going home to meet him. "Since you see everything, God, could you please tell me how that jerk Frankie Barker knew what Marvin said to Mary Frances as he was running away? Marvin said there wasn't anyone else around to prove that Mary Frances was mad as a wet hen but alive and well when he left. Frankie must have been there too, if he overheard their conversation, don't you think? Why didn't Marvin see him? I'll have to remember to ask Grandpa that question too. Well, God, I'm really tired, so please bless all those I love, and I'll talk to you soon." Yes, the summer and Cricket's stay with her grandparents was almost at an end. This would be the last visit she would ever make to Everett and the last summer she would see her lifelong friends, but the story of the events of this summer was far from over. A surprise awaited the whole community.

What's This?

"WHAT SAY YOU WE have one last picnic on the boat before you head for home, Cricket?" said Grandma. "We can pack a scrumptious lunch and sail around the islands. What do you think?"

"Great idea, Grandma," said Cricket. "Let's ask Grandpa just as soon as he gets home."

When Thad got home from work, he barely had time to take off his coat and hat before Cricket was all over him about Grandma's wonderful suggestion.

"What do you think, Grandpa? Can we?" Her face glowed. "You know, I think that is just perfect," said Thad. "We could

all use a day of fun after these last few weeks. When would you ladies like to go?"

"How about tomorrow?" said Cricket. "Can we go then?" "You know," he said, "that would work out just fine. I had a luncheon meeting scheduled for tomorrow, but it was canceled, so the timing is excellent."

It seemed that just about everyone living on Puget Sound owned a boat of one size or another. Thad's boat, the *Miss Makyla*, was a beautiful little cabin cruiser that they took out often during the summer and sailed through the San Juan Islands that dotted the edges of the sound. There were 172 islands in the group, and the four largest were accessible by ferries. The others were only accessible via small boats or air, and a few were owned and lived on by individual families. Cricket's favorite was Orcas Island with all its many coves, bays, beaches, and the half-mile-high Mount Constitution. Her mother had told her many stories about exploring this island with her father when they were first courting. They would drop anchor in a small bay and take the dinghy to shore, where they spent the afternoon exploring, swimming, and picnicking.

"I'm looking forward to getting a little sea air and salt in my face, and it will be a great way to end our summer," said Grandpa. "Yes, a great way," Cricket echoed her grandfather. "And I can steer the boat and be your second mate, huh, Grandpa?"

"I couldn't sail her without my second mate now, can I?" said Grandpa, giving Cricket a sly wink as he leaned over the table and kissed Grandma hello, a love habit he performed each time he returned home.

The next morning, they began their preparations for one of Grandma's special picnics and an afternoon of sailing. Grandpa headed out to make a quick stop at the office and gas up the boat, and Cricket and Grandma prepared the food. They made Grandpa's favorite sandwiches of tuna salad, tomatoes, and lettuce on homemade bread, a few salami and Swiss cheeses, and of course, Cricket's favorite, peanut butter with Grandma's homemade jam. Grandma whipped up a wonderful macaroni salad, and she always packed her special cupcakes with chocolate frosting. Included were two thermoses, one of coffee and one of hot cocoa. The marina always had a certain smell, a mixture of fuel, fish, and saltwater. As the engine revved up, they enjoyed the clean scent of pure saltwater and the fresh wind that splashed across their faces. About an hour out, they arrived at Orcas Island. They found a calm, secluded bay, dropped anchor, and took the dinghy to shore. Once landed, they chose a wide sandy beach that met the forest's edge. It was loaded with trees all dressed for fall in their electrifying display of shimmering gold leaves. Grandma went about setting out the picnic, while Grandpa and Cricket took a short hike into the woods to explore. There were amazing collections of a variety of birds. Unlike the Cascade forests that were filled with the distant sounds of scurrying animals and only a few birds, this forest was a chorus of the avian residents all auditioning for the star role. Grandpa and Cricket came upon a wide freshwater pool that was fed from the gently sloping hills beyond the forest. They could see fish dashing between the sunlight and shadows, swimming in the crystal clear waters. Cricket's mom had told her of this place many times and of the camping she and her brothers enjoyed with many a fresh trout dinner. Farther upstream, Cricket and her grandfather came across a wide meadow covered with the last of the wildflowers, the last splash of summer. She gathered a large bouquet of flowers to take back to her grandmother.

"Let's take a break, Annie," said Grandpa. "I'm a little tired." "You okay, Grandpa?" Cricket studied his face, concerned. "I'm fine, sweetie. I must have lifted something the wrong way.

Have a slight pain in my back and here in my chest. It's nothing. Just getting old, I guess."

"Grandpa, can we talk for a minute?" "Why, sure, honey. What's on your mind?"

They stopped and straddled a large fallen log.

"I'm feeling . . . sort of . . . well, different, not like myself. I mean, not like I used to feel, you know . . . before Mary Frances was killed."

"I think that's pretty normal under the circumstances, don't you?" said Grandpa.

"I just don't know anymore. Things that I used to be so sure of . . . I'm not so sure about anything anymore."

"Sometimes when things happen when you are a little too young to understand, particularly something as horrible as the situation with Mary Frances—it feels unsettling even to adults—it feels strange and scary. In a little while, when this is more of a memory, things will start to feel normal again." "You really think so?"

"Yes, of course they will. I promise. But there is a lesson to be learned here."

"And what's that, Grandpa?"

Grandpa cupped her face in his hands and said, "Don't you ever grow up any faster than you have to. Just enjoy being a kid as long as you can. Promise?"

"Sure, Grandpa, I promise. That's good advice. Feel better already. How about you?"

"Still a little pain in my right arm, but I'm good. I wouldn't mention anything about any pain to your grandmother. You know how much she worries. She'd have me in the hospital over a splinter if it were up to her."

The two of them laughed and had started on their way back when Cricket stopped and said, "Oh, I almost forgot. I was thinking when I said my prayers last night. At the fair, remember when Frankie was making fun of Marvin and they got into a fight? They got into the fight because Frankie was laughing about Marvin's last conversation with Mary Frances. How did he know what they were saying to each other if he wasn't there? Marvin said there was no one around to witness the fact that when he left Mary Frances, she was alive and well."

"What's that again?" asked Grandpa.

"Marvin said in the sheriff's office that Mary Frances was really mad at him and she kept laughing at him and making fun of him. How did Frankie know that if he wasn't there too?"

"Good question. One I sure intend to ask Mr. Frankie Barker when we get home. You'd make a great little detective, Annie Jordan."

"Thanks. Sort of like Nancy Drew, huh?" said Cricket with a big smile.

"That's right, just like Nancy Drew. Now, let's get back to your grandmother, or she'll think we've been eaten by bears." They walked hand in hand through the forest back to the seashore. The sun had started her slow descent into the cool blue sea just as they pulled the *Miss Makyla* into the marina and tied up at the dock. They cleaned up her cabin, secured all the covers, and headed for home. Cricket had just finished clearing the dinner dishes when there came a knock on the front door. Grandpa opened the door to find the sheriff standing on the front porch.

"I need to talk to you, Thad," said the sheriff. "Something has come up that I think you should know." "Funny you should say that," said Thad.

"I was just about to call you about something too."

"Come on in. How about a cup of coffee?" asked Grandma. The sheriff smiled and shook his head no.

"Thanks, Arvilla. I just need a moment of your husband's time." He and Thad headed to the living room. "It's about Bertha Perkins and Mrs. Landry," said the sheriff. "Miss Perkins took a nasty fall a few days ago, and Doc Miller put her in the hospital for observation. Last week, during the last night of the fair, there was a break-in at her home, and some money and jewelry are missing. That same night, vandals broke into Mrs. Landry's greenhouse and destroyed all her prizewinning plants and flowers. Not a plant left undamaged. Senseless destruction. Two of the four kids seen running from Miss Perkins's house were caught with some stolen goods, and they were covered with potting soil and mud from Mrs. Landry's greenhouse. They were Sam Lock and Barney Swanson. The other two were probably Walter Mode and Frankie Barker, since they all seem to be joined at the hip."

"What's this got to do with me, Jim?" said Thad.

"Sam Lock says he has some unknown information about the day Mary Frances was murdered, and he's looking for some sort of a deal to lessen any jail time."

"You have any idea what this so-called information could be?" "No," said the sheriff, "but he says he has firsthand knowledge of what happened and has proof he's telling the truth. We're having a meeting in the morning with the prosecutor at the courthouse. I thought you might want to be there. You don't think there's something Marvin is holding back, do you?"

"No, Jim, I don't believe Marvin has anything to do with these kids. Come, I'll walk you to the car. I have something odd to tell you that Annie brought up today concerning something Frankie said to Marvin at the fair. Something that's worth looking into." The two men walked out the front door and down the walkway.

"What's all that about?" asked Arvilla when Thad returned to the kitchen.

"I'm not sure," said Thad. He was scribbling notes on a large yellow pad for the next day. "But there's something very suspicious going on here, and we need a few answers from Frankie Barker's friends."

"Is it something the Waters or Maggie should know?" asked Arvilla.

"No, I don't think so. Not yet," said Thad.

"I'll wait and see what tomorrow brings first. Annie shouldn't mention anything about Frankie to anyone until we have a few more answers. Okay, Annie?"

"Sure, Grandpa. My lips are sealed."

The next morning, everyone in the Bane household was up early, and there was a certain whir of anticipation and excitement in the air. What was this mysterious, astonishing information that would shake up the investigation into Mary Frances's murder? And how did Frankie Barker overhear the last conversation between Marvin and Mary Frances? While Grandma and Cricket were on edge with curiosity, Grandpa sat casually drinking his coffee, eating his breakfast and finishing the newspaper.

At 8:15 a.m., Grandpa finally rose from the table, kissed them both, and left for the meeting at the prosecutor's office. When Thad arrived at the courthouse, the prosecutor (Avery Morris), Sam Lock, his parents, and Sam's attorney, Vernon Fender, were present and waiting. "Good morning, gentlemen," said Thad.

"Now, what's this all about?" Mr. Fender spoke first.

"My client has information that leads to proof that the death of Mary Frances Toomey was committed by someone other than Adder Toomey, and that someone is still at large in the community. Considering the importance of this information, we feel Sam is due some leniency for his cooperation."

"And just what might that information be?" asked the sheriff. "What sort of leniency and reduced sentence are we talking about, Sheriff?" countered Mr. Fender.

"Well, as I said," interjected the prosecutor, Mr. Morris, "that depends on what Sam has to say, where that info leads, and just how believable it is."

"Hypothetically," said Mr. Fender, "let's say my client heard the confession of the crime in person and has knowledge of physical evidence only the murderer could have obtained. Would that be pertinent enough for you, Mr. Morris?"

"If that's the case," said Mr. Morris, "I could ask for a lesser charge on the burglary case and perhaps some form of restitution, like rebuilding Mrs. Landry's greenhouse and replacement of her destroyed plants . . . restitution. Sam has a fairly clean record up till now. He could get little or no jail time, possibly just probation, but there again, that depends on his statement.

"Mr. Morris sat back in his chair, crossed his arms, and looked over the top of his horn-rimmed glasses, awaiting Mr. Fender's response. Sam and his attorney stepped over to the corner of the room, where they exchanged words in hushed whispers. Finally, Mr. Fender and Sam returned to their seats.

"We trust in your sense of fairness. It's a deal. Sam will tell you everything he knows."

All eyes in the room turned to Sam Lock, waiting for him to start his incredible story. Sam cleared his throat several times, looked around the room with great discomfort, and began. "Ever since Marvin beat the crap out of Frankie in the park that day, he's been obsessed with getting even. He's been following Marvin and his friends, like Mary Frances, Kat, Cricket, all those kids, everywhere they went, all summer long, just looking for a chance to get back at Marvin. "On the day of the Shingle Weavers Picnic, Frankie shadowed them everywhere. After a while, Barney and Walter got real bored, so they took off, and it was just me and Frankie. It was pretty creepy. Frankie lurked around like some kind of a spook, in the shadows, watching, tracking, stalking everything they did and everyplace they went. I mean creepy and very boring. I don't know what Frankie thought was going to happen, but I finally got fed up with following him around, so I took off. "Just before the fireworks, Frankie came running up to us really excited. He said he had finally gotten Marvin real good, that he had fixed Marvin for sure by making it look like he had done something pretty awful. He said Marvin was going to get the blame for something Frankie had done and that he had planted something just to make sure.

"'Look,' Frankie told us, 'I got a trophy.' In his hand he was holding a gold locket with a diamond in the center. We didn't really know what he was talking about until we heard the news about Mary Frances being murdered and Marvin's knife being found under the body. Then we thought, holy shit, Frankie killed Mary Frances just to set up Marvin. He was so excited that he wanted to celebrate, so we busted into Miss. Perkins's house, stole a few things, and then had a ball messing up Mrs. Landry's greenhouse."

"Do you know where the locket is now?" asked Mr. Morris. "Yeah," answered Sam. "Frankie keeps a treasure box of stuff from places we broke into, up in a hole in the attic over his bed. He likes to pull it out and look at it all the time. Makes him laugh."

The sheriff got on the phone. "Dan, I want you to get over to Frankie Baker's house right away and bring him in for questioning. Take another deputy with you and search the house, particularly in the attic over Frankie's bedroom. Look for a tin box filled with stolen objects and money. Let me know when you've got Frankie here. Thanks."

"Wait a moment," said Thad. "I'd like to verify something before we go off on a possible wild-goose chase, if you don't mind, Mr. Morris. Sheriff?"

"Not at all, Mr. Bane. Please proceed," said the prosecutor. Thad picked up the phone. "Miss Millie, this is Thad Bane, would you please connect me with the Waters residence? Thank you. Kat, this is Mr. Bane. Is Marvin at home? Put him on the phone, please. Thanks. Marvin, I have a question to ask you, and please be as detailed as possible. It's very important. Describe everything about Mary Frances the last time you saw her . . . yes . . . everything . . . what she was wearing, what she had with her . . . like a purse or sunglasses, that sort of thing . . . ahhmm . . . yes . . . uhum . . . anything else? Okay, Marvin, thanks. I'll be talking to you later."

Thad turned to the other men and said, "Marvin just described everything Mary Frances was wearing, including the locket. She was wearing the locket when he left her." The once-quiet office was abuzz with activity. Sam was returned to his cell, the sheriff prepared to bring Frankie Barker in for questioning, and the search was on for Frankie's treasure trove of stolen items. Thad headed for home and lunch, knowing full well a word-for-word account of this morning's events would be demanded upon his arrival. And so it was, one question after the other, until Cricket and Grandma heard the whole tale. Or most of it. He kept the details of Sam's story to himself for the moment. Both Cricket and Grandma felt sick to hear of the damage done to Mrs. Landry's greenhouse and the loss of all her beautiful flowers. It seemed like the mystery surrounding Mary Frances was never going to end. First, it was Marvin on the hot seat, then Mr. Toomey, and now with Frankie being brought into the mix, would Marvin be in trouble again? Could Frankie possibly have an explanation for his involvement? Everyone was on the edge of their seat, waiting to hear Frankie attempt to wiggle out of this one.

CHAPTER 25

Frankie's Story

FRANKIE WAS BROUGHT IN for questioning. He had very little to say. His parents requested a delay to hire an attorney before any further questioning took place. The search of Frankie's house did, however, take place, and just as Sam had said, a box filled with stolen items from several local robberies was found, along with Mary Frances's gold locket. The first several sessions of questioning finally began. Frankie was represented by an attorney, but not much was accomplished. The evidence was piling up proving he was involved in a string of robberies and the trashing of Mrs. Landry's greenhouse. He saw the ridiculousness of stalling. Frankie's friend Walter was eventually arrested, and now all four of the suspects were in jail and willing to sell their souls for leniency and a lighter sentence. Sam had already made his deal with the DA, and now Walter and Barney were scrambling to make their best deal before Frankie decided to talk and their testimony would no longer be needed. All three of Frankie's so-called friends agreed to supply evidence against him, and you could hear the scratching of the vermin's feet as they ran for shelter, leaving Frankie to face the music as alone as a skunk at a wedding reception. Eventually, Frankie, tired and worn-down, decided to talk, and what a tale it was. Spending several nights in jail was just the come-to-Jesus meeting he needed. Frankie entered the prosecutor's office with his parents and a young attorney from Marysville, a Mr. Luther Dodd. You could feel his exuberance in finally having a headline case, unlike the boring land use cases he was accustomed to. He apparently lived alone, with no wife to subject him to a once-over before leaving the house, judging by the price tag that was hanging from the cuff of his new suit. Once he took notice of it, he quickly removed it and stuffed the offending object into his pants pocket. He carried a rumpled white linen handkerchief that he used to constantly wipe away the perspiration that annoyingly and repeatedly appeared on his forehead. Frankie took a seat the sheriff offered him, and the room took on a hushed sound, like everyone was holding their breath.

"Now, Frankie," said the sheriff, "I understand that you are ready to tell us the entire story and answer all questions. Is that true?"

"My client has offered to be completely forthcoming and answer all questions, and I want it noted for the record that my client is cooperating fully," said Mr. Dodd, whose ears had begun to turn a bright, cheery red with the excitement of the moment.

"So noted, Mr. Dodd," said the prosecutor. "Now, can we get on with the statement, please? Sheriff, continue."

Frankie sat slumped in his chair, with a cocky attitude and a smug look on his face, hardly the contrite, eager-to-cooperate suspect all present were hoping for. He might have agreed to finally give up his stalling and tell the truth, but that obviously had no effect on his smart-ass demeanor. As the first of many questions were placed in front of him, he sidestepped, acted vague, and made jokes. Finally, the sheriff removed the cigar he was chewing on, walked over to Frankie, and placed his hands on the chair's armrests, with his face within inches from the boy's.

"Listen to me, Frankie Barker, and listen well. This isn't a joke or a game. You either straighten up, answer what I ask, or I'm going to throw your good-for-nothing hide back in jail, and you can stay there until you change your attitude or die of old age, whichever comes first. Are you reading me, young man?"

Frankie's smirk and swagger slowly slid off his face and body, and he took on an air of contrition as he straightened up in his chair with a new attitude.

"Now, let's have it from the beginning. No more bullshit or your smart-alecky remarks or punk attitude. I want the truth, and I mean I want it *now*!" barked the sheriff.

Frankie looked around the room and squirmed uncomfortably. His father glowered in his direction, clearing his throat to gain Frankie's attention. Frankie's bearing adapted a whole new, humble approach.

"Yeah," began Frankie, "I was pissed that Marvin beat me up. He doesn't even fight fair, and all over some seven-year-old kid who's not even his family. I just knew if I followed them around, sooner or later, I'd have a chance to get even. So ever since that day in the park, I followed them all everywhere they went, and they didn't even know I was watching them."

"Just who are the *them* you say you were following?" asked the prosecutor.

"Marvin and the other kids in his neighborhood. You know, Tommy, Chris, Myrna, Mike, Kat, and Cricket. They did everything together as a group, always together," said Frankie. "It was easy to follow them at the picnic. With so much going on and so many people everywhere, no one even noticed what I was doing, not even the high and mighty Marvin. All day long, I watched Marvin and Mary Frances fooling around, holding hands, Marvin picking her up and whirling her around, laughing together, making a big deal of the trophies Marvin, Tommy, Chris, and Mike won."

"What other things did the group do?" asked the prosecutor. "They watched the log-rolling contest, the greased pig race, and they ate a ton of ice cream. Then they strolled down to the boat dock. They just sat around the dock, laughing and throwing stones on the lake, until just before sunset, when they all headed back to the picnic grounds. I was hiding in the closed concession stand near the dock, and I was just about to run into the forest edge so I could watch them on their way back when Marvin and Mary Frances suddenly turned around and went back to the dock and the others walked on. They were looking for something. They looked all over the place and finally checked under the dock. "While they were under the dock, they started fooling around and laughing. That turned into kissing and making out, and when Mary Frances took off her bathing suit top, things looked like they were going to get very interesting. "Then, all of a sudden, an argument started. Mary Frances was hopping mad about something, and she hauled off and smacked Marvin right in the face. I couldn't hear what all the fuss was about at first, and then Mary Frances started laughing at Marvin, laughing that he didn't know how to do *it*, that he is a virgin, and Marvin didn't think it was very funny. Not at all. When she wouldn't stop laughing, he smacked her right back, told her he was done playing her little games, and turned to leave. "Mary Frances got really pissed—I mean *super* mad—when Marvin started to leave. She cussed at him at the top of her voice. She could cuss like anything, and then she yelled at him really loud and screamed she was going to tell everyone that he raped her and he'd go to jail for making a fool out of her."

"Did you hear what they were looking for?" asked Mr. Morris. "Yeah, they were talking about a knife, something that belonged to Marvin," said Frankie.

He asked for a drink of water and received it. He drank it slowly as he glanced around the room at all in attendance, like he was putting off the next part of his story. He finally set the empty glass down and continued. "Well, I thought that was it. After Marvin ran off, I figured, just as soon as Mary Frances started to head back, I'd slip into the woods and go back to the picnic grounds unnoticed, but she didn't leave right away. She adjusted her bathing suit and brushed all the sand off her body, then out of the blue, Mr. Toomey showed up, drunk as a skunk and mean as a junkyard dog. He grabbed ahold of Mary Frances and began screaming at her, and she screamed back. Then he tried to kiss her, and she kicked him in the shin. That didn't stop him. They struggled for a while, with Mr. Toomey ending up on the ground, dragging Mary Frances with him. Now, Mr. Toomey had the advantage, being so big and all. He held her down with one hand on her throat and yanked her bathing suit bottoms off with the other. Then he held her by her wrists and started kissing her chest, then her stomach, then between her legs. 'Tell me what I want to hear. Tell me you want it,' he said to her. Stupid stuff like that. "Then Mary Frances spit in his face, screamed that he was a loser, disgusting, pathetic. He tossed her over on her stomach, and he nailed her right there in front of God and the world. He nailed her from behind, and he took his time. All the while, Mary Frances was screaming at him to stop, that he was hurting her, to get off."

"What do you mean he *nailed* her?" asked the sheriff.

"I need you to be specific, Frankie." Frankie began to squirm with discomfort.

"Ah, Sheriff, you know what I mean. Do I have to say it?" "Be specific, Frankie," said the sheriff.

"Okay, Sheriff . . . specific. He fucked her right there on the beach, and he enjoyed every minute of it. He moaned and groaned like an old bull stuck in the mud. He kept talking to her, like, 'I know you like it. Every time it gets better, and the night's just starting.' Gooey love stuff like that." The room fell eerily quiet as those present let Frankie's description of events sink into their minds. The picture of a young girl fighting for her life and forced to submit to the drunken advances of Adder Toomey was horrifying. "And what happened next?" asked the sheriff. "Mary Frances struggled to get one arm free, and she grabbed him by the nuts, and he let out a scream I thought would be heard in town. Then he fell to the side, holding his nuts and cussing. Mary Frances got to her feet, and just as calm as could be, she shook the sand out of her hair, pulled back on her bathing suit just as if nothing had happened, walked over to Mr. Toomey, and kicked him right in the groin again, again, and again. That did it, the fight was over, and Mr. Toomey let out a wail of pain, staggered to his feet, and went limping away like a flogged mutineer. He disappeared into the woods, and I stayed hidden for a while just to see what Mary Frances was going to do. Finally, I stepped out from where I was hiding, like I was just walking past the dock and happened to notice her."

"Was anyone else in the area? Did you see anybody?" asked the sheriff.

"No, just Mary Frances and me," said Frankie. "It was freaky. She just sat there on the edge of the dock, looking out over the lake. I walked up to her and started talking to her. I told her I'd seen what just happened and if she was still passing *it* out. 'How about passing some my way?' I reached over and touched her arm, and that was when she went berserk. I mean, she really went nuts . . . all-out crazy nuts . . . screaming, yelling, and calling me every dirty name in the book. Then she came at me like some sort of wild animal. Christ, all I did was touch her arm, and she went after me like I was Mr. Toomey or something . . . like she wanted to kill me, swinging, kicking, hitting me with her fists. I tried to grab her, but she was unstoppable. She just kept swinging and hitting me until I finally hit her back . . . I socked her in the jaw and gave her a big shove to get her out of my face." Frankie lowered his head, and his hands began to shake at the memory.

Finally, he lifted his head, looked around the room, and in a soft voice, said, "That was when it happened. She fell backward really hard and hit her head on the side of the dock. I didn't know what to do. She didn't move, and she wasn't breathing . . . I was scared to death she was dead. I tried to revive her. I called her name and shook her, but she didn't respond, then I knew I was in real trouble. I didn't mean it . . . I didn't mean to hurt her." Frankie began to sob, and this time, they were honest tears. The room went silent, and you could feel the astonishment circulating among the awestruck adults. "Pull it together, Frankie. What happened next?" said the sheriff.

Frankie wiped his eyes and blew his nose. "I was . . . I didn't know what to do. I didn't think anyone would believe me when I said it was an accident. I knew they would think I did this awful thing on purpose. Then I spotted Marvin's knife lying in the sand, and I got the idea to make it look like Marvin had done this to Mary Frances . . . the perfect way to get even was right in front of me. So I put the knife under her body and pulled down her bathing suit top. I grabbed the locket she was wearing, and I ran like hell away from there as fast as I could. I never meant to hurt her . . . I just pushed her too hard to get her off me, that's all."

Frankie began to break down again, accepting the enormity of his actions. He placed his head in his hands and sobbed. The story that had just unfolded caught everyone off guard. It seemed like minutes before, anyone could speak. Finally, the sheriff got up from his chair and walked to the window, lit his cigar, and gazed off into the distance in deep thought. Mr. Morris was the first to speak.

"Well, it looks like we have to rethink this situation. Is there anything else whatsoever we should know about what happened?"

"No, sir," said Frankie. "That's it, all of it."

"Very well," said the sheriff. "Looks like we're done here."

The deputy took Frankie from the room and back to jail; the prosecutor gathered his briefcase and coat and mentioned to the sheriff he would call him later that day with formal charges against the four boys. Thad and the sheriff shook hands, and Thad headed for home and the waiting inquisition. When Thad arrived home, he and Arvilla had a private talk in their bedroom about the details of Frankie's story. Cricket was given the G-rated version over dinner. Not only was Marvin innocent of having anything to do with Mary Frances's death, but it also seemed that even Mr. Toomey, as despicable as he might be, was innocent, at least in her death. That summer, Cricket learned the meaning of "Some things are not always what they seem to be" and just how complex life and its twists and turns can be. The law became a fascination for her in this summer of her awakening to the real world, a fascination that only grew and intensified as she got older. That night, after all were in bed, Cricket started her nightly ritual. She reached under her pillow, retrieved her precious wrapped wings, opened them, and lovingly held them in her small hands. "Dear God, Cricket here. Thanks so much for helping Grandpa prove Marvin is innocent. I just knew he couldn't do anything as horrible as kill someone. It looks like you were pretty kind to Mr. Toomey too, although I think he should be punished for picking on someone so much smaller than he is. Maybe you can reconsider this a little bit. And a big thank-you again for sending us my baby brother. You answered our prayers. I know some people say prayers aren't answered. Well, if they ever took the time to talk to you, they would know better.

"I'm so glad you're my friend. Life sure would be hard without you. I would like to add Mary Frances to my 'bless them' list. At first, it was so hard for me to talk about her, but just as Grandpa said, when I got older, it would be easier. Well, I'm older now, and I'd like to send her my love, if that's okay with you. Bless Grandpa George, Mom, my brother Max, Grandma and Grandpa Bane, my friends, and special love to my dad and Mary Frances. Good night, God, and pleasant dreams, if you ever get a chance to sleep, that is."

Happily Ever After? Maybe

"HAPPILY EVER AFTER" IS a matter of opinion. Mrs. Parker, once cleared of all charges in the shooting of Adder Toomey, took her daughter and grandchildren back to live with her in Seattle. She never did return to Texas, and her philandering, abusive husband eventually died from lung cancer and a monumental case of the clap. Maggie ultimately divorced Adder and remarried years later to a kind, gentle veterinarian who loved her children. They lived in the countryside outside of Tacoma, where he practiced his career, and they expanded their family with the addition of two little girls. Adder Toomey was committed to the psychiatric ward at Walla Walla. He was deemed unfit to stand trial for the rape of Mary Frances, and since her murder had been solved, it all became a moot point anyway. He was never found to be capable to aid in his defense, and his mental condition deteriorated into a catatonic state. He died several years later without ever uttering another word after his tirade the day he was shot by Mrs. Parker. Marvin's release from jail and exoneration of all criminal charges didn't repair the damage done to the rather-reclusive Waters family. Their comfort level in the community was never the same. Seeking anonymity from all the publicity, they put their house up for sale before Christmas and joined the thousands of people relocating to Southern California to take advantage of the booming job market and the pleasant climate. Frankie was charged with manslaughter instead of murder, three counts of burglary, and one count of malicious vandalism. He was sentenced to Langton Juvenile Center until he turned twenty-one, a rather light sentence under the circumstances. Sam Lock did get off with just two years' probation for his cooperation, while Barney Swanson and Walter Mode both were sentenced to eighteen months in a juvenile center for their part in the robberies. Cricket returned to her life with her mom on the ranch with Grandpa George, and she fell head over heels in love with her new baby brother. He did remind her of her dad, with a laugh so much like his that it could almost bring her to tears just hearing it. The grandfather Cricket so adored died of a heart attack that winter. It was a cold, windswept winter day when he came home for his usual lunch and decided to take a short nap before returning to work, some case concerning a new movement that twenty years later would be known as a civil rights action. When Arvilla went to wake him, he had died in his sleep. Cricket was inconsolable. She thought the pain she felt when she lost her father was the most anguish a person could feel, but she was wrong. The loss of her grandfather left a chasm of grief that seemed to have no bottom, no end. Arvilla, Cricket's grandmother, came to live with her, Makie, Grandpa George, and Max. Having her around did make the loss of her grandfather a little more bearable. Cricket could never bring herself to return to Everett, even as an adult. Too many memories of people who had scattered to the wind. For a while, she and her summer friends exchanged letters several times a year until they were well into their thirties. After high school, Kat went on to the Parsons School of Design, and upon her return to Southern California, she became a well-known Hollywood costume designer. Cricket and Kat would meet every now and then to catch up with each other. Kat, the young adult, was indescribably beautiful with her crystal blue eyes that could stop traffic at a glance. She was still the shy, quiet person she was as a child, hated the glitz and bright lights of Hollywood, and eventually married someone not in the business and moved to the East Coast. Cricket heard that Kat was the mother of three and very happy living on a small farm outside Charleston. The whole gang was right in their estimation of the heights that Myrna might aspire to and, perhaps, surpass. She didn't go into law, as they all expected. Instead, she chose the medical field and ended up being a noted surgeon specializing in neurology and chief of staff at the famed Mayo Clinic. Tommy stayed in Everett and followed in his dad's footsteps, working in the family's lumber yard and hardware business. He married his high school sweetheart, and they adopted three children. Chris married a very earthy young woman who loved animals, herb gardening, and composting. They moved to Montana, where Chris fulfilled his lifelong dream of being a cattle rancher. There they raised a large family of six children, two of whom were twins. Then there was Mike Toomey. Of all the Toomey kids, Mike took the circumstances surrounding his father the hardest. The damage done followed him well into his adulthood and hung like a black cloud over his every endeavor. Just like his father before him, his attempt for a normal life seemed to fail time and again. Alcohol eventually took over his life, which seemed to languish in a painful limbo forever. Cricket eventually lost track of her summer friends, as happens in life. Who got married to whom, where they moved, who got divorced, who died. But she never forgot that last summer or the events that changed her whole perspective of the world and the humans in it. You could only imagine her total astonishment and surprise when, years later, she encountered Marvin's handsome face staring down at her from a large movie screen in the company of such well-known actors as Rita Hayworth, Katharine Hepburn, Spencer Tracy, Humphrey Bogart, and Ann Bancroft. He had taken his mother's maiden name and changed the color of his curly dark hair to blond, but his rugged good looks, intense brown eyes, and deep, husky voice remained the same and was undeniably that of Marvin, her childhood friend and hero. She made a point to see every movie he appeared in. Marvin's star burned brightly through the fifties, declined in the sixties, and turned to dust by the seventies when the Hollywood gossip magazines reported he had become an emcee for a strip club on the outskirts of LA. One day, Cricket unexpectedly received a letter from Kat. Her letter was written with a pen of pain and sorrow that intertwined with each word she wrote. Marvin had been killed in a motorcycle accident where drugs were suspected to have been involved. How ironic that his life challenges began with a motorcycle accident and ended up, in the long run, with a similar event taking his life. He died just two weeks short of his fifty-second birthday, alone. On Cricket's return from that last visit to Everett, she was oh-so happy to see her mom, Grandpa George, and her pup, Sheila, and meet her new baby brother. Home and life in general had never felt so good before. Still, her now-and-then recall of the dark and terrifying past lurked just below the surface and brought back some of the confusion and bewilderment that had filled her with a rainbow of emotions that her youth found difficult to dispel. Her love and adoration of Grandfather Bane and the exemplary life he had lived (as seen through the adoring eyes of a child) was the single most motivating incentive that propelled Cricket through college and onto law school. She graduated summa cum laude, the top of her class, along with a brilliant young man by the name of Ramsey "Jock" MacGowan. She saw him as the perfect combination of her cherished grandfather and the father she lost way too soon—men of principles, compassion, honor, and a keen sense of human kindness. Cricket and Jock were married the day after graduation in a quiet ceremony in the hills above the ranch, with just close friends and family. They went directly from graduation, right past a multitude of exceptional offers from several prestigious, high-paying law firms, directly to the public defender's office, where they took on the legal distress of the poor and downtrodden. Right after the twins, Thad and Max, were born, Jock and Cricket made the big move into private practice, where they stayed until retirement, and then their sons took over the firm of Jordan and MacGowan. From time to time, Cricket would allow herself to travel back to that summer in her prayers with her best friend, God. They would discuss her feelings of confusion and bewilderment, and although her mirror didn't show her as changed, she felt like a stranger to herself, like some odd pieces of different beings thrown together in a rush. A dog without a tail, a cat with duck feet, a fish with wings. Nothing seemed to match what she observed of herself and how she felt inside. Something that was once a part of her was gone, missing, left behind, and she deeply mourned its departure, like a long-lost friend, a favorite doll, a fading memory of her dad. Could it be lost somewhere in the enormity and remembrances of her childhood ghosts? Or perhaps it wasn't lost at all but had simply found a cordial place to live in quiet anonymity. Eventually, as her grandfather had predicted, the ordeal of that last summer in Everett did find a soft place to fall in Cricket's memories. She credited her grandfather's wisdom and her deep, continuing friendship with God to shepherd her through the halls of childhood, the turbulence of puberty, onto the comprehension of maturity. The lessons learned were invaluable. Growing up was a difficult task for everyone, but compared to those less fortunate who had little love, protection, or family, she was indeed a blessed child, one who had become capable of surviving anything life had in store. Whatever the mystic answer might be, Cricket visited this memory less and less as the years rolled by and her life rolled on. But there always remained a tiny little part of her soul that continued to search for this lost piece, this missing fragment of her innocence, a longing she only discussed with God, and he alone knows she continues to mourn it still.

"Well, there you have it, Max. The whole story of that summer so long ago. It was a more innocent time. Acts of violence and the darker side of humankind were felt deeper than today, where our children grow up witnessing over six thousand acts of violence on TV, movies, or video games before they even start school."

"Thanks, sis. It makes a lot of things in my past make sense now. I only wish I had the chance to know our father and Grandpa Bane as you did. We were two lucky kids to have the family we did while the whole world was falling apart around us. I love you, you know. I think I would even if you weren't my sister." Max gives Cricket a huge hug as they head for the kitchen.

"Right back at you," says Cricket with a smile of pride.

The sun begins its retreat from the day, painting the distant clouds in vibrant hues of pink and purple. Her husband, Jock, pulls up in the gravel drive, and Cricket feels an inner joy that Max will be staying for a while.

"Join us for dinner?"

"I thought you'd never ask," says Max.

They both laugh, and he begins to pour three glasses of wine. Jock saunters through the kitchen door and immediately kisses Cricket—their favorite ritual—and presents her with a bouquet of wildflowers.

"Well, what a nice surprise, dear brother-in-law. I thought you were headed for home," says Jock, giving Max a big bear hug.

"I couldn't leave Miss Bumble Bee here to finish this last, sad piece of business alone, now, could I?" says Max. "I've got a few days to spare."

"Miss Bumble Bee, huh? That sure describes her to a tee," says Jock, turning to Cricket.

"Speaking of which, why don't you *buzz* that glass of wine in my direction, and Jock and I will get the fire going in the living room?" And the two men disappear out of view.

"Hand me that small log on top. Thanks," says Jock. The fire begins to take hold, filling the room with its dancing light. Jock and Max lean back into the comfy sofa, staring at the mesmerizing flames. Jock breaks the silence, saying, "Sorry about your mom. Everyone that ever knew her loved her dearly. She sure will be missed."

"Thanks," says Max. "I don't think it's all sunk in yet. I still see my mom around every corner of this cottage."

"How long can you stay, Max?"

"I've got a late flight tomorrow," replies Max. "Illness never takes a holiday. My office is in total crisis mode rescheduling appointments as is, and I've only been gone a few days. My usual stand-in was on vacation when I got called home."

"Ah, I'm sorry. We'd love to have you stay for a while. Cricket will really be sad to have you leave so soon."

"Well, I have something I think will cheer her up. Julie is pregnant. We're expecting a baby girl this summer. After three boys, finally a little girl, and we are going to name her Makyla Lara, after Mom."

"Congrats! What great news! You're right, this will send Cricket over the moon with joy," says Jock.

"I never thought I'd be a repeat Dad in my fifties," says Max, "but we couldn't be happier. I'll tell Cricket after dinner to soften the news I have to leave tomorrow."

"Speaking of little girls, grab your glass," says Jock with a big grin on his face. "I've got something to show you. Hey, Miss Bumble Bee, while you're buzzing around the kitchen, mixing up that amazing aroma on the stove, I'm taking Max to the barn to see the new foal. How much time we got before dinner?"

"Okay, you two, get going. Dinner goes on the table in about thirty minutes," says Cricket.

She leans against the doorjamb, sipping her wine, watching two of the four most important men in her life (her sons being the other two) enjoying their bond created so long ago. Just before they reach the edge of the yard lights, where the beginning of evening meets the incoming fog, they turn to wave at her, and for just a nanosecond, the briefest of moments, she sees Max become her father. She hears her father's laughter, imagines the smile that can warm the soul, and then they disappear into the dusk. Cricket reaches for her bracelet and tenderly runs her fingers over her father's aviator wings. Her heart fills to overflowing with treasured memories of the past.

"Thanks, God. You always know how to smooth over a rugged day like this one." She quickly adds, "You're welcome to stay for dinner, or at least for grace. Here, I'll set a place for you."

She goes into the living room to stoke the fire and is looking around the room like saying goodbye to an old friend when her eyes come to rest on a picture on the mantel of her mom and dad sitting on a rock by the ocean. She fights back the tears she has been holding all day long.

"Get a grip, girl," she tells herself. "Not in front of Max. Mom would want it that way. Back to the kitchen."

Eventually, the kitchen door swings open and in come Jock and Max, who must have raced from the barn to the house.

"Just in time, gentlemen. Dinner is served," states Cricket. "Max, you want to say grace?" says Jock as everyone sits down. "Sure," says Jock.

"Are we expecting another guest?" asks Max, observing the extra place setting.

Cricket smiles. "Well, you never know."

"Ah," says Max. "Sort of like that invisible friend you were always talking to at night when we were kids."

"Something like that," says Cricket. "Now, how about the blessing."

"Bless this table, this food, and the people who sit here in your honor." Just as Max finishes the blessing, the kitchen door blasts open, the gust of wind scattering leaves across the floor. Cricket gets up, closes the door tightly, and removes the extra place setting from the table.

Max teases, "Your guest not showing up?"

"Maybe he just had time for grace and was too busy to stay longer," Cricket says with a wink and a sly smile. They devour the meal, push back from the table when finished, and open another bottle of wine. Cricket is indeed overjoyed by the news of the new baby. They toast the expected child and enjoy one another's company long after the candles have melted into small swirling puddles of wax. Soon, Max will be on his way back to the East Coast, and Cricket will miss him dreadfully until he is next free to visit. Privately, both Max and Jock ponder the odd event of the extra place setting and the door bursting open, one of many such curiosities surrounding Cricket over her lifetime that friends and family simply accept without question. Each promises himself that one day he will press her for an explanation. Maybe one day, but not tonight. Not tonight. The End (Or Is It?)

ABOUT THE AUTHOR

P. C. Smith was a well-known stained glass artist in Carmel- by-the-Sea, California, for over fifteen years, creating custom pieces for celebrities and clients all around the world. Upon retirement, she took up her second love, writing, and has published poetry and short stories before writing this, her first novel. She is a mother of two, a grandmother of four, and a great-grandmother of six. She lives on the Monterey Peninsula, California and in Darby, Montana, with her loving husband and two dogs.

REVIEWS

"She was about to be deported from Never-Never Land, and her life would never again feel as absolute."

Seven-year-old Cricket is standing on a precipice, though she doesn't know it yet. It's the summer of 1942, and just as the country is waking up to the losses and horrors of World War II, Cricket is struggling to make sense of her first tragedy. Her mom, Makie, heavily pregnant, sends the young girl on her first solo train journey from the San Joaquin Valley, California, to rural Everett, Washington, to stay with her grandparents for the summer. Braving the trip alone is only the first of many times Cricket will have to swallow her fears and put on a grown-up face as she navigates the confusing world of adults.

Cricket reunites with the gang of neighborhood kids with whom she spends every summer. Though she is the youngest of the group, all the children are still innocent, content to build forts in the woods and pick wild strawberries. Even Marvin, the oldest at fourteen, is sweet and very protective of Cricket, defending her valiantly from some nasty town bullies. But when twelve-year-old Mary Frances comes to town to stay with her cousins, she shakes up their insular world. From the first time she pulls out a cigarette, she divides the group, as the younger ones refuse, but the older boys all try out smoking. Cricket decides Mary Frances is a free spirit and is alternately baffled and intrigued by her new adult behaviors.

But the idyllic summer is punctured by disturbing violence, domestic abuse, and rape—all of which the children of Everett witness. Cricket, in particular, gets drawn into the adult world of the police and lawyers who are investigating. Cricket's understanding of these incidents is limited. She often doesn't even have the vocabulary to describe what she witnesses. Her grandfather Thad Bane, a retired lawyer and judge, takes on the case of a controversial defendant, and the family suffers death threats and even injury as a result.

This lyrical and nostalgic tale of times and traditions of the past is often like listening to stories at your Grandmother's knee. There are evocative descriptions of the delicious foods Cricket's grandmother cooks, and the narrative transports sensory details of the beauty of country life. Cricket has especially charming nightly chats with her friend God, to whom she confides all of her secret fears and longings.

Smith's novel is reminiscent in many ways of *To Kill A Mockingbird*, the great American coming-of-age story that also deals with a young girl's loss of innocence, violent tragedy, and a controversial trial. And like Harper Lee's masterpiece, the narrator of this novel is simultaneously a seven-year-old girl and a grown-up version of herself remembering the events of that fateful summer. A large cast of characters is explored, with chapters devoted to Makie, Mary Frances, and others, providing context and developing the rich characterizations. There are multiple depictions of violence and sexual abuse that are all the more startling for their stark juxtaposition with the folksy, idealized portrait of small-town life in the last century. The author's book will likely appeal to nostalgic older readers and fans of stories of small-town life, such as *Our Town or Fried-Green Tomatoes.*

In this gripping tale of good and evil, a group of young children lost their innocence when their idyllic, small town is rocked by a horrific murder

In the summer of 1942, Anne Elizabeth Jordan, also known as Cricket, travels alone to Everett, Washington from San Joaquin Valley, California to stay with her maternal grandparents. Cricket's mother Makie is unable to go because she is heavily pregnant. Traveling alone is the first of the many unexpected things Cricket experiences in this fateful summer.

Arriving at Everett, an idyllic and picturesque small town, Cricket is reunited with her group of friends she spends every summer with. The kids are innocent and just enjoying their childhood. But their small and playful world is rocked by the arrival of Mary Frances, a free-spirited twelve-year-old who already knows how to smoke.

The seemingly peaceful summer, however, was shaken when one of the children is murdered. In a neighborhood once thought to be safe, the murder sent a shock wave throughout the town. Cricket is then drawn in the confusing world of adults. Her young and innocent mind has been muddled by a slew of disturbing violence she and her friends witnessed. The murder and the investigation that followed added more confusion to Cricket's mind.

PC Smith has written a superb and engaging mystery with a surprising twist. The story is fast-paced, and readers are introduced to multiple character with complex personalities. This novel is truly a page-turner and hard to put down as each chapter keeps us at the edge of our seats. Smith knows how to captivate her audience with her writing. Her beautiful and vivid description of an ideal and picturesque small town is conjoined with her graphic depiction of violence and domestic abuse. As shocking as some of the scenes are, they are needed to highlight issues that society is still afraid to tackle.

This novel is a must have for mystery fans who love a good twist. Well-written and entertaining, this a worthwhile addition to every book lover's collection.

PACIFIC BOOK REVIEW

Much of P.C. Smith's novel *The Shingle Weaver's Picnic* is told through the young eyes of Annie Elizabeth Jordon, a girl known best as Cricket. Most of the story is set in Everett, Washington, where Cricket is spending the summer with her wise and moral grandparents. The setting is nearly perfect, filled with small town joviality and scenic boat rides. Cricket, it would seem, shouldn't have a care in the world. However, as her story unfolds, we learn how she has many heavy cares for such a young child. Sadly, trouble so strong comes into her world, no bars of steel could ever keep out.

Cricket's first personal crises happens when her young father is killed in World War II. This makes her mother a single mother, with another child on the way. While mom is pregnant, Cricket is sent to spend a summer with her grandparents. We get the immediate impression this summer vacation is an annual one, as she has established friendships when she arrives there. It is there she is forced to try and heal from losing a father she so dearly loved.

The story is one where one would least expect to find acts of evil taking place. In fact, Cricket's second crises occurs during one of the happiest times of the year. It all develops during this small town's annual fair. The scene is taken right out of a Norman Rockwell painting. There are rides for the kids, logrolling contests, piemaking competitions and all the Americana trimmings. These are supposed to be events to build lifelong memories upon. While the happenings of this one summer did, in fact, create distinctive memories, these were also the kind of recollections she'd gladly forget – if she ever could.

It's a place where the greatest threat normally might have been the town drunk, instead the rape and murder of a young girl shattered the locale's picturesque view. Although it's likely Smith's main intention for her book was to tell a story about lost innocence, she writes it in such a way it is also presented as a murder mystery story. The reader is led to believe that a young boy murdered this young girl, at first. That is until the town's drunkard wife-abuser seemingly is exposed as the perpetrator. Yes, he was also involved in this crime, but he was the rapist, not the killer. Only toward the book's end do we find out who the real killer actually is. Smith does a good job of stringing the reader along before eventually revealing the final damning facts of the case.

The victim is not only Cricket's friend, but her grandfather is also a defense lawyer and becomes involved in the murder trial. She's connected to it all in many respects. Cricket is thrown into a situation where the kids in her peer group must act as witnesses, and a few even end up being among the accused. This is not the way any kid wants to live. These are usually adult crimes. Before all this criminal behavior rocks her community, though, Cricket has a conversation with her grandfather where he tries to help her understand war's evil that led to her father's death. Her grandfather was previously also involved in a case that involved Japanese internment camps during WWII. These war-related incidents, though, are mostly due to adults not being able to resolve problems in a civil way. The murder of her friend, however, involves a young boy killing a young girl, which can be even more difficult to comprehend – especially for a child.

Yes, *The Shingle Weaver's Picnic* is, well, no picnic, P.C. Smith is a gifted storyteller, though, and will keep you turning pages wondering what might happen next. It's a story as compelling as it is troubling, and most certainly a memorable one.

INDEX

L

M

N

P

www.ingramcontent.com/pod-product-compliance
Lightning Source LLC
Chambersburg PA
CBHW030132010826
48973CB00002B/518

* 9 7 8 1 9 6 4 0 9 7 4 5 9 *